EMPIRE REBORN

BOOK FIFTEEN OF THE EMPIRE OF BONES SAGA

TERRY MIXON

Empire Reborn

Published by Yowling Cat Press ®

Digital edition date: 10/27/2025

Print ISBN: 978-1947376403

Large Print ISBN: 978-1947376410

Cover art - image copyrights as follows:

NASA, ESA, Hubble Space Telescope, Orion Treasury Project Team, Massimo Robberto (STSci, ESA)

Luca Oleastri

Donna Mixon

Cover design and composition by Donna Mixon

Print edition design and layout by Terry Mixon

Audio edition performed and produced by Veronica Giguere

Reach her at: v@voicesbyveronica.com

ALSO BY TERRY MIXON

You can always find the most up to date listing of Terry's titles on his Amazon Author Page.

Note: the links below (ebook only, obviously) redirect you to my website where you can click a button to go to Amazon. This allows me to participate in Amazon's associates program and earn a little more. Sorry for any inconvenience.

The Last Hunter

The Last Hunter

Bonds of Blood

Alpha Strike

The Enemy Revealed

Command Authority

The Grand Conspiracy

Shield of Humanity

Fog of War

Ships of the Line

Operation Liberty

The Empire of Bones Saga

Empire of Bones

Veil of Shadows

Command Decisions

Ghosts of Empire

Paying the Price

Recon in Force

Behind Enemy Lines

The Terra Gambit

Hidden Enemies

Race to Terra

Ruined Terra

Victory on Terra

When Luck Runs Out

Gunboat Diplomacy

The Imperial Marines Saga

Spoils of War

Imperial Recruit

Enemy Action

The Humanity Unlimited Saga

Liberty Station

Freedom Express

Tree of Liberty

Blood of Patriots

Single Novels

Scorched Earth

Storm Divers

The Vigilante Series with Glynn Stewart

Heart of Vengeance

Oath of Vengeance

Bound By Law

Bound By Honor

Bound By Blood

Box Sets

The Empire of Bones Saga Volume 1

Want to get updates from Terry about new books and other general nonsense going on in his life? He promises there will be cats. Go to TerryMixon.com/Mailing-List and sign up.

DEDICATION

Empire Reborn is the 50th novel I've written or co-written under my own name. That makes it a big deal to me, so I'm expanding my normal dedication to more fully capture those who helped get me to where I am today.

First, this book would not be possible without the love and support of my beautiful wife, Donna. Your unwavering backing made this possible. I love you more than life itself.

To my daughter, Felina. Your encouragement was also a big help to me. Thanks for being there for me.

I'm also dedicating this book to my ex-wife, who told me that I would never publish a single book. You did your part to get me to where I am, too, so thanks. I guess.

ACKNOWLEDGMENTS

I want to thank the folks that support me on Patreon. You got to read this book as I was writing it and that kept me working. You have my deepest thanks.

In particular, I want to thank those patrons that supported me at the $10 level:

Bryan Barnes
Robert Broadly
Tony Craven
Bill Colston
Dave Dolan
David Goldstein
Eugene Humbert
Mark I Marcum
Christian A. Michelsen
John Page
Carl Rumbolo
Lisa Slack
Dale Thompson
Raymond Wang
Clark Williams

Finally, I want to thank my readers for putting up with me. You guys are great.

1

Admiral Jared Mertz let his gaze roam around the empty flag bridge of the superdreadnought *Invincible* and sighed. She'd been a good ship, and he was sorry to be leaving her behind, but the engineers had determined she wasn't repairable. The final battle with AI-controlled warships protecting the master AI had done her in. Even so, she'd stood strong and protected most of her crew, and that's all one could really ask for in the end.

Marcus had moved the ship into a parking orbit over the second planet orbiting Alpha Centauri A. Alpha Centauri was a complicated bit of galactic geography in that it was a system with three stars and three different sets of planets. The two larger stars orbited one another in a binary system, with Proxima Centauri orbiting both of them at about a fifth of a light year. Alpha Centauri A and Alpha Centauri B were both similar to the star Terra orbited and had individual planets orbiting each at very close approaches, and there were several planets orbiting the pair of them much further out.

There was an alien base buried beneath the surface of the hot planet he now orbited, but they didn't have any bandwidth to send explorers down or, frankly, the desire to do so. Whatever was there had been there for millions of years since the crablike aliens who had mapped the flip points throughout the galaxy had disappeared, and it would still be there when they finally got around to looking at it. He had more pressing things to deal with.

Such as getting his new fleet organized around a different flagship. They'd relocated Marcus to a new superdreadnought, and he was once again online. The AI had quickly determined that it was suitable for Jared's flag, so the surviving crew from *Invincible* had already moved over. Now, it was his turn.

He shouldered his bag, having waved off any of the crewmembers who had wanted to help him collect his personal belongings, and headed for the cutter that would take him across. There would still be a few engineers aboard *Invincible* for the next couple of hours to shut the fusion plants down and make sure everything was secure before they departed, so he wasn't turning the lights off on his way out, but it sure felt that way.

It had only been three weeks since the climactic battle that had finally seen humanity triumph over the master AI that had brought the old Terran Empire down. It felt like it had been months, but events were still moving at a breakneck pace.

The AIs had had a large number of robotic warships that had been defending the system, and he'd decided that it made more sense to relocate his people to new homes. None of the ships had names, so they'd be naming them as they went along.

When it came to basic firepower, he already had more at his command than when he'd arrived in this system. The problem was that he'd lost so very many people. Out of his original fleet, half the vessels had been destroyed outright and the others badly damaged. When the tally had finally been completed, they'd lost in excess of two-thirds of his people for this victory. It hurt deeply to suffer those kinds of losses, but if he'd had to trade his own life and the lives of every single person with him for that victory, he'd have done so without a moment's hesitation. Taking the AI's heel off of humanity's neck had been worth paying any price.

Thankfully, since Marcus was an AI of greater capability than those that commanded battle fleets for the master AI, he was completely capable of running those automated vessels. There wouldn't be a single fully crewed ship in this new fleet—dubbed Alpha Fleet by Princess Kelsey—because there just weren't enough bodies to go around.

Besides, with the automated systems able to operate the ships and do damage control, there was no need. It made more sense to put human beings where their judgment and experience could come into play, so that's what they'd done. Everyone was exhausted, but they were finally beginning to get everything back under control.

The last action that he'd had the master AI do before they'd shut it down and sent it toward Proxima Centauri in normal space had been to order all the hidden warships and those under complete robotic control to come here so he could figure out how to deal with the invasion of the Rebel Empire by the Clans. He still wasn't sure what he could do to turn them back without killing them all, but at least he had the firepower to make even that happen. One way or another, their threat would be ended with just as much finality as the master AI.

Kelsey had already gone back to the Home system to confer with the leadership of the resistance inside the Rebel Empire. He hadn't gotten any word from her since then, and he didn't expect any. She'd be on her way home to the New Terran Empire by now. She was now almost seven months pregnant, and there was no way he'd allow the heir to the Imperial Throne to put herself in danger by remaining in a combat zone even a moment longer.

Elise would also be on her way back to Pentagar. It was important to him that his wife and their children were safe. It was a huge load off of his mind and allowed him to focus on the war he still had to fight.

Once he boarded the cutter, someone at the front leaned into the control area and informed the pilots, and they disconnected from the derelict superdreadnought and began the journey toward his new home. It was floating in orbit just in front of them, so the journey would take less than ten minutes. He'd have looked out through his implants using the cutter's cameras to get a look at the robotic superdreadnought, but he knew very well what it looked like.

The ship was virtually brand-new and had never housed humans before. That had proven to be an unexpected challenge. Moving beds and other supplies that people required had taken longer than getting the ship under their control. Thankfully, that work was now done.

Once the cutter docked, he stepped out into the ship and was greeted by… well, no one though he knew he wasn't alone as soon as a voice spoke from the overhead speakers.

"Welcome aboard, Admiral."

"I'd say I'm glad to be aboard, but that's not exactly true, Marcus. What's our status?"

"All of the crew is currently aboard, and *Gauntlet* is prepared for operations."

"So that's the name you decided on? I approve. I assume my flag staff is set up in Admiral's Country, but what about the rest of the ship? What did you decide for crewing levels?"

As he was asking that, he walked down the corridor, dodging a couple of the robotic remotes that the ship used for repairs and maintenance, and entered one of the lifts and instructed it to take him to the flag bridge. It was really weird coexisting with the signs of the AIs being so blatant, yet that was the price one paid for having a ship this size with as few people running it as he did.

"All departments have senior personnel that will be directing their 'mechanical minions' in regular operations and combat. It was necessary to relocate the vast majority of our crew to other ships so that they would have enough people to perform oversight duties. Regretfully, trust is low, and I fully understand that, but it means that we require people everywhere. That won't be realistic once more ships arrive, but that's a problem for later."

The lift doors opened, and Jared stepped out onto a flag bridge identical to the one he'd left less than half an hour ago. One of his stewards was standing there, so he handed the man his personal belongings. Everything would appear in his new quarters and be set up before he had an opportunity to get there. Having stewards was an amazing thing.

Unlike the flag bridge aboard *Invincible*, the one on *Gauntlet* was fully manned, and every station was occupied. The plot at the front of the compartment showed the area where they were assembling the fleet, and there were already a large number of vessels in formation. Even more were beginning to slot themselves in place as he watched. Unless he missed his guess, Alpha Fleet was twice as big as the fleet he'd arrived with and only growing larger as more ships trickled in.

"How will this work, Marcus?" Jared asked as he took a seat behind his console. "The fleet is still coming together, and we're getting ready to move out. Do we have any idea how many ships will arrive after we depart? What do we do with them? How could we do anything with them?"

"The simplest answer to that, Admiral, is that we will leave enough personnel behind to assume command of these vessels. They will answer to the instructions they are given, but they will be at a disadvantage when fighting as units since there is no AI capable of controlling them as a group. I believe that any additional ships that arrive need to be transferred to where we can take direct control of them. I think the Home system would make an adequate Fleet base."

Jared wasn't certain what the resistance would think about that, but he also didn't know what Kelsey had set up before she'd departed for Avalon. As far away as they were—even with the full map of the flip point network—it would take her months to get home. If his calculations were correct, she'd arrive just before her daughter was born.

What that meant in practical terms was that his sister wouldn't have a lot of time to negotiate everything that would need to be done. The resistance wouldn't just kowtow to the New Terran Empire, of that he was certain. There would need to be negotiations and deals struck, and that meant he'd have to rely on Justine Bandar. The ex-Empress was not his first choice for that type of work—or his second or third—but he'd have to make do.

"We'll see how that works out, but I wouldn't hold my breath if I were you," Jared said. "That still doesn't answer my question about how many additional ships we can expect. We did pull that data from the master AI, didn't we?"

"We did. While there will undoubtedly be losses as the robotic ships converge on this location, there will be approximately a quarter of a million ships once they have all gathered. The vast majority of them will be destroyers, but there will also be a levy of cruisers, battlecruisers, and superdreadnoughts in decreasing numbers as the ships grow larger. At this time, we have only taken possession of sixty ships. The force that will eventually gather will dwarf our present firepower by many orders of magnitude."

That was a lot of ships. Even if the Clan destroyed some of them en route, it would barely make a dent in the overall firepower they were talking about. The only problem was that there weren't enough people to run that kind of fleet, and without having AIs like Marcus to accompany them, they would be unable to fight effectively as a unit, and their force would be wasted. That was something he'd have to figure out before he attacked the Clans.

Jared nodded. "And what will their orders be when they arrive? In fact, how long will it take the most distant ships to arrive?"

"Travel times across the Empire are quite lengthy, so I expect the most distant ships to arrive six months from now. We have to take into account the time required for destroyers summoning them to arrive and then for the ships they're summoning to return. While there are a large number of systems in close proximity to Terra, we can only anticipate about thirty percent of the listed ships arriving in the next six weeks."

"What about the next two weeks?"

"No more than ten percent."

Ten percent of 250,000 ships was still a very significant number. They'd need to find a place where they could create a massive Fleet base that could service that number of ships or co-opt one that already existed.

"Marcus, where is the closest major Fleet base that we could utilize for operational control of the ships?"

"That would be in orbit around Terra. There are twenty-seven orbitals that have power. The AI formally in control of the system is aboard the largest, and it has all the capabilities of Orbital One around Avalon and many more in addition. If we were to download the information from that AI for later perusal and historical purposes, we should be able to create a new AI that will run the Terra system for us. Even with all the systems that are no longer functional, there are hundreds of orbitals that could be brought into service.

"None of the tremendous industrial capacity of Terra was destroyed during the Fall. It would be trivial to have the ships remain there rather than making the final transition to Alpha Centauri. That would also serve to keep anyone from looking too closely at the events in the system if they do penetrate the area."

The idea of utilizing the AI that once watched over that system to defend Terra against all comers was certainly appealing. It meant that they'd have a formidable redoubt that the Clans would be unable to savage.

While it would take a long time for the debris from the battle here to scatter to the point where no one would know what had happened, that really wasn't important for what they were doing right now.

"All ships are to set course for Terra once we are ready," he ordered. "We'll spread out and make sure the flip points are well-defended and that we aren't showing any signs that the system is occupied. I want FTL probes on the other sides of the flip points leading out of Terra keeping an eye out for anyone coming our way while we keep the hammer hidden behind our backs. How soon will we be able to get all the ships that can travel there?"

"It will take a couple of hours to pull the last of the personnel off the ships that are being shut down. I suggest that we leave some vessels behind to take everyone aboard and join us while we take the majority of our force there and begin setting up. There's no telling what condition the station is in, and the sooner we can get my new associate up and running, the faster we can deploy our fleet and go after the Clans."

"Make it happen."

Leaving that to his flag captain, Jared considered the next steps they needed to take. Keeping a grip on Terra was a good way to start this off. It was the home of humanity and the seat of power of the old Terran Empire. Possession of that strengthened their claim to the Empire as a whole.

He'd still need to send someone to get the situation with the resistance under control. He'd work with them as much as possible, but he wouldn't let them steamroll him. He'd also take steps to make certain it didn't look like he was intimidating them into doing his bidding. If they were ever going to have a peaceful reoccupation of the Rebel Empire, it would have to be through cooperation and accommodation.

He wished he didn't have to do this diplomatic dance in the middle of an invasion by the Clans. There was no telling how much force they'd brought with them, and he already knew from prior experience that they wouldn't surrender. He'd have to chase down every single warship to cripple or destroy it.

Then he'd have to deal with the worlds settled by the Clans after the Fall. They'd continue to foment war against the Empire even after he and his people had freed it from the AIs. They were, in their own way, completely and utterly mad. The terror of being controlled had turned them into ravening beasts, and they'd have to be stopped by force.

So be it. That had to be the next thing on their to-do list. If he couldn't go directly after the invading ships, he might have to settle with their worlds first. That could be done though it would be a bloody and terrible thing.

For now, it was time to occupy the Sol system and see if he could send down enough people to chivy out the squatters in possession of the Imperial Palace. They weren't nearly as bad as some of the others they'd met on Terra, but if he was going to take possession of the system, he wasn't going to leave that most sacred of places in the hands of others.

2

Elise stood beside Angela Ellis on the bridge of the Marine Raider strike ship *Persephone* as they made the flip into the Terra system. She'd originally expected to find Jared and his people at Alpha Centauri, but the only thing there was wreckage from the battle. Even the master AI was gone.

She'd been afraid that her husband had already left and she wouldn't be able to give him the information about what they'd been doing, but a glance at the plot told her that there were a lot of ships still at Terra, and that meant he was probably still there as well.

Some battlecruisers were patrolling the system, and a few were stationed at the flip point leading to Alpha Centauri. Angela and her people had spotted a couple of FTL probes watching the flip point, so she wasn't surprised to find them waiting for her and was gratified to see that they didn't react hostilely.

In fact, one of the officers turned to report an incoming signal, which Angela ordered them to put on the screen. Moments later, Jared was looking at them. Rather, he was looking at *her*, and he didn't look very pleased.

"While I'm happy to see you, I thought you were on your way back to Pentagar, Elise. Is something wrong?"

"No, but there have been developments that we need to talk about, and I'd rather not do it over an open communication channel," she said. "Are you in orbit around Terra?"

He nodded. "We've been waiting for more of the summoned ships to arrive, and Marcus and I have been working aboard the orbital space station to repurpose the system AI into being a real person. We didn't want to leave all the ships under the command of someone who wasn't in control of their cognitive functions."

"Then we'll head that way as quickly as we can. I'm eager to see you, and we've got a lot to talk about."

"No man ever likes to hear his wife say that they have things to talk about," Jared said. "We're getting close to sleep time here, so I'm planning on hitting the sack shortly. Don't rush on our account, because we'll be back up in about eight hours."

"That should work out just fine for us, Admiral," Angela said. "We'll see you then."

Once the transmission ended, Elise shook her head. "He's going to be so angry."

"He's not going to be angry," her friend said with a smile. "He'll be worried about you, and he'll be concerned about your children, but he's not going to be angry."

"I suppose we'll see. How long will it take us to get into orbit around Terra?"

"What you think, Jack?"

Senior Lieutenant Jack Thompson, their helm officer, turned to face them. "The position of the flip point leading toward Alpha Centauri and Terra aren't well aligned at the moment, so it's about a seven-hour trip in. If we dawdle a bit, we can arrive after they've woken and deliver Her Highness in time for breakfast."

Angela nodded and made a shooting gesture with her finger. "Make that happen." Then she turned back toward Elise. "Get a good night's sleep. You'll want to be fresh for this meeting."

"I certainly don't want to come in exhausted, but sleep isn't coming easily these days. I dread having to explain everything that's happening. Still, I suppose you're right. Catching a nap is better than going in tired."

"You bet it is. Now, get out of here. Oh, and be grateful that you can sleep in a real bed rather than one of the bunks we use."

That made her smile a little. "I wish there was a way to communicate back and forth so that I could take you back with me and bring you here if there were any issues, but there's not. Try not to get the ship blown up, because I'm pretty sure that appearing in vacuum would do me no good."

"It certainly wouldn't, but you'd be able to see conditions on the other side of the portal before you stepped through. All you need to remember is that vacuum won't instantly kill you. Don't try to hold your breath; just let it go, or you'll get an embolism in your lungs. Then, use your powers to get yourself back somewhere safe. Not that we'll be attacked here and now. We're as safe as we could be. Now, shoo."

Elise touched a dark spot on the outside of her left wrist and willed into existence a portal connecting to the strange realm that she alone could access. One step, and she was through it, and the portal closed behind her.

The room she appeared in was the one she'd arrived in the very first time she'd entered this realm. It was something like a small study, with shelves and a desk made of an elegant wood that was not of a grain that she was familiar with. It had required some cleaning and polishing to get a good look at it, but now that she had, it certainly fit in with the rest of this place.

The building was made of closely fitted stones, and if she walked out into the rest of it, she'd get a good look at the strange, alien space that it floated in. She didn't want to deal with that particular issue right then, so she didn't. Instead, she opened a portal to her quarters aboard *Audacious*.

She'd been sleeping there the entire time *Persephone* had been traveling toward Terra. Honestly, she'd expected this strange motive power she had to go between places to be limited by the distance, but she hadn't found an upper range yet.

Carl Owlet had been tearing his hair out about how it could be powered since it wasn't drawing energy from her body, and it didn't seem to be pulling it out of the building she had access to. It made no sense to him, and she could commiserate with that. It didn't make any sense to her either.

Oh, well. He'd figure it out eventually.

The strange robot that had attached itself to her when she'd visited the crab aliens' strange city was waiting for her and seemed excited at her return. It bounced up and down slightly on its crablike legs, which was pretty much the only indication she had of how it felt. The damn thing wouldn't communicate with her by any means she could understand, so she was left trying to parse out its behavior.

It didn't like it when she traveled somewhere it couldn't go, but it seemed to be learning to accept that if it waited where she left it, she would return shortly. That was the best that could be hoped for, and she was pleased to see that it hadn't torn up anything while she'd been gone. Sometimes, it did, and that was annoying.

She'd prepared for the possibility of having to spend another night without her husband, so she'd laid into a snack and a bit of a sedative. Getting to sleep was more difficult these days, and having something to assist her was okay with the doctor as long as she did so in moderation.

After she'd eaten and taken the medication, she stripped and climbed into bed. There was a lot of tossing and turning, but she eventually fell asleep, only to wake up what felt like just a few minutes later, still tired as she checked the time via her implants. It was about ten minutes before the alarm was set to wake her, so she rose, showered, and dressed.

As she was planning on eating with Jared, she didn't take any time to feed herself. Instead, she went back to her house in the alien dimension and then opened a portal to the cargo area aboard *Persephone* that had been cordoned off for her use.

Angela was waiting, so she stepped through. "We've just entered orbit around Terra and are right behind the big station. Admiral Mertz sent a message that he's already up and waiting for us."

"Then let's head over and get the yelling done with."

Her friend laughed. "It's not going to be that bad. Come on."

The two of them headed to the stealthed pinnace attached to the Marine Raider strike ship. One of the other crewmembers would do the flying and take the pinnace back to *Persephone* after they'd been dropped off.

The flight over took less than fifteen minutes, and she passed the time by linking her implants to the pinnace's scanners and watching the approach. That space station was ten times larger than the one over Avalon, and that had dwarfed anything she'd ever seen before. Pentagar had been technologically behind the New Terran Empire when they'd been liberated from the incessant attacks that the Pale Ones had continuously launched at them, and it showed.

She could hardly imagine what they'd use all of this space for, but when the Terran Empire had been at its height, it had no doubt been a very busy place. Now, it was a derelict that held an ancient AI that had helped exterminate most of humanity and enslaved the rest.

The pinnace made its way to one of the massive hatches leading into a small craft bay that was literally packed with old cutters and pinnaces that had been sitting there for hundreds of years, but there was a cleared space off to one side, and she could see Jared standing there.

Once the pinnace settled to the deck, Angela led the way down the ramp at the back and out to meet Jared. Elise resisted the urge to run over and hug her husband. She wanted to, but she would behave with the decorum befitting the crown princess of Pentagar.

Thankfully, Jared pulled her into a hug and squeezed her tight. "I'm happy to see you, but I have to say that I'm worried by what you wouldn't want to speak about over the com. Is Kelsey okay?"

She nodded. "She's fine. Nothing I have to pass on is terrible, just inconvenient and irritating. Is there a way we can get something to eat in a private setting so I can lay this all out for you?"

He gestured toward the large hatch leading back into the station. "There's not much that's been refurbished, but I had my people clean out a couple of sets of quarters we can use. My steward has set something up for us, so we'll have fresh food and coffee. This way."

"You said that you were resetting the AI so it would have a real personality," she said as they walked. "How's that going?"

"We decided to hold off until I heard what you had to say. I didn't want that level of uncertainty hanging over me before I made a big choice like that. Whatever name the AI picks for itself once it becomes a real person, Marcus will help it understand the situation we're in, and I feel confident that it will be just as helpful as Marcus, Harrison, and Fiona have been. Having an AI watch over Terra will be a huge weight off my mind."

He led them into one of the lifts and up an incredible number of levels before they got out and walked down a bare corridor into what had probably been VIP quarters at some time, based on the number of rooms. She knew that Jared would prefer to have something less ostentatious, but if someone else was picking his quarters, it was likely those belonging to whatever admiral had commanded this station at one time.

In any case, whoever had done the work had located some tables and chairs so they had a place to sit while the steward served them breakfast. There was even a tablecloth. She wondered where that had come from.

The steward excused himself and withdrew, leaving them alone. Jared wasted no time in taking a sip of his coffee and having a couple of bites of eggs before he faced her. "So what's going on? What's happened?"

"Would you believe that I managed to get more alien tech inside me?" she asked in a disgusted tone. "Nothing harmful, but I feel like an idiot."

He seemed to relax slightly. "While I'm not exactly happy about that, on the traditional scale of our troubles, that's pretty light. What about the kids?"

"I sent them on to Pentagar without me because the crablike aliens' alien tech keeps trying to infect them," she said tiredly. "Carl got them cleaned out, but every time I came into their presence, they got infected again. He thinks that that will stop as they get a little older, perhaps even before they're born. I hope that's true, but I'm worried that it's not."

He took her hand in his and squeezed. "Whatever happens, it'll be okay. Carl will figure out how to get around this problem. Trust him to make it work."

"There's a difference between trusting that someone can do something and having an emotional response that they can't. What if I can't ever see our kids?"

He squeezed her hand harder. "Carl will solve this problem. Having hope is much better than despair. So, you must've found something else that was alien in the Home system or somewhere nearby if you run into more nanites. What was it?"

"A crashed ship. It was pretty small and had three crab alien shells inside. I found something that looked like a bracelet and picked it up. It melted and flowed right through my glove and into me. Carl thinks that it was used to control a gate that was at the back of the ship. That was significantly stranger than finding anything else that I've seen thus far. He thinks it responded to me because I already had their tech inside me."

Jared took a bite of his toast and gestured for her to continue as he sipped his coffee.

"This wasn't anything like the gates that were in the facility that transported you across the universe. No, this was much stranger. It worked a lot like the transport rings that we have, only it connected to a completely different universe. Not something like Julia's universe, but one that was radically different than anything you could possibly imagine. One where the laws of physics don't seem to play by the same rules as they do here. And, of course, I got myself into trouble there too."

He crossed his arms and mock scowled. "I can't let you out of my sight for five minutes."

"You need to get all the way off my back about this," she groused. "It wasn't my fault."

"If you only knew how many times I've heard variations of that where it was indeed the person's fault. What happened?"

"I turned off the gate when we got to the other side, but there was no power, so we couldn't open it again. We were stuck over there for days until we could get the power system functioning, and no one could come and rescue us because I was the only one who could activate and deactivate the gate. It was only pure luck that we solved the problem and got ourselves out without somebody getting hurt."

"Well, if that's the only thing that came out of it, you definitely got lucky."

She dreaded telling him this next part, but she knew that she had to. She might as well get it over with because it wouldn't get any easier if she waited.

"About that. While we were there, we found the wreckage of an alien ship that didn't look like it was part of the crablike alien civilization. It was like a sailing ship made to fly through those strange skies on gossamer wings. It had crashed a long time ago, but not millions of years. There were still desiccated bodies, so maybe decades or perhaps a hundred years. The medical staff aboard *Audacious* is working on the bodies to try to figure that out."

She took a deep drink of coffee and kept going. "So, Kelsey talked me into exploring the ship with her, and while I was there, we found a bunch of stuff that we brought back for everyone to look at. I didn't think anything about it, and I stuck a bracelet on my wrist, and it got absorbed, too."

Jared considered her for a few seconds and then shook his head. "I'm definitely assigning you a marine guard to be sure that you don't touch things. I'll give him a ruler to smack your fingers if it looks like you're reaching for something."

"You think you're funny, but you're not," she assured him. "Besides, you've got other things to be upset about that don't involve me. For example, Kelsey isn't on her way back to Avalon. Circumstances dictated that she remain in the Home system, as well as travel to a nearby location to do some work there. The resistance won't give up their dream of controlling the Terran Empire unless we manage to get five systems peaceably under our control."

Her husband sighed. "I suppose it was too good to hope for. Still, she's hopefully keeping herself safe, and no doubt, her mother will be absolutely certain that she doesn't stick herself into a troublesome spot. Why don't you fill me in on exactly what's been going on?"

As the two of them continued eating, she let him know about how they'd infiltrated the Devon system and how the resistance there had betrayed Justine Bandar, Olivia West, and Veronica Giguere, as well as how Justine had been tortured for days and how they'd eventually helped defend the system from the Clans when they'd invaded. He sat there and listened with a thunderous expression as she explained the situation to him. By the time she finished, they'd both polished off their meals.

"That's definitely a lot more than I expected to happen," he eventually responded. "We can't let this pass. As much as I dislike Kelsey's mother, she was acting as an ambassador for the New Terran Empire, and we have to make an example of the people that crossed us."

"That will be taken care of shortly, and you'll have some input into it. Kelsey wants to go over everything that's happening there with you."

He shook his head. "I don't have time to travel there. Things are happening too quickly, and we won't be able to deal with the Clans if I take a break, so she'll have to figure this out for herself. She's more than capable of doing so. I've seen some of the examples she's made of other people, and only an idiot wants to cross her."

Elise smiled a little lopsidedly. "Actually, you *do* have time. Remember that other bracelet I absorbed? It gave me new powers, and I think it's time for a demonstration. You'll want to tell someone that we'll be away and that I'll have you back in a couple of hours. If you need to leave instructions for anyone else, please do so."

He gave her a look that said he had no idea what she was even talking about, but when she gestured toward the door, he walked over, stuck his head out the hatch, and spoke briefly with one of the marines on guard.

Angela walked over to the hatch. "I'll leave the two of you to it and head back to *Persephone*. If you need me, you know where to find me."

Jared clapped a hand on her shoulder and then returned to stand next to Elise. "Now what?"

She touched the dark spot on the back of her left wrist and willed the portal to open to her getaway inside the alien dimension. It opened directly in front of her and showed the crablike robot waiting for them. "It's perfectly safe. Step on through."

Instead of doing that, he walked around the portal and stared at it. "What's creating this? Where is it going? How do we even know it's safe?"

"I've used it enough to know that it's safe. As for where it goes, step through, and I'll show you. Have you ever wanted to have a getaway home where you wouldn't have to worry about people bothering you? I certainly have, and now we have a place that no one else can get to."

Once he stepped through the portal, she followed him and closed it behind them. The lights inside the building illuminated the wood and stone that it was made out of, and she gave him a brief tour, starting with the upper floor where there were views of everything. The wide windows showed another strange reality, and he stared at the clumps of matter that floated past them in their multicolored glory.

"You installed life support?"

She shook her head. "This entire reality—at least the parts here—seems to have an atmosphere we can breathe. As for the matter you're seeing outside the windows, it's roughly twice as dense as soil even though it looks like it's made of cream. It's a very strange material and not even close to the oddest thing that Carl has found here while we were stuck on the crabs' base. This, by the way, isn't that facility. That's a different one though it's in the same universe."

"That's utterly crazy," her husband said, never taking his eyes off the alien landscape. "How does getting here work? What powers it? Surely, that takes a lot of energy."

"I haven't got the slightest idea, and neither does Carl. He's been wracking his brain and coming up empty. There's no power generation in this building other than what keeps the lights on, and that's provided by power supplies in the lights themselves. We'll have to build something once we start renovating."

"Renovating? Are you seriously saying that we should use this as a getaway home?"

"Why not? The ability to get here and not be disturbed has to be worth something, right? We'll want to do some work on understanding how this works so that we can develop other ways of getting in and out, but having some peace and quiet is useful. Also, this place has been very helpful from a tactical sense. I can pack the basement full of people with weapons and armor, and no one will see anything until I open a portal and everyone comes rushing out."

"It's going to take me a while to get my head wrapped around this. You say it has a basement? What else does it have?"

"Let me finish the grand tour. It's got everything that a mansion of this size might have, and even though it isn't furnished, it wouldn't take me much work to open portals of the necessary places for people to bring things in. That's for the future, but before I take you to Kelsey, you'll want to see everything here."

She spent the next half hour showing him around, and he took particular interest in the ship on the lower level. He walked its decks and stared at the gossamer sails.

"It's beautiful. As a pilot, one of these days, I think I'd want to take it out."

"When you have time, you're more than welcome to. Carl will want to go with you because he's itching to dig into this thing and figure out how it works. For now, we should probably go meet Kelsey. If I'm to get you back to Terra in the next few hours, we don't have that much more time to spend sightseeing."

In the middle of the basement, she opened the portal leading to her quarters aboard *Audacious*. As far as she knew, the ship was still in the Devon system, but it was always possible it had left to go elsewhere if needed.

Her husband blinked as they appeared aboard the carrier. "And just like that, we've gone all that distance? I'm not sure I'll be able to wrap my head around that."

"We'll have time to figure it out, but right now, you need to focus on your meeting with Kelsey. There's a lot going on, and we could certainly use your help. When we're finished, I'd be happy to show you around the alien facility, or perhaps we could find time for lunch."

He smiled. "Food sounds better to me right now, and maybe you could spend the night with me at Terra."

"Count me in."

3

Kelsey stood as Jared and Elise walked into her quarters. She gave her brother a big smile and opened her arms for a hug. "It's good to see you again. What do you think of Elise's new ability?"

He gave her a look that said he wasn't buying everything she was selling but returned her hug. "I think it's amazing, and I can't wait to figure out how that works and what capabilities it'll give us. Before we start that, though, aren't you supposed to be headed for Avalon? Talbot won't be happy when he finds out you're still here in the middle of all this."

That soured her expression. Her husband wouldn't be pleased.

"Have a seat, and I'll explain. I've been on pins and needles ever since Elise left because I knew this moment would come, but it couldn't be helped. First of all, everybody conspired to make sure that I didn't leave. I cannot begin to tell you how many medical exams I've had in the last few weeks. Frankly, the number of restrictions that have been put on me is excessive."

He chuckled as he sat. "So, Elise said that you made a deal with the resistance. If we could capture five systems, they'd acknowledge the New Terran Empire's claim to the old Terran Empire?"

"Not capture," she corrected. "They want us to get buy-in from the local governments, whoever they may be. Now, admittedly, there has been some capturing going on, but I'm not counting those systems toward our total, and neither are they. The system coordinator at Devon has agreed to allow us sovereignty, so that's our first and only sign-off. There was a disabled battlecruiser left at the gas giant, and we've got it back in operation. Veronica has assumed command and has been promoted to captain with Don Sommerville as her executive officer."

Jared nodded. "That sounds like a good call. How badly was the ship damaged?"

"The computer core failed. It was a manufacturing defect, and we've already moved Fiona in to take command of those operations. Carl had time enough to expand the computer center and armor it more heavily to protect her. Once we get more ships, she'll be able to use the codes we have to command those vessels in combat."

"That works. So, you had a fight here? Which system did you have to invade?"

"The Ritali system," she said as she leaned back and propped her feet up on the small stand she had at hand. "They sent a heavy cruiser, two light cruisers, and four destroyers to capture the Devon system. We were able to circumvent them and send them packing without taking any damage, and they ran into a Clan task force at the flip point. In fact, the two groups ended up face-to-face at point-blank range, and it was a slaughter."

"How much was the damage to our forces?" he asked with a frown.

"The Ritali force was totally destroyed, and we jumped the Clan vessels. We didn't take any losses and virtually wiped them out. We captured a badly damaged battlecruiser and heavy cruiser and then sent people to go over them once we pried the crews out. They didn't want to surrender, so that wasn't a simple task. It's all sorted out now, but there was needless loss of life on both sides. Luckily, the ones that ejected themselves in escape pods were easier to handle."

"It sounds like you had a lot to deal with. What about the attack on the Ritali system? How did that go?"

She sighed. "Not as easily as I'd have liked, but we have control of the system. They sent the vast majority of the ships under their command to seize Devon and were left wholly unprepared to deal with a carrier and her escort. Oh, did I mention that Devon has six destroyers? We left four back to be sure the system was protected, but Zia said that two were more than enough protection with the fighters she had and Veronica's battlecruiser."

"I was along for the ride and watched everything from the flag bridge," Elise said. "All they had left in the system were a couple destroyers, and even though it took a bit of work to chase them down, they made the harsh discovery that when your enemies know where all your flip points are—especially the ones you don't know anything about—it's easy to get ambushed by a bunch of fighters on a ballistic track."

Kelsey grinned. "That part of the fight went to plan. We found a one-way flip point that we could use to get in that came out far enough away that no one noticed our arrival. Using FTL probes, we got all the data we needed about the disposition of their ships. They had the two destroyers near the two flip points, so we just had to get fighters into position to disable them before they could do anything hasty. The destroyers we brought with us followed them up and seized both vessels when they surrendered. Then *Audacious* and *Artemis* strolled into orbit and intimidated them."

Jared's eyebrows rose. "And they surrendered?"

"No, but they're penned in, and we've seized the orbitals. The system coordinator and his Rebel Fleet lackeys are hiding on the planet in some command bunker or another, but they're not a direct threat to us at this point. We don't have the manpower to dig them out now that we've lost virtually all of our marines and Marine Raiders."

Her brother grimaced. "And these aren't people we can negotiate with?"

She shook her head. "Not a chance. These are the kind of people we don't want in charge when we take control. Everything I've heard about them is bad, and the resistance on the planet is working on trying to locate where they're hiding. When they do, we may just turn it into a smoking crater and call it a day. Honestly, that sounds like the best idea to me, but I want to know what your opinion is."

"Planetary bombardment is usually a bad idea, and there are all kinds of restrictions about doing it, so I'll say, as tempting as it might be, you should probably come up with another idea. What about the other systems in this area? Are we going to be able to negotiate with any of them?"

"We've sent people to talk to some of them, and a few of them are willing to consider the offer, but none are eager to commit," she said. "I'm afraid that the Rebel Empire has come apart. Everyone has seized power in their own systems, and they're not willing to let it go. We made a mistake in how we went about doing this, and that's my fault. We should've left the AIs in control until we arrived to assume command."

He shrugged. "It doesn't do any good to cry over spilled milk. We'll find a way to make this work. Since you knew I was going to be here, I assume you've got reports of various kinds for me to take back and study at my leisure. I'll put Marcus to thinking about it, and you can do the same with Fiona. Maybe together, they'll come up with something we can use. We'll need a base of operations to strike out at the Clans and stop this invasion before it tears everything apart. Is Devon willing to provide those services?"

She nodded. "They don't have a lot of orbital infrastructure built for that work, but they'll provide what they can. How many ships are we talking about?"

He grinned. "Far more than we can actually put crews aboard, so I'm not sure exactly what we can do to split up the groups any more than we already have. We need AIs to command the various fleets. Otherwise, we have to send task forces to various locations with general orders to subdue any resistance, and that always leaves the opportunity for something to go terribly wrong."

"You didn't answer my question," she said. "How many ships have arrived at Alpha Centauri?"

"We've relocated to Terra, taken over the big space station, and are slowly bringing it back online. I can send a hundred ships right now and still have plenty left to provide protection for the system. We're talking a dozen superdreadnoughts and the rest battlecruisers. Everything is computer controlled, and I've relocated my people to a new superdreadnought, *Gauntlet*, because *Invincible* isn't repairable. We took the AI in command at Terra and reformatted it. His name is Arnold. He can run the system defenses after we leave, so I can take what ships we have and head here. We'll need to send another ship with an AI in command to pick up the reinforcements."

"Why would you need to do that?" Elise asked. "You've got the command codes, and Arnold is right there. Or you can have trusted individuals utilize those codes as the ships arrive and send them here to Devon."

He nodded. "I suppose I could, but that would leave them somewhat vulnerable on the way. Maybe if we sent them in a large pack, they wouldn't be assaulted by the Clans. You said you have a lot of Clan prisoners. What are you doing with them?"

"We stunned the lot of them and transported them down to an island. That seemed like a great way to keep them from escaping. There was enough infrastructure there that we could provide food and medical attention as needed, but they're so xenophobic that they just attack everything that comes near them. They won't surrender, and they won't comply with orders. I'll be damned if I know how we're going to solve that particular problem."

She watched him rub his face. Kelsey sympathized with how he felt because she felt exactly the same way. The Clans were as human as they were but had been poisoned by the Singularity. She was absolutely certain that the other polity had been working behind the scenes to make certain the Clans were as extreme as they could be made to be even though they'd already been ravening beasts.

Jared shook his head. "I suppose isolation right now is the best thing. I'll bet it didn't take long for them to start building rafts."

"You're not wrong," Kelsey grumbled. "We've been able to deal with their attempted excursions, but it hasn't deterred them in the slightest. Their sense of superiority is as outsized as their egos. They won't accept failure."

He pinched the bridge of his nose and shook his head again.

"They're like rabid dogs. I hate to say that, but it's true. Whatever solution we come up with for them will have to restrict them to the worlds they came from. They aren't suitable to mix with the rest of the Empire until some of their xenophobia can be diluted. Thankfully, I don't have to figure out how to solve that particular problem. I just need to beat them in space and let the rest of it sort itself out."

She rose to her feet. "And we'll figure out how to do that, but I'm starving. It's not exactly mealtime, but why don't you join me and my mother for brunch? Maybe she'll have some insights for you."

Kelsey chuckled at his expression. "She's really trying, Jared. I ask that you set aside everything you think you know about her and give this a try. She's had a hard time, and the stability will be good for her."

His expression darkened. "Elise told me they tortured her. That needs to be answered for."

"I couldn't agree more," Kelsey said. "I didn't want to take any steps until I'd spoken with you, but I intend to see the people responsible tried for their crimes and executed. How do we want to handle that? They were members of the resistance, but the leadership here has washed their hands of them and said we can do whatever we want to them."

"Oh, there will be a trial," he said grimly. "I think setting up something to happen in a few days would be worthwhile. People need to know that when the Empire sends someone as their ambassador or negotiator, if anything happens to them, the sky will fall on them."

"I'll make sure that happens," she said. "You'll probably want to get some input from my mother on what she thinks because I'm not sure how badly testifying about this will destroy her. She has an acute case of PTSD, and she's fragile."

"Then I think having dinner and discussing this is probably the best plan. I feel bad that she'll have to go through it again, but this is the only way the guilty can be punished. I'm sorry that she'll be punished alongside them, but she'll get to see the results for herself. That's got to count for something."

Kelsey sent a message to her mother, letting her know that Jared was there with Elise and that they were all having dinner. She then added that Jared needed to discuss what happened with her on Devon.

She expected her mother to dither a bit, but she simply responded that she'd be there shortly. Her mother was stronger than she'd given her credit for, and things between them had changed for the better. They'd get through this, and once it was done, they could move forward together.

As for the people who had tortured her mother, she'd space them. Or maybe they'd choose death by firing squad, and Kelsey would cheerfully pull the trigger. The people who had harmed her mother would die by her hand, and Kelsey wouldn't lose a single moment of sleep over it.

4

Talbot stepped off the pinnace's ramp and looked over the ruined megacity of Frankfort on Terra. It hadn't changed since he'd seen it last, but the circumstances of the citizens here—as well as his own—had in the intervening months.

He'd chosen to land outside the city near where the horde city that had been preying on it had once been. As they were looking to bind the friends they'd made here even more tightly to themselves, he'd taken it upon himself to fly down once they'd beaten the master AI and warn the people in the horde city that they needed to depart.

They'd ignored him, of course, so he'd been forced to use his weapons to vaporize their walls and set them fleeing. The level of technological difference between the New Terran Empire and the horde was inconceivably vast, and one pinnace had been more than enough to drive them off.

That accomplished, Marcus had kept an eye on everything from orbit, and anytime it looked like the savages wanted to come back around, Talbot had been there to drive them away. Now, they were distant enough that he was confident they weren't coming back, so it was time to move to the next stage of his plan.

Leader Mordechai and his son Jebediah were waiting near the perimeter of Frankfort with at least a score of others. They were dressed for war, but he knew that was not their intent. This was simply their way. He'd chosen to dress in unpowered combat armor and had a rifle strapped across his back as well as a pistol on his hip. Marines were in short supply, but he'd still brought a couple of them with him.

In fact, the very lack of marines was one of the reasons he'd chosen to intervene at Frankfort. They needed people, and he was less than picky about where he was going to get them. Mordechai and his people had taken a chance on them when they could have imprisoned him and his friends, and Talbot would now repay their assistance with a chance to elevate their people.

Of course, some of them would be at risk when the fighting with the Clans picked up again, but that couldn't be avoided. There was no way he could reconstitute either the marine complement or the Marine Raiders. This was a stopgap measure, no matter how one chose to look at it.

With his eyes roving over the pinnace, Mordechai and Jebediah stepped forward. The older man extended his hand in greeting. "Well met, Talbot. Your circumstances have certainly improved since the last time we spoke. I take it that your quest was successful. Is the artificial intelligence that destroyed our world truly gone?"

"Yes and no," Talbot said as he shook the other man's hand. "The AI is physically still there, but we have erased it and reconstituted a new artificial intelligence that is friendlier to humans. I won't say that the war is over because there are still problems to be dealt with, but Terra is safe."

"It's still very hard to believe," Jebediah said. "I suppose seeing this magnificent machine should be proof enough that things have changed. Did it truly come from space? How does it fly?"

Talbot grinned. "Would you like to find out for yourself? Admiral Mertz and Princess Kelsey have tasked me with making an alliance with your people that stretches beyond Terra. If you're willing, I'd like to take you to the space station in orbit where we've taken up residence so that we can speak."

"I *should* say no and send my son to do the speaking for us, but I have to confess that I want to see these things with my own eyes," Mordechai said with a smile. "How long would we be gone?"

"I can bring you back this evening if you'd like. I suspect that tomorrow would be better because I imagine there are a lot of things that you'll want to see, but you are free to depart at any time. I or one of my people will see that you are promptly returned home when you are ready to go."

The older man looked at him for a few seconds and then nodded. "Your word is good here. If that's what you say will happen, I believe you. Frankly, I want to know more about what happened after you left our city. I'm sure there is a tremendous saga that our people would want to hear, and I wish to see many of these machines that you have working. As you know, my people's lives are hard. We live among the wreckage of giants, but we don't know anything about how to fix anything. Will improving our lives be part of the arrangement you wish to seek?"

"Absolutely, though we'll give you what assistance we can no matter what you decide. We want to see Terra restored to her former glory. Perhaps none of us will be alive to see that goal accomplished, but if we don't start taking steps now, it never will be. Raising the standards of living for your people and bringing this city back to life once more is important to us. Perhaps almost as important as it is to you."

"Then let us speak to your admiral and princess. Jebediah, take a moment to let everyone know what's going on so that no one worries. Tell them that we will be back tomorrow by midday. It's always possible that we will once again depart to go up and continue our conversations, but I, at least, will be remaining here at Frankfort once these initial conversations are finished."

The younger man inclined his head and headed over to the other people. The conversation was short, and Talbot could see the worry on some of their faces, but Jebediah looked confident that he could handle any trouble that came up. It wasn't true, but Talbot would see that no harm came to them and that they were returned as promised.

Once that was done, he escorted the men into the pinnace. While his associates strapped themselves in at the back, Talbot led the other two toward the control area. The pilots already knew what he intended, and they'd made certain there was enough space for a couple of people to hover over their shoulders. Three would make things crowded but not impossible.

Once Talbot was in place, he took a knee so that the other two could see more clearly. "Take us back up to the station, slow and easy."

"You got it, sir," the woman flying the pinnace said.

She lifted off gently and retracted the landing gear even as she pulled the ramp back in. After a few moments, the necessary indicators turned green, and she circled the city. The view from up here was magnificent and gave the two visitors a bird's-eye view of their home. It was even better than the one from the top of the building they used for their council meetings.

It was certainly easier to get here in a pinnace than climbing all those stairs. Doing that without the benefit of his augmentation had been a huge pain in the ass.

The two men said nothing, their attention focused on their city. The pilot circled around it twice and then lifted higher into the air. The ground fell away, and the curvature of the planet became evident. Very quickly after that, they reached the edge of space, and everything began to darken as the stars came out.

Once they were in orbit, she assumed a course for the giant station, and they were quickly catching up with it. As he watched it grow larger in front of them, he knew it was easy to underestimate its size. It looked so tiny at a distance, but that was an illusion. The space station was titanic.

Mordechai and Jebediah said nothing as the station grew large. Off to the left-hand side, the superdreadnought *Gauntlet* floated, looking tiny in comparison to the massive station. Once again, the two wouldn't know anything about how large the ship was, but seeing the station and the superdreadnought floating there had to have an impact on them. How could it not?

"Were these left here from before the Fall?" Jebediah asked, his voice a hushed whisper.

"The station was, but the ship beside it is one we captured in battle. The admiral's original flagship was the same class as that vessel, but it was so badly damaged that we had to abandon it. Once things are done, we'll have her towed here and turn her into a museum. She's a big part of how we won. His original ship was named *Invincible*, and this new ship is named *Gauntlet*. They're what we call superdreadnoughts. The biggest warships the old Terran Empire ever created."

"I feel like a fly looking at a towering building," Mordechai said. "Human beings are insignificant compared to something like this."

"I couldn't disagree more. These are nothing but tools and are useless without human beings to design, build, and use them. We're the most important factor in everything you see here, and at some point in the future, we'll have to rule Terra once again, and that means restoring peace and prosperity to all who dwell there. Take us around *Gauntlet*, Lieutenant."

"Yes, sir."

The pinnace circled the superdreadnought, and he pointed out the pinnaces nestled against the other ship near Marine Country. "Those are the same as the pinnace we're in now."

"And they are as small against that ship as it is against the other thing," Mordechai said.

"It's an orbital station. Now, let's get aboard it."

None of them said anything more as the pinnace made its way to the station and into the small craft bay. The pilot found a parking location and set down gently. Once she started shutting the pinnace down, Talbot stood and showed his guests out the back and into the station itself. The monstrously large compartment they stood in was easily the size of a number of blocks in Frankfurt. The ceiling towered over their heads.

A party of Fleet ratings stood by, and at their head stood Admiral Mertz and Princess Kelsey. He'd expected her to be here after he heard about Elise's ability to travel so far across space, but it'd been a long time since he'd seen his wife, and he drank in her presence. She was getting close to giving birth, and being pregnant with her small frame made her look ungainly. She was still beautiful, though. Maybe even more than before.

Behind the two of them stood Princess Elise. He hadn't noticed her at first, but he was happy to see her there as well as he took their two guests forward to meet everyone. The side party came to attention and saluted as Mordechai and Jebediah approached.

"Welcome to Terran Orbital One," Jared said as he extended a hand to the two men. "Mordechai, Jebediah, it's good to see you both again. You already know Elise and Kelsey."

Hands were shaken all around, and Mordechai turned to look over the grand chamber. "Your circumstances have certainly improved, Jared. This is an imposing structure."

"People far greater than I built it. All we're doing is bringing it back to life. If you don't mind, I'd like to take us to where we can eat and talk a bit more comfortably. Once that's done, I'd be happy to see that you get a tour of everything you'd like to see. I'm afraid that a large amount of the station is currently locked away because it's not fit for habitation, but I think we've got more than enough ready to show you a bit of what has been restored to the people of Terra."

Jebediah raised an eyebrow. "But has it truly been restored to the people of Terra? Talbot said something about unifying the people here, but that will be no simple task and will take lifetimes. Our people won't even be able to comprehend things like this. Perhaps the youngest of children can be taught and grow up accepting these marvels, but I know that I will never understand even a fraction of what is around me now."

"I don't know that I'd sell myself short if I were you," Kelsey said. "When the circumstances are a bit more in our favor, we'll be able to bring people to educate your people about technology like this. You've got a city that can be renovated and brought back into some form of operation. We can talk about how I'd imagine something like that would work, but if you don't mind, I'm starving."

Mordechai chuckled. "As I recall, you're *always* starving. It seems to be a continual state of being for you. I cannot help but note that you are with child. My congratulations to you and Talbot. I hope that your son or daughter is healthy and grows up to be as strong as their parents."

"It's a little girl, and I certainly hope so. As for my appetite, now that my augmentation is back online, I have to eat a lot to keep it in operation."

The older man frowned. "I know that you spoke of machines inside your body, but I still confess that I don't understand how such a thing could be possible. What do they do?"

She smiled at him. "Would you like a demonstration? I promised my doctors to keep everything low-key, but I should be able to show you an example of what the physical augmentation I have can accomplish."

The man nodded. "If it causes you no harm, I am curious."

Kelsey bent toward the deck and curled the fingers of her hand to create a stirrup. "Put your foot in this and hold onto my head for balance. I promise I won't do anything too out of line, but I don't want you to fall over because you're surprised."

Somewhat hesitant, Mordechai did step forward, put a foot into her hand, and rested both of his hands against the top of her head. She stood up and lifted him easily into the air with one hand, raising her arm so that it was extended fully in front of her. That forced the man to have to bend at the waist, but the demonstration was certainly made.

Then, with a grin on her face, she extended her other hand toward Jebediah. "You're next."

The younger man was obviously gobsmacked. Whatever he'd expected to see, this had *not* been it. Nevertheless, he put a foot in her other hand and rested his hands on top of his father's.

Kelsey lifted him up beside Mordechai and then began walking slowly forward. "As you can see, my augmentation gives me the ability to lift great weights. There are a lot of other things it does for me, but I can't demonstrate those without having my doctors get on my case."

Having finished saying that, she lowered the two men back to the deck so that they could stand staring at her, agog.

The older man recovered. "I'm having difficulty believing this just happened. How can someone as small as you lift so much?"

"Technically, I have roughly the strength of ten men if I can put my full ability to use," she said. "The machines inside me greatly enhance my strength, and I have a coating on my bones and joints that gives me much greater leverage. I'm also significantly faster than anyone you've ever met. The machines inside me were what the old Terran Empire did to create their greatest warriors. I certainly wouldn't count myself among their number, but I at least have some of the training and the hardware."

"That's… rather terrifying. I suppose our first meeting would have turned out quite differently if you'd had this technology available to you then. I'm unsure if I completely understand why you didn't have use of it, but I think I'm grateful."

She laughed. "There's no need to be worried about it now. I promise that I would have behaved. Tell them, Talbot."

"If you're to look for somebody to lie for you, you need to find someone that knows you less well than your husband," Jared said. "Or any of your close friends. Possibly anyone that's ever met you."

"You're a riot. So, if you two would come with us, we'll show you something very interesting, and then we can eat and have a heart-to-heart talk. My brother and I have a deal that I believe you'll be interested in. Talbot already knows about it, and he'll have a part to play in pitching it, but I don't want to rush things."

Talbot fell in with the two men as the group walked deeper into the station. A lot of it was in ill repair, and it showed. They just didn't have the personnel to perform any of the cleaning operations. The AI that had controlled the station hadn't put any stock in keeping it ready for human habitation. It had all been in vacuum when they'd arrived, and they were still turning up the occasional skeleton of a defender that had died here during the fighting.

They'd cleared them out from the areas they would visit, but it would be an ongoing effort to recover the dead and see that they were properly interred. All the stations in orbit around Terra would have to have a thorough check before they could be certain there were no unpleasant surprises left to find.

The history of the Terran Empire was glorious before the Fall, but it was a gruesome task to bring it back to life.

None of the lifts worked, but the two men with them were used to climbing up stairs without number to reach the tops of some of the tall buildings. They had to go up a dozen levels to reach the one they were interested in and then go almost halfway across the station to where a very fancy restaurant had once operated.

As they entered through the front doors, everyone's attention was captured by the view of Terra through the wide viewports overlooking the planet. This wasn't information transmitted through a viewscreen. It was actual light reflected off the world of humanity's birth.

The engineers had done a thorough check of the plassteel windows and found them to be just as strong as the day they'd been cast. Such large panels must have been hideously expensive even at the height of the Terran Empire, but for what must have been the premier dining establishment aboard the most important of the Terran orbitals, nothing was too good.

Most of the tables within were barren, but one had been placed so as to have the best view of the world below them. The blue-and-white globe hung in front of them with the North American continent laid out before them.

Even though the visitors had no eyes for the table, Talbot took a moment to examine it and nodded. The wood that was visible was dark and well polished, and even the intervening centuries hadn't seemed to cause it too much damage. Someone had probably taken the time to oil and wax it again before covering it with a blindingly white tablecloth. The plates seemed to be of the finest china, and the utensils were polished silver. Everything gleamed, and Talbot was more than willing to bet that Jared's steward had seen to that.

The food wouldn't have been prepared in the kitchen here but rather aboard *Gauntlet*. There was no need to try to fix a kitchen that had been left to rot for five hundred years. That was very low on their priority list, though if everyone who was staying to work on the station came here to eat, that might be taken care of faster than he expected.

There was one other person who would be present at dinner, but he wouldn't be saying anything, at least not audibly.

The system AI that had once ruled Terra with an iron fist and exterminated the vast majority of its population was no more, but its hardware had been repurposed so that a new being could come into existence. As this station was his body, he had everything they needed to monitor what was going on inside of it. Talbot was certain that Arnold was paying close attention.

The test that theory, he initiated a call to the AI via his internal com. *Feeling nervous?*

One could say that, General Talbot. While I personally had nothing to do with the extermination of everyone on this world, the people dining with you today certainly wouldn't see it that way. Even if they somehow came around to understanding that I was a different kind of AI, they would rightly distrust me. For that matter, I couldn't blame them if they hated me and demanded my execution.

Talbot sat at the table. *I don't think you need to worry about it, buddy. While they'll have a say in what happens here, no one will allow any harm to come to you.*

Perhaps. Or perhaps not. In either case, I'll have an eye on things in case you need any information that I can provide, but I think it best if they are unaware that I am listening in. The fact that they are not technologically advanced means they don't understand how unlikely that is, and I would prefer to keep it that way for the time being.

Good call. How goes the work on the station?

While he was waiting for an answer, Talbot accepted the glass of water that one of the servers filled for him and looked over its rim to where their guests were still standing at the window with Jared, Kelsey, and Elise. They wouldn't be dissuaded from looking at their home world for the next few minutes. Unless he missed his guess, Jared was pointing out where Frankfort was. He was certain that neither Mordechai nor Jebediah would have ever envisioned seeing their city from so high above.

The work is proceeding apace, Arnold said. *The critical systems, such as engineering and the weapons arrays, are still fully functional, and I have a large number of remote repair drones to take care of bringing everything else back into operational status. It will not happen overnight, but I am working diligently to restore life support to all sections of the station. My estimate is that that will take at least a month. There are a number of hull breaches from debris that was allowed to strike the station that will have to be repaired before all sections can maintain pressure.*

Talbot nodded. *What about the deceased personnel?*

Between myself and the personnel you have assisting me, we have recovered the bodies of seven hundred and forty-two persons. One of the small craft bays has been converted into a morgue, and they are being stored in vacuum conditions so that they will not deteriorate. Where possible, I am attempting to use the records from the original computer system to determine who they are so that they may be memorialized.

That was something Talbot wanted to see accomplished. It couldn't hold all the names of the dead, but they needed to be remembered for what they had died doing.

I'd imagine that number will grow as you continue your work and then grow again once we expand to working on the other stations in orbit. I've talked a bit with Admiral Mertz about where we can build a spire here on Terra. I know they used to have one that was used by Fleet before the Fall, but it was destroyed, so we'll have to rebuild it as well.

Arnold was silent for a few moments. *The task of reconstructing Terra seems to be a never-ending one. Do you truly believe that these people will be able to assist you in the work?*

I know they will. The question is, in what capacity? We could really use some help with fighting the Clans, but I don't think we'll get a lot of volunteers. Frankly, that's probably for the best. Terra is their home, and bringing it back under control and helping to restore what was taken from them is a task that I believe we can all get behind. We'll leave people here to help them if that's the case, but I hope at least a few of them will join us on our trip to see other worlds.

Even as he was saying that, the party at the window turned and came to the table. It was time to get something to eat and see exactly how much help the people of Frankfort could be and what was next for them. Then, maybe he could slip away for a little time with his wife.

They had a lot to talk about, and he wanted to know everything she'd been up to. He was certain she was doing things she shouldn't be, and though he knew he wouldn't be able to stop her, he might be able to moderate some of her impulsiveness.

If not, at least he could show her how much he'd missed her. The strange ability that Elise had to travel so far in the blink of an eye would prove *very* useful when it came to conjugal visits.

5

Jared sat at the head of the table. He'd made certain ahead of time that everyone would have an unrestricted view of Terra through the viewport, so one side of the table was empty. While he wasn't a politician, he certainly understood the necessity of good staging. Right now, with their attention split between him and the planet they'd come from, Leader Mordechai and Jebediah might be a bit more receptive to what he was about to propose.

Still, he wouldn't push to the point too quickly. This was far too important to screw up by rushing things. They'd formed a relationship with the people of Frankfort, and it was his job to leverage that into something that served the Empire.

The preparation for the meal hadn't taken place on the station. Even though they'd gotten this large dining room cleaned out, they hadn't had the time or personnel to go over the cooking equipment that had been abandoned for more than five centuries.

Instead, his steward had worked aboard *Gauntlet* to get everything prepared the way he wanted. They were much more skilled in that kind of work than him, and Jared was certain that he would be pleased with what they'd put together from the supplies they'd scavenged from *Invincible*.

The way they'd arranged the seating, Leader Mordechai sat to his right with Kelsey beside him. Jebediah was next to her, and Talbot was next to him. Elise was the anchor at the far end of their group.

The servers came out dressed in their white uniforms and began serving the food. The utensils and plating had been recovered from the restaurant and polished to perfection. That was certainly something that would make an impression on the Terrans because they'd been living in a city that had died during the Fall.

There was no attempt to try to make this a high-society kind of affair because his guests didn't have any knowledge about how the upper classes of society back in the New Terran Empire ate. For that matter, neither did Jared. That was, in his opinion, a good thing.

He kept the conversation light as they ate, and then only once they'd been served some alcohol did Jared dive into the subject that was high in his thoughts.

"I believe Talbot told you that it's our intention to reclaim Terra for the Empire," he said to Mordechai. "We'd like to enlist your assistance in that."

"Considering the tribes that live near us, I'm afraid that we don't have the kind of force that would be needed to do that," the older man said. "Your people managed to drive off the horde, but there are other threats that shouldn't be taken lightly. Looking down upon our world, I cannot imagine how anyone could tame it once more."

"One meter at a time," Talbot said. "It's not as difficult as you might think, though. One pinnace drove the horde off, so how well will the rest fare? They'd be unable to even threaten it and could be driven away if need be. We can and will arrange for the security of Frankfort, no matter what you decide to do about our request. We'll make certain that your people are safe."

"And we'll also make certain that we send some specialists down to help you begin recovering your city," Kelsey said. "Most of the buildings are unrecoverable, but temporary repairs will improve them while new buildings are constructed. We can see about providing equipment that would raise your standard of living significantly. Even having a single doctor with modern medical equipment would be a lifesaver in the most literal of senses."

Mordechai nodded. "I'm certain that everything you say is true, but the scope of the task you've broached is immense. Even if every single person in my city devoted themselves to absorbing the territory around us, we would be overwhelmed because no single person can do everything that's needed. The task is simply too great."

Jared took a sip of his alcohol. "You're not wrong about any of that, but the longest journey starts with but a single step. The people around you on the plains can be brought around with the right enticements. I'm not saying that everyone needs to be conquered though I'm certain there will be some fighting. Nevertheless, if we don't start bringing Terra back under control, it will never be raised back to the glory it once held."

"And no one said you had to do it all at once," Talbot said. "Even with all the technological improvements we can give you, they'll be useless if you don't know how to use them. What we're proposing is to take some of your warriors and help train them to the standards needed to be Imperial Marines. Then, once they're fully able to do the work, they can come back home and help you."

"And are you talking about changing them like Princess Kelsey?" Jebediah asked. "Even a single person like that could become a warlord."

Now, it was Kelsey's turn to shake her head. "Not like me. At least, not until they prove themselves to be worthy. You're right that someone like myself or Talbot could do terrible things if we weren't honorable people, and we need to make certain that only the very best gain that level of enhancement. Even so, there are things that can be done to improve their ability to fight without utterly changing them."

Mordechai raised an eyebrow. "Such as?"

"Now that the artificial intelligences have been overthrown, I'll suggest something that you might be hesitant about. I ask that you hear me out before you make a decision, and even then, maybe take some time to think about it. Each of us has an implant in our head that allows a small computer to assist us in tasks that range from fighting to interfacing with Imperial equipment and even communicating with one another. The people that will be coming to repair Frankfort will have that as well, and it would help your warriors interface with Imperial weapons if they also had the implants."

Mordechai's expression closed down. "You're speaking of the mechanical things inside people's heads that turned them into slaves. Our people—more than most—understand how dangerous that is. Why would we repeat the mistakes of our fathers? For that matter, why would you?"

Kelsey spread her hands on the table and nodded. "Everything you say is correct. The Empire made a terrible mistake when they assumed that nothing bad could happen with these cranial implants. We've had our security people go over the equipment and software —the things that make up the implants themselves and control how they function—and made certain that no changes can be made without the explicit permission of the person with the implants. If they are under duress, the equipment can tell and won't allow itself to be updated. We'll certainly make additional mistakes as we go forward as a people, but we won't repeat that particular one."

"And you believe that the benefits granted warrant the risks?" Jebediah asked, obviously as skeptical as his father. "Perhaps it's because your people didn't have to live on Terra, but I don't believe you'll find many people that will agree with those sentiments."

"Maybe not without seeing the benefits for themselves," Jared agreed. "Nevertheless, the people that live on every other world inside the Terran Empire have these implants, and they won't go away. Nothing we say or do can convince you that this is absolutely safe. Nothing in life ever is. Even so, that's what's coming to Terra, whether you like it or not. Will the people of Frankfort be left behind or grow to meet the challenges that are coming?"

"And here we come to the bargaining," Mordechai said with a slight smile. "You've laid out what you want—at least in a general way—but you've been light about what's in it for my people to take these risks. It's time to put your cards on the table, Jared. If you want my people to do as you ask, the rewards will have to be worth it. And I'm not talking about some generalized statement that they would be left behind if they don't take what you offer. If you wish the assistance of my people, you must be willing to pay for the service."

Jared considered that and nodded. "You're absolutely right. When one is bargaining, it's always best to set out the initial parameters of the deal. I've said what I want, and now it's up to you to tell me what the price I'll have to pay to get it is. The problem is, you don't really understand the coin which I can pay with."

"Before we make any deal whatsoever, there will have to be some kind of proof that having these implants is worthwhile. Once that is established, then we can move forward with the rest of the deal. I'm not in the habit of buying a cow unseen."

Jared considered that. These people had no frame of reference to understand what he was offering, and perhaps utilizing Elise's talent could get them the information much better than him simply talking about it. At the very least, seeing a city that wasn't dead might show them what they'd gain in the future.

"Then I think that's the first step we should take," he said, tipping back the last of his drink and setting the empty glass on the table. "We have a means of showing you what a city like Frankfort would be like if it were restored. Would you care to see it?"

The older man looked at his son. "And this is some kind of technological means of seeing how things once were? I'm not certain that I would completely trust such a representation."

Jared shook his head. "No. I'm talking about visiting a real city in person. We have a means that can allow us to go visit another world in the flesh, and you can see what we're talking about. I think that would be a much more visceral experience for you than simply being told about it or seeing a recording."

"I see. Or rather, I don't. How long would we be gone?"

"We can still have you back in time to get you home as promised. Or, if you'd like to see more of what we have to show you, then you could arrange to stay longer. In the end, it's your call."

The two Terrans spoke softly to one another for a few minutes—stepping away so Kelsey wouldn't overhear but not realizing that she likely could—before Mordechai returned to his seat and nodded. "I would be a fool not to take advantage of your offer. I will tell you, though, that there is only so far that the trust you have earned with my people can carry you. Showing me things that are simply far beyond our imagining will not reduce the price that would have to be paid for our services."

"I wouldn't expect anything less," Jared said as he stood. "Elise, where do you think we should do this?"

"Why not here?" his wife asked as she gestured toward the area closest to the viewports.

He walked over to stand where she indicated, and slowly, everyone else did the same. He could see that Mordechai and Jebediah were utterly confused by what was going on, and he imagined that what was about to happen next would make them feel even more flummoxed.

Elise touched her arm, and an open portal emerged in the air before them. The view on the other side was the large room in the basement of that strange alien building or, as she liked to put it, their home away from home.

Even having seen it before, he was still utterly astonished. That didn't hold a candle to the open-mouthed stares of the Terrans.

Mordechai walked over to the portal and stared through it. "What magic is this? Even the wildest tales that have undoubtedly grown with each retelling never suggested anything like this. What is on the other side of this thing, and how is this possible?"

"In this case, it's actually alien technology," Elise said. "I wish I could explain it better, but I can't. We don't understand how it works either, but it allows me to arrange for us to travel from one place to another, seemingly no matter the distance, so long as I have been in both those places and take a trip to this building as an intermediary step. By going through here, we can then open another portal and go to visit a world of the Terran Empire so that you can see for yourselves what Terra could one day be like."

That obviously put the two Terrans in a more uncertain mood, but Mordechai nodded his agreement.

To make certain they knew things were safe, Jared stepped through first and waited for Kelsey and Talbot to join him. Mordechai and Jebediah hesitantly stepped through next, followed by Elise, who dismissed the portal as soon as they were through.

Not giving them an opportunity to get sidetracked, she immediately opened another portal leading into a room that looked relatively generic. "Gentlemen, please step this way, and see the capital of a world inside the Rebel Empire. Welcome to the Devon system."

Once everyone was through, Jared saw that they were in what appeared to be an apartment. It was furnished decently enough though everything was a bit worn. He wondered whose place it was.

His wife answered that question with her next words. "This is an apartment that I lease here so that I can have an unobtrusive location to come visit without everyone being aware of what I'm doing and also make sure that no one sees me arrive. That tends to freak people out."

He'd imagine it would.

She considered the two men. "Your clothing, while absolutely suitable for Frankfort, will stick out like a sore thumb. Perhaps the first place we should go is somewhere to acquire clothing that will stand out less. After all, you'll want to see everything this world has to offer, and it would be best if everyone wasn't staring at you. I'll rent a van, and we can load up in the parking garage. No one will be the wiser."

Personally, Jared wasn't so sure. The two men held themselves and moved differently from regular folk. They'd stand out, though maybe not enough to raise too many eyebrows. Time would tell.

They took the lift down to the parking garage, and he watched

Mordechai and Jebediah walk down the line of vehicles, examining them. They'd seen the wrecks of such vehicles before, but these were in pristine condition. Well, okay, they were operable because this wasn't the most affluent section of the city, and there were plenty of dings, dents, and more than a bit of rust.

After about ten minutes, the van arrived. It was on autopilot and parked in a space marked for such, and Elise led the way over and slid open one of the doors. "If everybody will get in and secure their seat belts, we'll be on our way. I took the liberty of finding a place where we could buy clothes for the two of you. On reflection, I think we should do the same for my husband and brother-in-law. Military uniforms may not get a very positive reaction here since you would undoubtedly be associated with the Rebel Empire Fleet rather than our own. This planet just went through some trouble with people from that organization, so it's best not to take chances."

The Terrans were obviously enamored by the fact that the vehicle could move on its own and even lift itself into the air. Also, the fact that Elise could control it so easily had them transfixed.

"How difficult is it to learn to use one of these things?" Jebediah asked. "Is there something like this that will happen on Terra?"

"This is only the beginning," Jared said with a smile. "You can't begin to imagine the number of things that will change with technology. So many things that are difficult and time-consuming will become easier, and even the nature of what someone has to do to make a living will change in time. Some of those changes will be good, but I'm certain that others will be met with uncertainty and maybe even rejection. That's part of what you'll have to navigate as Terra once again becomes a technological world."

When they exited the parking garage and began rising up above the ground level, the city came into sight, and he could see how it was so much like Frankfort yet so different. This city was alive and filled with people going about their business. None of the buildings were wrecked, and there was technology scattered about, being used by people just going about their day.

There was no way that Mordechai and Jebediah would be able to take all this in and understand it. This was simply a chance for them to see what a living city looked like and to imagine what technology could grant them. That would be very ephemeral knowledge because there would be no way to explain how any of this worked until they learned to use the technology themselves.

Yet they needed to be exposed to this. They might never be able to fully understand, but their children and their children's children would—perhaps not as well as those raised here, though, if they were brought to a place like this for an education that would make a world of difference for them.

He had to be honest with himself. Terra would never be brought back to fully being the leader of the Terran Empire without an incredible amount of work and time. It wouldn't be decades before things were better; it would take centuries to repair the damage that had been done and raise the people up to be fully contributing members of society. Even so, they'd never be like the people on the rest of the worlds in the Empire. What had been done to them would linger for many generations. Perhaps forever.

Elise landed in a parking area near a clothier. Jared could read the sign well enough to grasp that it wasn't a high-end location, but it did offer fittings. He supposed that was for the best as the Terrans were rugged and muscular people. Clothing in generic sizes wouldn't fit them correctly.

In fact, going through the fitting process would probably be educational. It would show them how technology changed even the most basic things. They undoubtedly had someone in their society that made clothes by hand, and seeing how alterations were made was something they were familiar with. Now, he'd be able to add technology to the mix with something they at least had some familiarity with.

The six of them trooped inside the building and were met by a salesperson ready to direct them to the various locations in the store, depending on their needs. Elise informed her that they wanted to select men's clothing to fit all four of the men in their party and that she wanted to be certain everything was tailored to fit.

The woman smiled and nodded, giving them a curious look as she led them to the men's section. There were racks of various kinds of clothing, and they let Mordechai and Jebediah look over the various options while the saleswoman considered their strange clothing.

"Are those handmade?" the woman asked somewhat hesitantly.

"They are," Jared said. "We just arrived on planet, and they are from a world that's more of the frontier than Devon. We didn't have an opportunity to pick up more suitable clothing and were just trying to get everything set up."

"And you're in Fleet? I don't know much about the service, but with all of those insignia, you must be somewhat high-ranking. Maybe I should go get my manager so she can be certain everything is to your liking."

"That's okay," Jared said with a smile. "I'm certain that everything will be just fine with your help. My associates and I would just like something that's relatively casual and automatically tailored for our sizes. Once our friends make their selections, then they'll go through the same process, and that'll be fine. No need for any fuss."

She showed them a couple of options. He quickly selected one that he approved of, and Talbot did the same. She showed them back to a scanning chamber, and he stripped off once inside and let the machine measure him. That done, he waited and was rewarded by his clothes being delivered about five minutes later. He dressed quickly and used a bag that had been provided to hold his uniform.

Everything fit perfectly, even the shoes. Satisfied, he headed out and met up with Talbot on the way out to where the others were waiting. Mordechai and Jebediah seemed impressed.

"The clothing looks good for having been fitted in such a short period of time," Jebediah said. "It usually takes us quite a bit of effort to get ones that can be utilized in hard labor that won't rip a seam. Even the experts that we have occasionally get things wrong. To have you pick up clothes and be dressed in mere minutes is astonishing."

"You only think it's astonishing now. Wait until you see the process you go through to get it. Have you selected the style of clothing and shoes you want?"

"With the lady's assistance, we have," Mordechai said. "We know what they should look like, but what happens next?"

"The woman that brought us here will take you back to a chamber where you will close the door, strip off your clothing, stand on the marks on the floor, and let a machine scan you. It will have you perform a few actions—like squatting and raising your arms—to get the full range of motion for you, and then it will tell you to wait. It should only take about five minutes for your clothing to be delivered. You can dress and put your original clothing in the bag that's provided. We'll be waiting here for you."

In less than ten minutes, their associates were back and dressed in clothing in the styles that had been suggested for them. They looked just like anyone Jared would've expected to see out on the street, with the exception that they were both rugged and muscular.

The two seemed completely stunned. He imagined the idea of selecting a specific style and having a machine do all the work of tailoring them in mere minutes was something amazing to them. Not only that, everything had been done so precisely that it was right the first time, better than a master tailor could do. Or at least, that's what Jared assumed. He had no experience with *real* tailors. They might surprise him.

"To see such a mundane task done so quickly and so precisely is a marvel," Mordechai said. "If this is how even a common task such as creating clothes is done, I can only imagine how many other things are different on this world."

"You haven't seen anything yet," Elise said with a grin. "Let's go to the center of the city and see what a bustling metropolis looks like."

She paid for their clothing, and in a few minutes, they were back in their vehicle and flying toward the tall towers at the center of the city. That wasn't to say that the rest of the city was low to the ground, only that the center of the city went hundreds of stories into the air.

The buildings here were significantly taller than even those that rose the highest in Frankfort. All the air cars circling around and even the ships lifting off from the spaceport lent everything an air of technological prowess.

Elise found a place to park, and they spent the next four hours wandering from location to location, seeing how people lived their lives in a modern world. She demonstrated how she could use her implants to communicate with the stores that they passed and find out information about them and even to consult the databases available to the public and get information on interesting places they could go. Every step of the way, she explained what she was doing and how her implants were assisting her.

When they were done, they returned to the apartment and sent the van on its way. Elise took them back through her portal and into the strange world in the alien landscape before moving to her quarters aboard *Audacious*.

From there, they spent another two hours taking a tour of the carrier and showing the men how the implants could be used to work the ship. They also made sure that they got a very good idea of how large and powerful the warship was and took pains to explain how, one day, Terra would once again have vessels like these at her disposal.

By the time they were done—even though the two still had very little understanding of the capabilities of the implants—Mordechai made the decision that he would allow volunteers to go through the process. He asked Jebediah if he would be the first, and while Jared would certainly not call that volunteering, the big man agreed.

They stopped by the medical center and had the physician on duty run through the specifics of what was involved. Jebediah and Mordechai listened closely and asked numerous questions. Once they were satisfied, Jebediah agreed to have the procedure done, and the doctor escorted him away with the explanation that he would be done in a couple of hours.

As they sat to eat an evening meal, Mordechai looked uncertain. "I'm not sure I'm making the right decision. What if I am opening the door for something to crush our people?"

"I can't tell you that's impossible, but I can say for sure that it's extremely unlikely," Kelsey said. "At the very least, you'll give your people a better life, and if trouble does come calling, you'll be better positioned to handle it."

"That's really all anyone can do," Jared said. "Once Jebediah has his implants, we can spend part of the morning showing the two of you how Imperial weapons work and how his implants will make the use of them easier and more effective. Then, we can take the two of you along to watch us liberate the Imperial Palace. You won't be doing any fighting, but it's time we evicted the current residents and took possession of it for ourselves. It was the seat of Imperial power, and that makes it important to us."

"That and the fact that the people there were jerks," Kelsey said with a scowl. "They deserve what's about to happen to them."

Jared didn't disagree. Those people had been cruel and deserved some of what was going to happen. He wouldn't see them thrown out with nothing to eat and no cover, but they'd be evicted from the Imperial Palace, and he'd use the marines aboard *Audacious* to do that. With them in armor, there wouldn't be much danger to his people.

That was the true lesson he wanted to teach Mordechai. With Imperial tech and assistance, they could liberate and control all of Terra in a much shorter time frame than anyone would expect. It wouldn't turn the world into a homogenous society, but that wouldn't happen easily or quickly in any case.

People would have to accept that Imperial authority existed and that when a representative of the Empire said to do something, they'd better do it. Beyond that, they'd have to live their lives, and the ones who were worthy would get assistance.

The ones that weren't worthy would find themselves disarmed. It wasn't the way he'd have preferred, but Terra was his responsibility too. He wouldn't shirk doing what needed to be done.

Talbot didn't know it yet, but he'd be the one assigned to oversee everything on Terra. He'd be responsible for coming up with the procedures and plans they needed to accomplish their goals. As long as they could turn the area around the Imperial Palace and Frankfort into safe zones, that would give them bases of operation to rebuild civilization there.

And while his brother-in-law did that, Jared needed to see about securing the rest of the Rebel Empire and kicking the Clans to the curb. Honestly, he had the more difficult job, and he wasn't looking forward to figuring out exactly how he could make it work. Yet one way or the other, he'd free the old Terran Empire, no matter what it took.

6

Elise spent most of the morning with her husband and then took Mordechai and Jebediah back to Terra. Talbot would see about getting them down to the surface after he'd had an opportunity to work with Jebediah and help the man begin the process of integrating his implants.

The big man tried to keep his emotions in check, but she could tell that he was awed by the access to the equipment the implants gave him. She suspected they secretly delighted him, and if things worked out the way she expected, he'd become their biggest cheerleader when it came to convincing others to get them as well.

Talbot would have that well in hand, she was sure. The overall plan was to see that a temporary fusion plant was installed in the city while one of the primaries was being refurbished and then begin bringing in other equipment that would help to remove debris.

Personally, she expected that the buildings would have to be torn down completely. There was just no way after all this time that they would be savable. It was a pity, but it might be best to begin construction of a brand-new city directly next to Frankfort. The old city could be scavenged for materials and eventually completely razed. On reflection, that made more sense.

Once they were gone, she took Kelsey and Jared to the Home system. It was time for him to meet Coordinator Gatewood and the rest of the resistance's leadership. There would undoubtedly be diplomacy, but Jared needed to establish himself as the senior military commander inside the Rebel Empire.

The resistance had insisted they wouldn't recognize the New Terran Empire's sovereignty unless they convinced five systems to join them willingly. Thus far, they'd managed to convince one and isolate another. They had some diplomatic feelers out to a couple of other systems, and she believed they could convince them. Eventually.

The place that she had a connection to inside the Home system was her quarters aboard their primary station. She was convinced that the locals weren't happy that she could just appear there with no warning. Still, other than the bedroom and bathroom, she allowed them to install monitoring devices to give them a warning when she appeared. By this point, they had to be relatively certain she wouldn't bring an invasion force in, but she understood their concern.

Just to be certain that she did have some unmonitored locations to come through, she'd opened portals in a couple of out-of-the-way locations before they'd been aware that she could do so. She didn't intend to ever bring an invasion force onto their station, but getting in and out without being noted was one of the biggest benefits of this new power of hers, and she didn't intend to waste it.

They arrived in her living room, and she took a few minutes to make certain everyone had an opportunity to visit the bathroom and take care of their business. That also gave their hosts an opportunity to prepare to receive them.

When she opened the front door to her apartment, there was someone waiting for them. She didn't know the man, but he looked like an aide of some kind.

He bowed slightly. "Princess Elise, Princess Kelsey. While I don't know you, sir, I'll assume from your uniform that you are Admiral

Mertz. Welcome. Coordinator Gatewood has asked me to escort you to her office."

Elise smiled at the man and gestured for him to lead the way. After traveling through several corridors and down a lift, he delivered them to the coordinator's office, and they were shown directly inside.

Coordinator Gatewood rose from behind her desk with a smile. "Your Highnesses, welcome back. And you must be Admiral Mertz. Welcome to the Home system. I'm Coordinator Sara Gatewood. Please, call me Sara."

"It's a pleasure to finally meet you, Sara," Jared said. "Call me Jared. I've heard a lot about you. I'm sorry to be visiting under these circumstances, but we've got unpleasant business to discuss."

If his words caused her any stress, it didn't show as she gestured toward the seating area off to the side of her desk. "If you'll have a seat, I'll have one of my people bring refreshments. Tea or coffee?"

"I'll take coffee," he said.

Everyone else gave their preferences and took their seats. She took a moment at her desk and passed on the orders before joining them.

Once she'd settled into her seat, she focused her attention on Jared. "I assume this is about the attack on Justine. As I've told Their Highnesses, the resistance repudiates the actions of those people in the *strongest* of terms. What they did was criminal and morally repugnant. They've earned whatever punishment you choose to inflict on them."

Jared leaned forward, his expression serious. "The New Terran Empire has very strong opinions about what needs to happen to those that harm our ambassadors and diplomatic staff. Let me be frank. They've earned the death sentence, and I want to know exactly how much grief that will cause us. Your people and mine need to continue working together, and this is a delicate situation where I want to see them punished to the fullest extent, but if that's going to be problematic with the resistance, then I'm willing to at least consider alternatives."

"I've had an opportunity to discuss what happened with the

senior leadership, and we're in complete agreement that they've earned whatever happens to them, including death. Their actions were horrific and put the entire resistance in danger because of their lust for power. I won't shed one tear over their passing, and neither will anyone else. I will ask that if you put them to death, that it be done in a manner that is humane."

"I'm not the kind of person that believes in tormenting anyone, so their ends will be as quick and painless as possible. I intend to sit in judgment on them today, and this will be a rather short trial as I believe none of the facts are in dispute. That being the case, they'll be taken from their hearing and immediately executed."

Sara looked over at Kelsey. "Will you be carrying out the sentence?"

"You're damned right I will," Kelsey growled. "After what they did to my mother, I don't have the slightest bit of guilt in doing so, either. I've killed plenty of people in combat, and this won't cause me worse nightmares than that."

"I can't imagine how you could live with that," Sara said with a shake of her head. "If it was me, I'd be having nightmares every single night. I don't know that I could live with myself, having been through some of the violence you've experienced. That said, I'll observe the execution because that's what a leader does."

The door opened after a knock, and one of Sara's aides brought coffee and tea for everyone. It was quickly served, and the young woman departed.

Sara turned to Jared. "With that bit of nasty business out of the way, there are other things we should probably talk about. First of all, in addition to the Devon system, we received word yesterday that the Carthage system has accepted the New Terran Empire's authority. With Ritali subjugated because they proved to be too warlike, I'd say that has put your people well on the way to achieving your goal of five systems brought into your sphere of influence."

"I wouldn't exactly say that Ritali is subjugated," Kelsey said. "We control everything in space, but we can't force them to give up the planet. The best we can do is start working on forming a resistance to the leadership and supplying them with weapons. No matter how that plays out, it won't be quick."

Sara nodded. "Nevertheless, it's one problem removed from the board. You control their orbital assets, and that means a great deal of their manufacturing capability is now out of their control. Keeping them in isolation will certainly keep them from expanding their territorial grip, and funding and outfitting a resistance is something we have experience with. We'll take care of that angle and see what happens. What I'm curious about is what you'll do next."

Jared smiled. "I believe I'll bring a fleet here to begin operations against the Clans and securing systems. And by here, I mean the Devon system. Nobody will intrude on the Home system. This your territory, and I respect that."

"I was given to understand that your fleet sustained significant damage and lost a lot of people. Do you mind if I ask what that actually means?"

Elise watched as her husband grimaced. "We came on this mission with almost a hundred warships. Two-thirds of those were crippled beyond usefulness or destroyed outright. We lost about the same percentage of personnel. Even so, now that we've taken the Master AI out of the equation, we have control of its robotic forces. While it will take as much as six months to gather all the vessels that respond to the call, we have a significant amount of ships that we captured at Alpha Centauri, and a good chunk of those will be heading out to join us here today."

Sara nodded. "And how many ships are we talking about? Don Sommerville gave me an idea of what might be in the area, and even though I've seen how powerful your carrier is with my own eyes, it would be a stretch to imagine that by itself, it would be enough to make a difference."

Jared grinned. "The first group of ships that we're bringing will number about a hundred. Ten of them will be superdreadnoughts, and the remainder will be battlecruisers. I'd prefer to have some destroyers and cruisers to guard our flanks, but I sent all the destroyers out to summon the other warships. Until they return, we'll make do."

Based on Sara's facial expression, Elise was pretty sure that the other woman was having difficulty imagining that much firepower. Considering that most of the Rebel Empire systems had control of a handful of destroyers and perhaps a cruiser or two, that kind of fleet could crush any resistance. The Clans were better armed, but no single battle fleet would overpower Jared's. Even so, Elise still didn't think that the coordinator realized the numbers they were talking about.

"Jared, Marcus was telling me about how you are summoning the other ships scattered throughout the Rebel Empire," Elise said. "Do you mind if I give the Coordinator some raw numbers?"

"Go ahead."

She turned to face Sara. "The Rebel Empire is a big place, so it will take about six months for the most distant units to get back to Terra. The closer ones will respond much more promptly. Marcus indicated that there are more than 60,000 hidden bases that contain stations with warships. He estimates there are 3,000 superdreadnoughts, 22,000 battlecruisers, 55,000 cruisers, and 170,000 destroyers that will answer the call. That is a quarter of a million warships. Ten percent of that force will arrive at Terra within two weeks. Thirty percent will arrive within six weeks."

Now Sara looked flabbergasted. Elise understood her reaction. That was an absolutely ludicrous amount of firepower.

"I… see," the subdued woman said. "And how do you intend to control that many ships?"

"Any of the AIs we've freed from their bondage will have the capability to manage them," Jared said. "Marcus is aboard my flagship, and he'll be controlling the ships we're bringing. Fiona will be here as well and can control a number of them. When we liberate a system and take control of the AI hardware, we can create more AIs that should be willing to give us a hand. The one in Devon can operate the Fleet base we'll be establishing there. The other two systems that we've established control over will provide hardware for two more, and using Elise's talents, we can send them back to Terra and put them aboard superdreadnoughts. Then those can control smaller fleets to perform operations as well. The more systems we free, the more flexibility we'll have."

"I can't imagine how anyone can stand up to that kind of firepower," Sara admitted. "Even if all the smaller vessels that are scattered throughout human-occupied space tried to fight that, they couldn't. It's mind-boggling."

"The people of the Rebel Empire don't have anything to fear from us," Jared assured her. "All we want to do is reestablish human control over human space. We have to fight the Clans, but we don't want to exterminate them either. Sadly, I suspect we'll have to kill a significant number of them."

Kelsey sighed. "That will be a challenge. I don't think I've ever run into a more xenophobic people. How former members of Fleet could turn into something like that, I can't imagine. They'll fight tooth and nail against us because we have the AIs on our side, and I'd imagine they'll fight to the death."

"We'll figure something out," Jared said. "One way or another, we have to get our own space under control, or the Singularity will slide through the back door and try to crush us. That's what they've been doing since they were ejected from the Empire so long ago. They are the real enemy here."

That left everyone quiet for just a little bit. Then Elise raised her glass of tea. "To the Terran Empire. May she crush her foes."

Everyone else joined in the toast.

"I think at this point that I have to admit defeat," Sara said. "There is absolutely no way that you'll fail to bring five systems under your control. The resistance will acknowledge the sovereignty of the New Terran Empire. I have no idea how things will work going forward, but it's time that we admitted that we don't have what's necessary to bring all of human space back under peaceful control by ourselves."

Kelsey leaned forward. "Don't think that you won't have an important part to play. Trust me when I say that the New Terran Empire needs every good, competent person to step up and do their part. Most system coordinators will have worlds full of people to rule over in the name of the Empire. You don't actually have that here, but I've got an idea about that if you're willing to listen."

Sara raised an eyebrow. "You've got my attention."

"Now that Terra is liberated, we'll be helping a friendly group of people in one of the cities there to begin bringing the planet under control. It'll be hard work as they don't have a technological base because they've been living in the ruins of a dead city for five centuries. How would you like to be the Coordinator of Terra? It's not much to look at, at the moment, but it will be the capital of the New Terran Empire at some point in the not-so-distant future. Let's just say that you've got a lot of room to grow."

Sara blinked. "That sounds like an extremely difficult job, and while I have nothing against hard work, shouldn't I be helping you in the areas of space we can access near the Home system?"

"You'd be doing that as well," Jared said. "I see what Kelsey is aiming for, and once this war is settled and Terra becomes strong again, you and your people will have a very powerful voice in the governing of the Empire. Admittedly, it will take time, but with the advanced medical nanites that we have access to, there's no reason that you couldn't still be there in a century or two."

"You've given me a lot to think about, so I won't give you an answer right now. I'll talk with the resistance leadership and see what they have to say. There is something attractive in the idea of being able to shape a world as it's brought back to life, but I'd imagine there are a lot of warlike people there who won't want anything to do with us. That will be a challenge."

"Just let me know what you decide, and if that doesn't work for you, we'll come up with something else," Jared said. "Meanwhile, if you could point us to a place where we could get lunch, I'm starving."

"Hey," Kelsey objected with a glower. "That's my line."

Everyone laughed, and they rose when Sara did. Whatever restaurant she had in mind would be delicious, Elise was sure.

It would take Sara a while to come around, but she suspected the allure of being in control of Terra would seduce her and the resistance. Things wouldn't be easy, but they wouldn't be impossible either.

Now, all they had to do was stop the Clans from rampaging throughout human space and make sure that they didn't open a gateway for the Singularity.

No pressure.

7

Kelsey decided the next morning that she'd eat breakfast with Talbot in the same restaurant where they'd met Mordechai and Jebediah. It was more like a picnic because they had to bring their own food, but the view was unparalleled. This time, there wasn't anyone else in the grand room, and it felt like they had the entire universe to themselves.

Being able to visit her husband from many systems away was an amazing thing, and she was grateful to Elise for indulging her. She wondered if the woman knew exactly how busy she'd eventually be, taking people from one place to another. For someone who was a crown princess of an entire world, this was an extremely pedestrian undertaking.

Unfortunately, they wouldn't be able to have anyone else do the same sort of thing unless they found more technology like what Elise had chanced upon. That would require searching that strange universe, looking for people, and finding out more about them. That was also something that they couldn't do on their own.

Well, that was a problem for another day. For now, she had other things to focus on: first, her husband; second, the trial of the people who had tortured her mother. Jared would handle that today.

She wanted to see the people who had done this pay the full price, and she would cheerfully do her part, but that might not be what Jared had in mind. He'd been quiet about the affair as he reviewed everything, so she wouldn't make any assumptions about his intentions. Whatever he did, she'd support it.

"You look like you're a million kilometers away," Talbot said with a smile. "What's on your mind?"

"A lot of things," she said with a sigh. "The trial, operations here on Terra, dealing with the Clans, figuring out what the Singularity is up to, and even how much work we're putting on Elise's shoulders. There's so much up in the air right now that it feels like we don't really have control over anything. And I'm still dealing with everyone we lost taking down the master AI. Oh, and I'm pregnant. That's never far from my thoughts either."

He gripped her hand. "I suppose things feel like they're overwhelming, but they don't have to pile up on top of one another. Some of the problems will solve themselves. Elise will figure out what's best for Elise, and you're not going to be pregnant forever. Soon enough, we'll have a little girl to dote on."

She laughed. "I've heard my mother tell stories about how little sleep she got after Ethan and I were born. If you think the first couple of years of dealing with a small child will be straightforward bliss, you're in for a very rude awakening. And I mean that in the most literal sense."

"I suppose that's true," he said with a chuckle, "but there's a secret weapon we can bring to bear. It's called a nanny. We're both busy people, and while I want to spend as much time as possible with our daughter once she's born, some of the more difficult aspects of this can be taken care of by other people. You don't have to be woken up at three in the morning to deal with a screaming child. This is manageable."

Kelsey frowned. "I'm not sure how much contact I want to give up. At what point does our little girl bond more with someone else other than ourselves? Being a parent is hard, but it can be the most rewarding thing we do in our lives. Having help is one thing, but farming out the care of our daughter isn't something I want to do."

"Being a parent is worthwhile," he agreed, "but so is freeing all of human space. I don't want to make it seem like I'm dismissing being a parent, but we've got a lot of really important things on our plates. We'll have to find a balance, and that means someone will have to help us. Probably a lot of someones. Whatever it takes, we'll do what we need to do, and we'll spoil our little girl rotten."

"No, we won't!" she said with a shake of her head. "Have you seen some of the entitled children that other people have? There will be an appropriate amount of spoiling, but we'll do whatever it takes to make sure she grows up to be a decent human being and not some pampered little princess. Believe me, I know what that feels like, and it's something I'd like to avoid for our child."

She took a bite of the breakfast burrito she'd been eating on and then a sip of her cooling coffee. She gestured out toward the world of humanity's birth. "How are things going down there? Are you making any progress with Mordechai and Jebediah?"

"Surprisingly, I am. Jebediah is very cautious about the implants, but he's learning how to use them and sharing how they work with his father. The two of them are coming up with a lot of ideas about how they could make their lives easier down below, and Mordechai is very impressed with modern weapons and how the implants interface with them. He said that might make liberating Terra a lot easier. They'll still be shy on bodies, but superior firepower and technology carry a lot of weight."

"It'll take a lot of time for them to get used to what the capabilities are, particularly since they're not a high-technology society," she agreed with a nod. "Even so, it'll make a huge difference in their ability to rebuild Terra. What are the plans for the Imperial Palace?"

"I've sent some scouts to check it from the outside, and it looks pretty much the same. I'd imagine they're still on high alert after our escape with their supposed god."

She nodded her agreement. Even though it had been months since they'd broken out with Major Jake Peters—the Marine Raider that had been both these people's prisoner and their god—that still likely had them stirred up. They were a cult, after all.

They retained some of the use of high technology, and the Imperial Palace still had power. That would make them a tough nut to crack, but she had no doubt that Talbot could manage. He was a Marine Raider, and now, he had all his hardware back online. While he might not be invulnerable in powered armor, he'd definitely be a lot more than they could handle. Backed up by other Marine Raiders from *Persephone* and Marines from *Audacious*, they could take out any resistance.

The goal would be to liberate everything without killing everyone resisting them. They just wanted to turn these people out and regain control over her family's ancestral home. If they chose to fight to the death, that was on them. She wanted them to have every opportunity to either surrender or flee. She didn't care which.

And if they decided to fight to the death, she wouldn't lose sleep over their fate. They'd kept Jake Peters imprisoned for five centuries. He'd been a Marine Raider before the fall of the Terran Empire. During the fighting on Terra, he lost both legs and an arm. He'd also suffered other injuries, but that was more than enough to give these people's ancestors an opportunity to make him into a pampered figurehead, though she wasn't sure exactly how pampered he'd felt.

She couldn't imagine living with the pain he'd been suffering under for five hundred years. While his existence drove home how long she and Talbot had to live together and raise a family—potentially a *very* large one—it was what the other man had been put through that stuck with her.

Even so, he'd stood back up using artificial limbs once they'd rescued him, and he'd participated in the attack on the master AI. When all seemed lost, he'd sacrificed himself to give them the chance they needed to achieve victory.

Kelsey would miss not having someone who knew everything about being a Marine Raider, but he'd done his duty—and far more—and would never be forgotten. Only now, they needed to liberate the place that had been his prison and turn his jailers out or kill them. That was what she needed to keep in mind.

"Since we got out through the tunnel used for small craft, I suppose we might get back in that way," she ventured.

He nodded. "That's one of the things we're looking at, but I wouldn't be surprised if they had someone watching it, and they'll be heavily armed. We've got the floor plans and can utilize them to find other points for ingress. With much of the technology either degraded or offline, there will be somewhere we can slip inside. Once we get in, that's when the fun starts."

"So you'll outfit Jebediah with unpowered armor and make sure he's well protected? I assume you don't intend to have him do any of the fighting."

Talbot shook his head. "Absolutely not. These people have modern weaponry—at least in limited quantities—and we want to make sure that he stays safe. What I want him to see is what it looks like when a technological society brings the hammer down on someone who isn't prepared for it. The people inside the Imperial Palace are more advanced than anyone else on Terra. If he can see us beat them like a drum, taking out those who are further down the food chain will be a lot easier for him and his people, so long as we provide a few military advisors."

"Just be careful. I've lost more people than I care to think about, and I'd like to see you come back in one piece. People like us don't need to lead from the front anymore."

He raised an eyebrow. "Who are you, and what have you done with my wife?"

That made her laugh. "I'm trying to be responsible here. Yes, I've taken a *lot* of crazy risks over the years. Now isn't the time to keep pushing. We'll free the Imperial Palace whether you're in the front or the back. Play the teacher rather than the warrior this time around. If I have to be good, so do you."

"I promise to be good," he said, raising his hands in surrender. "With a squad of Marine Raiders in powered armor, backed up by as many marines in powered armor as we need, this won't be a fight that's in doubt. If they have any weapons capable of piercing our protection, they won't have many of them. We'll strike at night and keep them off-balance. Anyone that shoots get shot though we'll use stunners where possible."

He took a deep drink of his coffee. "What will you do about the trial?"

"I'll attend and see that those people get what they've got coming. An example needs to be made of anyone who crosses the New Terran Empire. We'll take a lot, but if someone messes with our ambassadors and diplomatic staff, people need to know exactly what they have coming. Besides, these bastards deserve payback for what they did to my mother, and that makes it personal."

He squeezed her hand again. "And that's what I worry about. Whatever happens needs to be an impersonal projection of justice, not revenge. That's not the message we need to send to the Rebel Empire. If they see you carrying out bloody payback against someone who wronged your mother, that's the wrong message."

Kelsey ground her teeth but nodded. "I can see that, but it doesn't reduce my need to smash them. I promise that I'll be good. Whatever Jared tells me to do, I'll do. Whatever the sentence he lays out, I won't argue about it. At least not in public."

"Sometimes you need to be the avenging goddess of death, but not this time. We both know it. Jared will make them pay."

That brought the emotional temperature in the room down a fair bit, and now it felt depressing. She ate the rest of her food in silence as she brooded about what he'd said. She would be good, but oh my God, how she wanted to just grab a plasma rifle and incinerate that smirking bitch who'd tortured her mother. Or she could take her swords and chop her into little bitty pieces. Then there was the flechette rifle that she could use to punch so many holes through the woman that she'd look like bloody cheese.

Yeah, she probably didn't need to do that.

Talbot was right. This wasn't the time for revenge. The Rebel Empire needed to see what justice looked like and what the character of her people was. She'd behave, no matter how much it hurt her soul.

When they were done, she packed everything away and pulled

Talbot into a tight hug. "I won't make a scene, and I promise not to kill anyone that doesn't *really* deserve it."

He laughed. "That's the Kelsey I know and love. I'm headed down to the surface shortly, so I probably won't see you until all that is over with. By the time you get back, we'll have liberated the Imperial Palace, and you can once again lay claim to it. It's only a symbolic gesture at this point, but even those kinds of things have real meaning. I'd suggest considering how you'll use it to your advantage."

She frowned slightly. "I'm not sure what you mean."

"Once we have the Imperial Palace back in our possession, you could record something from the throne room. You are, in fact, the Crown Princess of the New Terran Empire. The right speech transmitted from there could change public opinion. That would be a lot better than sending troops down to the surface of places like Ritali and trying to free it by force."

"That's a good point, and I'll come up with something. How do you think Mordechai and Jebediah will react when they find out that Sara Gatewood will be the coordinator for Terra if she agrees?"

"That's a complication I didn't expect, but I suppose it's inevitable. There has to be an interface to the Empire that's fully conversant with modern technology. That's not Mordechai or Jebediah. On the other side of the equation, Coordinator Gatewood won't be doing any fighting down on the surface, so there will have to be a way for both sides to get some skin in the game and come to an agreement."

"The amount of rebuilding that's needed here is staggering," Kelsey said. "I'd imagine that many worlds will be more than willing to contribute people and equipment, but there will have to be someone with knowledge on the ground to make sure that the more violent groups don't do anything to disrupt things too much. It might be best if Mordechai and Sara get an opportunity to talk and see if they can come to an accommodation. They both want the same thing, but if there's going to be a power struggle, we have to figure out how best to make sure no one walks away dissatisfied."

"That smells like a diplomatic matter. That might be perfect for your mother. She needs to get her mind on something else, and she *is* our ambassador."

"That's a great idea. I'll talk to her about it once the trial is over. Now, we should both be on our way. We've got a lot to do."

She wasn't looking forward to having to sit still through this trial and accept whatever the final outcome was without raising an objection, but she'd be there for her mother. Sara Gatewood had told her that the resistance wouldn't tolerate this kind of behavior and that they would abide by the punishment the New Terran Empire called for.

Jared was her brother, and she had to count on him to do what was right. The day would be painful, but it couldn't be avoided. It was time to settle the matter once and for all.

8

Talbot walked down the ramp as soon as his pinnace landed outside Frankfort. Unlike last time, he was in Marine Raider powered armor though he had his helmet in the crook of his left arm.

Mordechai and Jebediah were waiting along with a number of others, observing as his pinnace disgorged a squad of marines. Unlike last time, there were a dozen pinnaces also packed to the gills with armed combatants in powered armor.

"Your people look quite dangerous," Mordechai said. "I suspect that none of my people's weapons would have harmed you inside this, and a single one of you could have routed us."

"You might not have been able to hurt anyone in powered armor, but a single person can't rout an army," Talbot said with a smile. "Not really. Insufficient numbers though they'd have a tremendous effect. Are you ready, Jebediah?"

The big man grinned. "Do I get to wear one of these?"

Talbot shook his head. "I'm afraid not. It takes a lot of training to be able to move effectively in this kind of gear, so we brought you some unpowered armor. It's not nearly as effective, but you won't be in the front anyway. That's what those brutes are for."

His last comment was accompanied by a gesture toward the marines in heavy powered armor that bulged even more than his own Marine Raider gear.

"They will be our guardians during this operation," he continued. "My wife has indicated that I'm not allowed to engage, so I'll be making sure you understand everything we're doing while we monitor the fight remotely. This shouldn't be too difficult because even though the people down in this facility have modern weapons, they're not trained in how to use them, and there's no indication that they have any armor whatsoever."

"If they have modern weapons, then why will they be ineffective?" Mordechai asked. "Shouldn't they be designed to fight people in armor like this?"

"Not really. What they likely have is designed to fight people in unpowered armor like what Jebediah will be wearing. Also, without having any experience fighting armored troops, they'll be at a significant disadvantage, and we won't give them time to adjust to what we're doing. This will be a lightning raid where we go in and smash all resistance before they can get their act together."

"Will our people be able to use this heavier armor at some point?"

"With proper training, yes. In the beginning, though, I think you'll find that it's a lot easier to use unpowered armor and handheld weaponry. Other than the people inside the Imperial Palace, no one else will be using weapons that have much of a chance of harming somebody who's protected. There will always be the occasional fluke chance that an arrow goes somewhere it shouldn't, but them's the breaks when you're fighting a war."

Two marines that weren't in armor came down with a set of gear for Jebediah. They'd taken his measurements when he was aboard the station, and everything would fit with some minor adjustments. It took only fifteen minutes to get him fully outfitted and get everything but the helmet locked in place.

The big man moved around and squatted. "This is a lot less restrictive than I expected. And it will protect against arrows and even primitive firearms?"

"It won't protect you against a cannon, so don't be wherever the cannonball lands, but it will be a lot better than anything else being used on Terra. While we're attacking the Imperial Palace, some of our other folks will be fitting volunteers with unpowered armor and starting their training on how to use stunners and flechette weapons, both pistols and rifles. You'll be back in time to play a role in that, but I wanted to be sure that we started by keeping up our end of the bargain."

"And our first target will be the horde?" Jebediah asked.

"I'm not sure. We'll give you all the intelligence we can about who is in the area and what they're doing. Once you have that, figuring out what you need to do—either bringing these people under control or driving them away—will be up to you. I'd prefer that we do everything possible to do this peacefully, but I understand that isn't always possible. The horde is a great example. I don't envision them surrendering."

"Neither do I," Mordechai said. "With their horses, they're very mobile. How will we pin them down and fight?"

"I think we have a surprise that you'll like. Something that will make them the ones unable to maneuver effectively while you're running circles around them. I'll save that for once we're done with the Imperial Palace."

The older man nodded. "I look forward to seeing what you have in store for us. As for the people inside the Imperial Palace, what are your plans for them? Do you anticipate that they will surrender?"

Talbot pursed his lips and shook his head. "No. They've turned the fact that they had a man who could live five hundred years into both a religion and a club to wield over their people. The leadership certainly won't give up.

"And the rest?"

"We'll probably have to burn them out. The people who resist will get themselves killed. The ones who aren't armed will be taken into custody and moved elsewhere. Somewhere they can try to rebuild their lives in a way that doesn't involve a theocracy."

"Then I wish you good luck, Talbot. I look forward to hearing how everything works out, Jebediah. If the circumstances turn so that you must fight, fight hard, my son."

The big man gripped his father's shoulder. "You know I will. Come, Talbot. Let's go see how well your crabs fight."

Talbot laughed. "We kind of do look like crabs, don't we? Let's go."

They went into the pinnace, and Talbot strapped the big man down in the seat next to his. Once he had done so, he attached his own helmet to the seat between his legs and strapped himself in. The rest of the marines did the same, and the pinnace was soon in the air.

"Here's where I get to show you some of the joys of modern technology," Talbot said. Then he shared the map they had of the Imperial Palace via his implants. "You should have just received an incoming communication request from me. Accept it and open the file."

The bigger man's eyes were unfocused, and he blinked. "This is… very unusual. I'm uncertain that I'll ever get used to it. The map is so detailed. How did you do that?"

"Kelsey had access to the map ahead of time. If we hadn't had our implants disabled in that EMP, we'd have been able to use it. This time around, we'll be able to leverage that knowledge to get into the facility and work our way around some of the fighting. If we can get into position in some of the better spots before the enemy knows we're there, this fight will be over pretty quickly."

"While I may not know much about your means of fighting, I think that sounds optimistic. You can't count on the enemy doing what you want, and anytime you assume you'll successfully infiltrate an area that you must get into, something will come up to spoil those plans."

"True enough. If that happens, we'll just bull our way through. Now, let me point out some areas of interest on the map. The first stage of the operation will be infiltration. When we escaped the last time, we went out through a set of hangars and a tunnel. Even though it's been a bit of time, I anticipate they'll still be watching them closely. There are a number of other potential ingress points, and we'll send scouts to see if those will work better."

He highlighted a couple of spots on the map. "Each of these particular points was made for the security forces that guarded the emperor and the Imperial Palace. They're not locations that would be easily accessible to those who didn't have the appropriate codes, and it's entirely possible that the people holding this facility are unaware that they even exist. We'll try to use them and see what happens. If all else fails, we'll blow a hole through the wall somewhere and go pouring in."

Because the facility had power, Talbot had ordered the pinnaces to come in low to the ground and set down far away from the facility itself. During the flight, the sun had already gone down, which would make their ability to slip closer significantly easier, but they'd still circle around and come in from a different direction just in case someone had noted their approach. The attack wouldn't take place until about three in the morning.

While these people had access to modern weapons, they weren't well trained in their use. It was more rote learning than anything else. None of these people had implants, and they didn't understand the security systems that they were relying on for their protection.

If he could guarantee it, he'd love to take every single one of them prisoner using the stunners and relocate them somewhere else, but that was unlikely. As soon as they knew intruders were present, they'd fight to defend their homes. He understood that, and to a degree, he sympathized. If they hadn't been total asses to Jake Peters, his sympathy would be a lot stronger. What they'd done to the man was inexcusable, and they were about to pay the price for it.

Moving on the ground was fast for the armored Marines. It was slower for him as he had to shepherd Jebadiah. Even so, he was able to keep pace well enough for them to settle into a hiding place. There were roving patrols keeping an eye out for trouble, so he let his people rest.

When they woke him before the attack, he took care of business and got a hot meal down. He made sure everyone else did too. Then they set out on the assault.

When they got close to the facility, the scouts led the way in and quickly spotted a number of people scattered throughout the facility, watching for trouble on the surface, but they didn't have access to night vision gear, and his people were invisible in the darkness as the moon had set a few hours ago. The scouts he sent in next weren't in powered armor and slithered in through the foliage to the entry point they'd selected for their first try.

"I'll share a video link with you just like I did the file," Talbot said to Jebediah. "It will allow you to watch what our people are doing. We can tap into anyone's armor, but the scout in question has a special camera just for this."

What they were looking at now was a man approaching a door that had been closed for five hundred years. For all Talbot knew, it might not open. It could be without power, and they'd have to look for a different location.

"Being able to see what any of your soldiers can see at such a distance is a great advantage for a leader," Jebediah muttered. "I can think of many times I wanted to know what my people could see so I could make plans. This gives you the ability to see one point along the battlefield."

"Once you're more skilled with it, you'll be able to tap into information from *all* your soldiers. You'll know who's injured and who's not—who's in combat and who is still disengaged. It's a game changer."

The scout finally reached the door and sent the access code through his implants. Nothing happened. "Negative access with the code," the woman said. "I'll see about physically plugging into the system and manually opening the access armored door."

There was an exterior code box, but it had been seriously degraded by the weather, and she simply broke it apart to get to the wiring inside. "No power. We're moving around to another potential access point, and we'll try again."

Getting to the next point took about twenty minutes, and it was just as unsuccessful as the first. Talbot suspected that someone had cut power to the exterior doors, and they'd have to do things the hard way.

"Proceed to Plan B," he ordered.

A fire team of Marine Raiders advanced while the other scouts scattered and began stunning guards that might hear what was coming. Two of the Marine Raiders began working on the door with short swords made of hull metal and their greater strength once the scouts declared the area as clear as it could be.

Talbot knew from personal experience that those swords were virtually indestructible, and even though the door was heavily armored, it could and would be forced. It was just a matter of time.

In this case, breaking through the locks took about ten minutes, and the doors were very hard to lever open, but his people managed it. As soon as they were in, Talbot ordered the rest of the attacking force to move into the area because they'd be using that single entry point to work their way through to some of the areas they wanted to access.

He and Jebediah were not the last ones through, but they were close to the back. A squad of marines would guard the exit to make certain that no one circled around behind them while he focused on monitoring the rest of the attack from this location.

The door they'd forced open led into one of the high-security areas used by the Imperial Guard back in the old days. It was in disarray and was obviously without power. Whether that was intentional or simply a failure of a system that should have kept things running, he didn't know. All that mattered at this point was that they were inside the Imperial Palace, and it was time to get everything taken care of before the enemy learned what they were doing.

With a full map of the facility at their disposal, his people had already planned out where they wanted to be, and now all they needed to do was adjust their plans based on the entry point. Within seconds, fire teams were moving through the Imperial Palace tunnels toward chokepoints that they intended to utilize.

"What do we do now?" Jebediah asked.

"We wait for the fire teams to get into position. Each one of them has a predetermined area of operations, and once they reach them, we'll kick off the general attack. If the enemy catches wind of what we're up to first, that means that some of the groups will have to continue fighting their way through to get to their positions, but that won't change things. It'll just make it harder."

And, of course, that's what happened. Not five minutes later, one of the fire teams ran head-on into a group of guards moving through the interior corridors of the Imperial Palace. There was a very brief and bloody firefight that his people won, but the noise spread the alarm to the general population, and the fight was on.

Talbot ordered the pinnaces to go airborne and provide covering fire outside if needed. Then he made certain he kept a good eye on everything that was happening via his implants and fed as much of the information as he could to Jebediah. The other man was plugged into the command circuit though he didn't know what anything meant, and Talbot showed him how to see the map of where their people were and to zero in on any specific individual to find out what was going on with them.

The occupants of the Imperial Palace swarmed like ants that had had their mounds kicked over. He supposed that made sense. This was the only place of safety they'd ever known, and they'd fight to keep it. Too bad it was important to his people too.

It irritated Talbot that he wouldn't be able to fight, but he'd given Kelsey his word. Besides, training Jebediah on how to use the systems was important. They wanted to convince more of the men inside Frankfort to join their forces. If they were able to use implants, pair up with weapons, and act as a coordinated whole, they'd be unstoppable, at least by the rest of the locals.

It didn't take long to figure out where the senior leadership lived inside the Imperial Palace because it was the most heavily guarded. That was where he sent some of his strongest forces, and they quickly broke their way in and stunned those that they could and obliterated those they could not. The entire facility was under their thumb in under two hours.

Only once he was relatively certain they wouldn't be ambushed did he lead Jebediah to the throne room. That wouldn't be where the vast majority of the enemy were being kept, but it was where he was setting up shop.

There had been heavy fighting here, and there was damage, but it was manageable. His people brought a table in, and he took a seat to go over everything that was happening and to get an eye on the senior prisoners as they were brought in. Many of them were unconscious, but others were wide awake and frothing at the mouth in rage.

That was fine by him. Let them rant and rave.

Even after securing the entirety of the Imperial Palace, Talbot didn't take anything for granted and sent his people through on several more sweeps to verify that they hadn't missed anyone. As usual, that policy proved its worth when they found holdouts both times. That caused him to send his people back through a third time just to be sure.

The end tally was that they had captured about seven hundred people. That was quite a bit more than he'd expected, but he supposed it made sense as many of them were children or elderly. There were a great number of women as well as men who were noncombatants.

They'd talked about whether or not they should hold a trial for the people who had held Jake Peters prisoner for so long and decided against it. Frankly, he wasn't even certain they would understand what they had done wrong. Many of them might not have even known that their supposed god had been a prisoner.

He turned to Jebediah. "The question now is what we do with these people. Without their high-tech weaponry, they're not much of a threat, and I'm caught between a rock and a hard place. If I just put them out in the open, the odds are good that someone will obliterate them or enslave them. Do you have any idea where they might be able to fit in?"

"We can take them back to Frankfort. We've had to take in others and deal with them over the years, and we have processes in place. Just like we told you when we captured you, we will make them part of her own society. If any of them prove to be too resistant to the idea or cause more trouble than they're worth, they will be dealt with. Those who fit in will be welcomed fully in time. They won't be enslaved, but they won't be allowed to leave."

Talbot wasn't sure that was the right decision, but there were very few options available to him. There would be a lot of work taking place in Frankfort, and having extra hands would probably be useful. These people wouldn't be murdered or enslaved by the horde or others like them, and even if they felt ill-used, his sympathy was limited. They'd never been good neighbors to those around them, and payback was certainly a bitch.

"I suppose that works. Is that what you'll do as you expand your area of influence?"

Jebediah shrugged. "I suppose we'll figure that out as we go. This won't be a process that happens immediately."

"It may feel like it will take forever to regain control over what's happening, but things might take place a lot faster than you imagine. Also, I probably should warn you that there will be a need for your father to find some accommodation with whoever is leading these people who are coming in to oversee everything. I trust him fully, but he doesn't have the necessary skills to create a high-technology world, so it will be a cooperative effort between the two groups."

The other man looked at him for a few seconds and then nodded. "I'm sure that my father won't exactly be pleased to hear that, but it makes sense to me. We have enough experience to control the city we have, but we will require assistance to advance. Or someone else will have to take that aspect of leadership, and we will have to find some way to fit into the new organization. What exactly do your people want?"

"I'm not sure that we want anything other than to see Terra back on her feet," Talbot said. "The problem is that it's a very difficult situation to deal with. We've already found someone who will take responsibility for representing Terra at the highest levels, but that doesn't have to be something that excludes your father and yourself. I'll see if I can get her to come meet you and Mordechai, and perhaps the three of you can come up with an arrangement that satisfies you all. If that proves impossible, then we'll have to figure out what's best and move forward to try to keep as many people happy as we can. No matter what happens, Terra will recover, and we'll do our part to make certain that happens expeditiously. No matter what organization you come up with here, Kelsey is in charge in the name of the emperor. She'll make the final decisions."

"She's a strong woman with a good heart," Jebediah said with a nod. "I feel confident that we will find an accommodation that suits everyone even if no one is completely satisfied. With life, you never get everything you want and have to hold tight to the things that are important to you. Don't trouble yourself, Talbot. We are your friends, and we will continue doing what we can to help those who need us."

Talbot grinned. "Good. It's time to make another sweep through the Imperial Palace, and there are a few things I want to show you. We'll have to bring some people in to help begin cleaning up some of this facility and make it ready for the Imperial family to once again call home. That will take a while, but if we're going to have Kelsey talk with you and Coordinator Gatewood, this is the right place to make that happen."

He sent out an order for his people to secure all the weaponry and to make sure the prisoners were as well taken care of as possible so that they could be transported to Frankfort when the time came. The operation had gone more smoothly than he'd had any reason to expect, but now that it was done, he was ready to move on to more important tasks.

It wouldn't be long before they moved against the Clans, and when that happened, he needed to have more marines at his beck and call. Hopefully, they would be able to recruit some of the locals to begin learning what needed to be done. The Empire might not be fully back in their hands, but they were closer than they'd ever been before. Now, they had to hold what they had.

9

Jared looked at himself in the mirror and nodded at how well his dress uniform fit. It had been a while since he'd needed to wear it, and he'd been concerned that he'd put on a little weight. Thankfully, everything seemed good.

He had to look his best today because it was time to oversee judgment on the people who had kidnapped Justine Bandar. People inside the Rebel Empire needed to respect the New Terran Empire, and he would be the stick that made sure they paid attention.

"Are you ready?" Elise asked as she walked into the bedroom. She wore a plain black dress with subdued jewelry to add highlights.

"As ready as one can be with this sort of thing," he said as he turned to face her. "This isn't something I look forward to, but it needs to happen. People like these have to be put on notice, and unfortunately, only stern measures will capture their attention."

His wife raised an eyebrow. "This won't be a long trial if I make my guess right. There's plenty of evidence against them between our own people testifying and statements made by them and their associates."

"I'm still half afraid that the resistance will take what I'm doing the wrong way, and it will cause us problems further down the line."

"Then you're reading the situation completely wrong. The resistance has washed their hands of these people. While I'm not privy to the innermost discussions inside the resistance, just listening to the various people I've run into has made it clear that they're not happy with how things were done, and they want to make certain it *never* happens again."

He pursed his lips and slowly nodded. "That makes sense. Are you ready?"

"Of course." She reached out and took his hand. "I know you don't like doing this kind of thing, but just think of it as a different kind of battle. These people earned everything that's happening to them, and you shouldn't lose one moment's sleep over giving them a just sentence even if it costs them their lives."

"I've killed better people for worse reasons, so I won't," he assured her. "I'd just rather be doing naval things. We need to get things in motion if we intend to fight off the Clans, and I don't like sitting in the Terra system, waiting to get enough ships to fight."

"It's been a week since you summoned all the ships, so you should be getting a steady stream of them right now. Didn't you say that you would have enough to send a task force here in about two weeks?"

"No. I sent a task force in this direction shortly after Kelsey departed. I'm waiting for a battle fleet to gather so I can begin hunting down the Clan task forces. The ships I sent are under autonomous control because there's no controlling AI to direct them. That should be perfectly safe, yet until they arrive and are brought under control, I'll be worried about them. It should only be another day or two, and then we can start spreading out and bringing the systems near Devon under our wing."

"Some of them won't cooperate," she said as she led him toward the front door to their temporary quarters. "Like that system where we've taken the space around it, but the planet won't surrender. Or rather, the dictator running it won't. How are you going to deal with systems like that?"

"We isolate them and come back around to deal with them when we have time. After we've subjugated their Navy, there's nothing they can do off planet. We can put a couple of destroyers in orbit and maintain control of the system while we deal with more pressing issues. Once everything is settled, then we'll figure out what we need to do to pry them out of their holes."

They stepped out into the corridor, and his marine guards fell in around them as they proceeded toward the area set aside for the trial. He didn't expect that anyone would try to assassinate him, but they were on high alert anyway. He didn't blame them.

"The old Terran Empire was huge, and even though the AIs reduced the number of worlds that were occupied significantly, the Rebel Empire still has a great number of systems we have to deal with," Elise said. "Even with as many computer-controlled ships as you have, this will take a while. Do you have any estimate of how long it might take?"

He shook his head. "This is one of those things that takes as long as it takes. We've been working toward this for so long that I'm not going to screw things up by rushing. We'll go step-by-step, and by the time we're finished, we'll be in control. Once that's done, then we'll do what's necessary to incorporate each of the systems into the New Terran Empire. Then I guess its name reverts to just being the Terran Empire. It's a little confusing, but thankfully, I'm not a politician and don't have to worry about it."

"That's relatively naïve, but if it helps you sleep at night, you keep thinking that," she said with a smile. "I'll leave you to what you need to do and join Kelsey. I know I don't need to tell you this, but stay strong. Do whatever needs to be done, and then put it behind you."

He reached out and squeezed her hand. "I will. Once this is over, we'll all go have lunch, and then we'll see about what comes next."

After Elise peeled off, he squared his shoulders and continued to the room where the judges would be gathering. This wasn't just his show, after all. It would be a tribunal with him at the head. Since Fleet officers were a little hard to come by, he'd tagged Zia Anderson and Don Sommerville to round out the trio.

When he walked into the compartment, both of them were

waiting for him. They both rose, but he waved them back down. There was a coffee service nearby, and he poured himself a mug. He'd have to be careful that he didn't spill it on himself, because that would be humiliating.

"Are the two of you ready for this?" he asked.

"I'm not sure I should be serving on this tribunal, sir," Zia said. "I might not have been directly involved in what was happening at Devon with these people, but they had their hands on my girl. I'm not a neutral party."

"And as a former member of the resistance, I'm not exactly neutral either," Sommerville said. "They betrayed all the oaths they ever swore and did something heinous. I have every reason to want to see them taken down."

Jared nodded. "And if you want to use that kind of yardstick, what happened affected my sister. Justine might not be my favorite person in the universe, but I like Kelsey a lot, and I'm not neutral either. Even so, we're the people that have to do this, and we will maintain decorum while being certain that no injustices are committed. I trust that we can do that."

"This sounds like one of those situations where we proclaim that there will be a fair trial after which they will be taken outside and shot," Zia said. "I used to always think that sort of thing was just a joke, but now I get it. The trial will be fair, and they'll be afforded every courtesy, but there's no way they'll dodge responsibility for what they did. They own this."

The three of them sat drinking their coffee and talking about the process for about fifteen minutes. Then there was a knock at the hatch, and a junior officer stuck his head in. "They're ready for you, Admiral, Commodore, Commander."

Jared stood, and once everyone else had joined him, he led the way out of the room, pausing long enough to rinse his mug and hang it back where he'd gotten it. The rest followed suit, and they moved under heavy guard to the courtroom, where they entered from the front. Everyone who was going to be observing was already seated though they stood as the officer acting as a bailiff called for everyone to rise. The bailiff also read off their names, so Jared and the others didn't have to introduce themselves.

Once Jared and the rest took their seats, he instructed everyone to sit down. With that done, one of the hatches to the side of the compartment opened, and some marines escorted the two former resistance leaders into the courtroom. Tranick had her jaw wired shut since Kelsey had broken it during her apprehension. They had a lawyer with them, and that person certainly had their work cut out for them.

Jared waited until the prisoners were standing behind their table, their arms cuffed behind them and their legs shackled, to order the bailiff to read the charges against them. The primary one was the kidnapping and torture of a duly credited ambassador from the New Terran Empire. There were other charges from the resistance about betrayal, but the ones that would see these two executed all related to Justine Bandar.

Jared leaned forward. "Rebecca Tranick, David Ensign, these are serious charges that you stand accused of. How do you plead?"

The lawyer opened his mouth to say something, but the man overrode him, his voice loud, clear, and defiant. "We did what was necessary to secure the world we were told to protect. We do not recognize the legitimacy of this court or your claim on our persons."

That wasn't what he'd been expecting, but it certainly added a level of drama to the proceedings. "Whether you recognize the legitimacy of this court or not is irrelevant," Jared said evenly. "We have possession of you, and you will answer the question. Are you guilty, or are you innocent?"

"This trial is a farce. You've already made up your minds what you want to do, so just get on about it."

Jared looked at the lawyer. "Do you have anything to add, Counselor?"

"Sadly, no," the man said. "My clients have chosen not to cooperate with my defense strategy."

"I'm sure you did your best, but sometimes we find ourselves in circumstances that make success difficult. Do you wish to withdraw from the case?"

"I do, Your Honor. There's nothing I can add if they don't want my assistance."

Jared looked at the other members of the tribunal, and they nodded. "This tribunal approves of your withdrawal and thanks you for your service."

The man inclined his head and walked back through the hatch that the prisoners had come through. His part in this drama was over, but the play was just beginning.

Once the man left, Jared continued. "This tribunal will enter a plea of not guilty on your behalf." He looked over at the prosecution's table. "You may proceed, Counselor."

The lead prosecutor, a slender woman with dark skin and black hair braided tightly against her head, smiled professionally. "Thank you, Admiral. The prosecution calls Justine Bandar to the stand."

Kelsey's mother rose from her seat in the front row behind the prosecution and walked to the witness stand, where she was sworn in.

As soon as that was finished, Ensign spoke. "Just pronounce your punishment. There's no need for us to sit here and listen through her crying about how she was mistreated."

"Your objection is out of order," Jared said sternly. "This court will hear from the witness. If that's uncomfortable for you, too bad. If you continue to be disruptive, I'll have you escorted to another compartment where you can observe the proceedings remotely and make objections via that method. If you want this trial to be speedy, then I suggest you allow it to proceed."

He focused his attention on Justine. "Please proceed, Ambassador Bandar."

The older woman swallowed and nodded. Then she launched into the story of how they landed to meet the resistance on Devon and had been kidnapped. She then proceeded to tell them how she'd been tortured again and again and been forced to fight for her life and kill to escape. It was a heart-wrenching story, and it took every ounce of his will to keep his face neutral as he heard her spell out in horrific detail what had been done to her.

By the time she finished, she was trembling. He considered

offering her an opportunity to step away from the stand and regain her composure, but he already knew that she wouldn't do it. She might not be very much like his sister, but she was going to finish this and wouldn't look kindly on him for dragging it out.

"And the people that carried out this torture, Ambassador," the prosecutor said, "are they the accused?"

Justine nodded. "Rebecca Tranick did the majority of the torture, but David Ensign was her willing accomplice and was present for some of the sessions. While she's the true monster, he was happy to watch."

"Do you have anything to add to your statement?"

"No."

"Then the prosecution is finished with this witness."

Jared looked at the two defendants. "Do you have any questions for this witness? I warn you that if you choose to badger her, I will bring that particular show to a swift and unceremonious end. Do not test my patience."

Ensign waved his hand as if Justine wasn't worth his time. "Let her go off somewhere else where she can cry herself to sleep. She was weak, and she deserved everything that happened to her."

Justine's features hardened. "If I were the kind of person that tortured others for enjoyment, I'd offer to torture you for as long as you did me and see who came out worse. As it is, I'll just have to watch you die when they find you guilty."

She then stood and walked regally back to her seat before sitting down with a stone face. Kelsey, who was sitting beside her, took her hand. Jared could tell that his sister was livid. She was more than capable of coming up behind the two prisoners and yanking their spines right out of their bodies before anyone could stop her, so he really hoped that she had a prodigious amount of restraint today. He personally wouldn't blame her for doing that, but it would make things messy in regard to both the trial and the cleanup.

The prosecution then proceeded to call Veronica Giguere and Olivia West. While they hadn't been present for any of the torture, they'd had to care for Justine after every session and had seen how injured she was. They also testified as to her mental state.

Once that was done, the prosecution rested. They really didn't need to present any more evidence. Everything they'd brought forward was completely and utterly compelling.

Jared looked over at the prisoners. "Would you like to call any witnesses in your defense? Perhaps you'd like to testify yourselves?"

Ensign made a rude gesture. "Just get this over with."

Jared shrugged. If the two wanted to get things done without doing anything to mitigate what might happen to them, he certainly wouldn't complain.

He leaned over toward Zia. "Thoughts?"

"Guilty as hell. Death."

Jared repeated his question to Somerville. The man also indicated a guilty verdict with the maximum penalty.

That done, he focused his full attention on the two prisoners. "The defendants will rise." They did so though they were surly about it.

"This tribunal finds you both guilty of all charges," Jared continued. "The sentence is death, to be carried out immediately. Let this be a warning to those who would harm the ambassadors or diplomatic personnel of the New Terran Empire. Marines, take them away."

He expected that there would be some type of demonstration or outburst, but the two said nothing as they were led out of the compartment. Even before they made it to the exit, Kelsey stood and stalked after them.

Her move wasn't a surprise. His sister might be gentle in times of peace, but when there was conflict, she was a warrior and wasn't afraid to shed the blood of those who crossed her. She'd already told him that she would carry out the sentence herself.

He thought that was a little bloody-minded, but that was Kelsey all over.

Jared stood once they were out of the compartment. "The New Terran Empire is just and fair, but we will not tolerate others harming our representatives. We're a good friend to those who want friendship and a terrible enemy to those who want war. We will free the Rebel Empire from the bondage of those who would enslave it, whether they be artificially intelligent or merely cruel and corrupt. Choose whichever side suits you best, but choose wisely. This court is adjourned."

He saw that Elise was standing next to Justine and helping her out of the compartment in the direction Kelsey and the prisoners had gone. It looked like she hadn't been kidding about wanting to see them die for what they'd done.

For his part, he was half tempted to watch the execution himself, but he resisted. He had enough nightmares already. No, it was far better for him to focus on what came next. The hard work was only just beginning.

10

Elise walked through the Imperial vault and goggled at the treasures stacked around her. The massive chamber under the Imperial Palace on Terra was packed with ten thousand years' worth of extravagant gifts from all over the old Empire to the reigning emperor of the time. Even setting aside the cultural value of the contents of this room, its monetary value was inconceivable.

Kelsey walked in front of her, stopping every once in a while to examine something. Her friend had decided to come back to Terra with her after the trial, and they'd been there several days, looking over the Imperial Palace and making modifications to their plans. It would take a lot of work to get this facility back into operation even though much of it was still technologically functional.

Frankly, it was filthy. The people they'd evicted hadn't been living in squalor, but they certainly hadn't taken care to clean up after themselves as well as they should have. Leaving aside the rot of five centuries, they'd certainly contributed their own mess, and now that had to be dealt with.

The two of them stopped in front of the three-meter-tall statue in pale stone. It looked to be hand carved and was absolutely gorgeous. She had no idea who the woman was, but based on the clothing, it was from a primitive society. The clothing was more revealing than she'd have considered appropriate for a gift, but it seemed in character for the person who was wearing it.

"Who is this?" she asked. "And better yet, why is she dressed like that?"

"It took a lot of digging around in the databases, but I finally figured it out," Kelsey said as she stared up at the woman's face. "This is Aphrodite. She was purportedly a Greek goddess. Greece was a country on Terra long before spaceflight. As one might guess from the way she's dressed, she represents love, lust, beauty, passion, and procreation. The database that Jared has indicates this was a gift for Empress Althea Bandar. She had a passion for the history of ancient Greece and their gods."

"I'm not sure that I'd say she's beautiful, but I suppose I'm not the intended audience," Elise said. "It's certainly a grand gift. I take it this was not a piece of artwork done in ancient times, but some kind of replica?"

Kelsey laughed. "I suppose it depends on one's definition of the word *ancient*. Empress Althea the First reigned just over eight thousand years ago."

"I suppose that does put things in perspective," she agreed as she walked around the statue and admired the carved roses and doves that adorned the pedestal, which she now realized was a gigantic seashell. How strange.

"Why didn't she display it somewhere?" she wondered aloud. "Why would she put it down here, where no one could ever admire it?"

"I suspect that it wasn't down here in the beginning," Kelsey said as she walked away from the statute. "I'm confident it was prominently displayed in the Imperial residence during her life and was relocated here once she passed. Almost everything down here would have been displayed somewhere for the citizens to see, or perhaps only the Imperial family, during the reign in which the person was given the gift. This is a gigantic storeroom where those items were placed afterward. With ten thousand years of history, that's a lot of rulers and literal tons of gifts."

"I wonder if our people ever sent anything? If so, to who? What would it have been?"

Kelsey turned her head and smiled back at her. "Of course your people sent things. Every world in the Empire sent something on each emperor's or empress's birthday. There are literally thousands of gifts from Pentagar in this room. Would you like to see some of them?"

"I would. I'm curious what my people would've seen as a worthy gift to a ruler of the Terran Empire. Pentagar was never a rich and powerful world, but I'm sure our people would've done the best they could."

As Kelsey stopped and looked around before heading off in a different direction, she chuckled. "The value of the gift isn't in how much it costs to make or how valuable it is, but in the regard the giver held for the recipient. A heartfelt gift can mean the most from a close friend even if it doesn't have any intrinsic value. When I was a girl, I tried to take up painting. Sadly, I wasn't well suited for that, but I still did my best, and on my father's birthday one year, I gave him a painting of himself."

"Oh? How did he like it?"

"He loved it, and it thrilled me that he was so pleased with it. Looking back, it was awful. Nevertheless, he had it framed, and it still hangs in his office in a place of honor. Love and friendship are what make gifts valuable to the recipient. I'd imagine most of these items inside this vault were simply things to the recipients, but there were undoubtedly some that weren't that valuable but something those rulers treasured. I'm sure many of the gifts from Pentagar—and most of the worlds—fit into that category."

Elise looked at the stacks of crates that rose to the ceiling twelve meters over their heads as they walked. "We'll probably never know this point. All of that history is lost. While you might have a listing of what sits in this vault, it will never tell us what the emperor or empress that received it thought about it."

"Sadly, that's true. Maybe there's something buried in one of the computers here that has more detailed information about that sort of thing. It wouldn't shock me if there were books written about particular emperors or empresses that talked about gifts they received that were meaningful to them. It's not exactly a high priority for us to find, but at some point, we'll have to try to figure it out. Well, we'll find historians that will do the work."

They walked for another ten minutes and eventually stopped at a stack of crates that looked like every other one around them. None of them were exceptionally large, but they were undoubtedly heavy.

"This stack has one of the gifts that your people sent," Kelsey said as she put her hands on her hips and stared up. "Now, we just have to figure out which crate has it and try to get it out without destroying everything. I'd like to avoid a repeat of what we did inside the treasure vault underneath the horde city. That was a *huge* mess and so damned destructive. We have to take care that nothing here is damaged."

Elise smiled. "If you ask Talbot, I'm sure he'd say that destruction and mayhem are your calling cards, and you should embrace them."

"I don't always destroy *everything*. Accidents happen."

"So if you don't want to destroy everything, how are you planning to get into these things? There has to be a machine in here that helped people stack them. Perhaps we need to look for that rather than testing your enhancements to move heavy crates while you're in such a delicate condition."

Kelsey sighed. "Part of me wants to argue, but you're right. I'm too far along to take that kind of risk. If there is something like that in here, it'll be along one of the walls. That's saying a lot in a place this big, so let's see if the inventory list has anything about that."

After a few moments, the princess smiled. "Got it. There's a series of machines used for that, and they're in charging stations in various places. It should only take us a couple of minutes to get one here if they work."

"This seems like an awful lot of work for just showing me a gift that came from Pentagar," Elise said. "We don't need to do this right now."

"I disagree. Now that we're invested in this process, I want to find out. I can see what the description says this gift is, but I'm not sure what it means. Once we find out which crate it's in, we can take that one back upstairs and begin tallying what's in it and examining it in greater detail. And by we, I mean somebody that's more professional at that sort of thing. Maybe an archaeologist or museum curator. I'm not sure."

"Then, rather than opening it here, we should move it into that transition place my gift takes us to. From there, it would be easy to find somebody on Devon who does this kind of work to begin the process. Once we use those artifacts to whet their appetite, we'll have them."

Kelsey grinned. "You're absolutely right. There's no way that somebody with a passion for this sort of thing could pass up an opportunity like this. We'll have to do a serious background check and make certain there are protective measures in place so that none of the gifts wander off, but that sort of thing would be enough to draw those types of professionals here to Terra."

"That's good, but how are you going to draw in the people that will clean up the entire Imperial Palace and its environs? If you ever intend to use this area to actually rule the Empire, it'll need a lot of work, and I'm afraid the cleaning staff isn't going to be nearly as enamored as a museum curator."

That made Kelsey laugh. "We'll come up with something. For the moment, let's work on one thing at a time."

It took about fifteen minutes to get a working forklift, get back to the stack in question, and locate the appropriate crate. Thankfully, it wasn't at the bottom of the stack. It wasn't at the top either, but it was farther up than their luck would usually allow for.

Learning to use the forklift was an occasionally hair-raising and mostly hilarious experience. Kelsey was being careful not to damage anything, yet she still almost dropped two crates while she was relocating things to dig into the pile until she had the crate she wanted. Once it was set aside, she carefully put the other crates back into the stack and made sure they were stable. There was no need to leave a mess when other people would undoubtedly try to get through this area sooner or later.

When they were finished, Elise opened a portal leading to the home in the strange other space, and Kelsey drove the forklift with the crate through it. Once she'd deposited the payload on the other side, she returned to the vault and got the forklift back where she'd found it.

"Let's head back to the space station," Kelsey said.

Elise nodded and opened a portal that took them to the compartment on the space station that had been set aside for her use as a portal area. It wasn't very large, but no one else would be putting anything in it, so there would be no danger of opening a portal into something that was packed in there.

She had no idea what would happen if she tried that and no desire to find out.

"We should've left the forklift in there," Kelsey said as they stepped out into the corridor. "I think it might be a better idea to set up an area to deal with that kind of stuff here where the marines can keep it under guard."

"That shouldn't be too much of a problem," Elise said as the two of them went into one of the functional lifts and started toward the quarters that her friend shared with Talbot. "Once we find the appropriate location for that, all I have to do is open a portal, and Talbot can push it through. It might scuff up the bottom of the crate, but that won't be a problem."

"So you're saying that my husband is basically a forklift."

"No. That's what *you're* saying, but I won't disagree with that assessment."

Kelsey laughed and they made their way into her apartment and found her husband on the couch, asleep. She walked over and smacked his foot. "Wake up."

He cracked one eyelid. "What if I don't want to?"

"Then you'll do it anyway because we need your help. Unless, of course, you'd like me to move something really heavy."

He sighed theatrically and rested the back of his hand across his forehead. "My work is never done. My wife is a slave driver."

She gave him a look, reached down, grabbed the bottom of the couch with one hand, and stood, flipping it over backward and dumping Talbot onto the floor.

He lay where he'd fallen face down. "I've slept in worse places, I suppose," he mumbled into the carpet. "At least it doesn't have any rocks."

Kelsey laughed and grabbed him by the ankle. "If I have to drag you to where I want to go, I'll do it."

"Okay. You win."

Once she released him, he stood and stretched. "You are a harsh taskmistress. What are we doing?"

Kelsey tipped the sofa back up until it was sitting correctly and then resettled the cushions. "We picked up a crate from the Imperial Vault, and we want to have a place here where we can move it. We'll need a location that's suitable for people doing artifact cataloging and restoration. It also needs to be under guard because everything in the Imperial Vault is incredibly valuable."

"Well, we've certainly got the space for that kind of thing around here." His eyes became unfocused as he accessed his implants. "I think I've found a location that will work. I'm not sure what it was used for before, but it's got a lot of large compartments and a series of smaller ones along the outskirts. All of them can be sealed off so that only one entrance is usable. In fact, it would probably be better to remove the hatches that we don't intend to use and make the bulkheads solid."

"That sounds good," Kelsey said. "Why don't we go take a look? If it's satisfactory, Elise will open a portal to her place in the other universe, and you can push the crate through. It's not that big, but I figured you wouldn't want me messing with it."

"If you weren't messing with it, how did it get in there?" he asked with a raised eyebrow. "The doctors said no lifting heavy things."

Kelsey held up her hand. "There were some forklifts down in the Imperial Vault. I used one of them. No risks were taken if you don't count the chance that one of the crates could've fallen on me or something."

"Knowing you, I'm not willing to rule that out."

She grumbled, and then the three of them made their way deeper into the station. Elise was continually amazed by how large it was. Admittedly, it was the primary orbital around the capital of the old Terran Empire at its height, but it was *huge*.

When they arrived at the area that Talbot had selected, it was obvious that it had not been used since the Fall. It hadn't been cleaned out, and there was a lot of junk still lying around. Just based on the number of tools and pieces of equipment, this had probably been some type of manufacturing area where they built equipment for use inside the station itself.

"This looks kind of important," she said. "We should pick a different location."

Talbot shook his head. "You have no idea how many different areas like this are scattered throughout this station. If they eventually get around to where we're so busy that we need this area, we'll figure something out. I wouldn't want to be the poor bastard that has to clean everything up in here, though."

The three of them found one of the smaller side compartments was mostly empty, and Elise declared it her new portal compartment for this area and opened a portal to where she'd stashed the crate. Thankfully, the hatches in this zone were large enough to move even something like the three-meter statue of Aphrodite through with room to spare.

Talbot eyed the crate. "Okay, that's not so bad. Let's get it in here and see what you've got."

The Marine Raider walked around behind the crate and pushed it through the portal. It made a relatively horrific scraping noise on the stone and then the bare metal of the compartment, but it didn't matter if the wood of the crate was damaged as long as nothing happened to the contents.

Once it was inside their new facility, Elise closed the portal and focused her attention on the crate. They didn't have any tools to open it, yet this manufacturing area was filled with tools. Surely, something would work.

It only took her a couple of minutes to find a prybar, and she returned triumphant with it to find that Talbot had already ripped the top of the crate off with his bare hands.

She scowled at him. "You know, there are times when you're a lot more like your wife than you would probably choose to admit."

He chuckled and continued pulling out packing material and items. "I can't argue with that. Still, it's good that you found that because other people won't have the strength in their fingers to do what I did. I promise I was careful."

The crate itself was about two meters on each side. That was a fair amount of storage area, but most of it was taken up by packing material to make certain that the contents were never in danger. By the time they'd emptied it, that crate had yielded several dozen items for their perusal.

Some of them were boxes that contained other things, while others were works of art that had been packed away without any covering at all: statuary, paintings, a small chest simply packed with exquisitely cut rubies that glowed a deep red, and all manner of other things. It was simply staggering. Aside from the massive vault, it was more wealth than she'd ever seen in one place before.

She looked from item to item and tried to figure out which would have come from Pentagar, and she had no idea. "Okay, I give up. Which one of these came from Pentagar, Kelsey?"

"How well do you like rubies?"

"What girl doesn't? So this little chest of rubies came from my home world? Not exactly a work of art or something from the heart, but it's definitely got my attention. I wonder where they mined them? I'm not familiar with that sort of thing on my home world."

"I'm just yanking your chain. The rubies—as beautiful as they are—came from somewhere else. According to the inventory, your people's gift is listed as a book. I'm not sure what the book is about because it doesn't say anything. Did anyone see a book?"

They searched around and didn't see any among the artifacts they recovered, so Talbot went back through the packing material and found the book had somehow gotten caught up in it. That made the three of them go back through all the packing material again just to be sure they hadn't missed anything else. It was a good thing they hadn't thrown anything away.

The book was a slender thing that hardly looked worthy of being a gift to a ruler of the Terran Empire, but when Elise cracked it open, she saw that the pages were of the finest vellum, and everything was inked by hand. The calligraphy was astounding, and the illustrations were still bright and vivid.

It was a history of Emperor Virgil the Seventh. It looked as though someone had written a biography of the person and then had it transcribed by hand. When she read the introduction, she saw why this was a worthy gift. The author dedicated the work to the emperor, and it said that the only copy of this work was in the emperor's hands. It would, therefore, never be printed again.

"What a magnificent gift," she said in a reverent tone. "Someone spent years working on this gift, researching everything and then writing a biography of someone, and penning everything by hand. Perhaps the person was the illustrator as well. Could this have all been done by a single person? It doesn't say anything here about the author other than their name, and I've got no way to look it up until the destroyer that's taking the resistance delegation to Avalon makes a side trip to Pentagar."

The cover of the book was of the finest leather, but even though it looked like it had been stored well, there were still cracks. This was one of those items that needed restoration though she wasn't sure how well that would be done. That was a question for an expert.

"When I go back to Devon and start looking for someone who might do this work, can I take this with me?" she asked.

"You can, but I was intending to gift it back to Pentagar. This is part of your people's history."

Elise shook her head. "That's a wonderful gesture, but this is the Empire's history. I certainly won't object to everything being scanned and sent back to my people so that they can enjoy it, but this item belongs on Terra. Maybe at some point, it can go home on a tour with other items. That's not for me to say."

"When you go back to Devon and hunt for someone that can restore works like that, I'd probably best go along," Kelsey said. "They'll be doing a lot of other work if they say yes, and it pays to make sure that we're getting the right people."

Talbot opened his mouth to say something and then frowned. "We've got trouble. I just got a report that a number of warships are in the system on the other side of one of the flip points. We've got hours before they get to this system, but I suspect we're about to have a fight on our hands."

"It's the Clans, isn't it?" Kelsey demanded.

He shook his head. "The ships are of standard Imperial design. The only way I know they're not automated warships responding to our call is that they just ambushed another group of ships that were on the way here and destroyed them. That probably means one of the AIs didn't surrender when instructed. Just like the mad AI that we ran into, I suppose."

"How many ships are we talking about?" Elise asked. "Do I need to go get Jared?"

"A lot. The range is still too distant to get a complete count, but we're talking several hundred vessels. They're continuing to pour through one of the flip points leading into the other system, so that's not a final count. We're lucky that we can use FTL drones to keep an eye on the other system without having ships there ourselves. It might end up being more warships than we've gathered so far, and we could be in real trouble."

Elise nodded. "I'll go get him right now. Once I get back, it might be best if we start evacuating the personnel off this station. If any of them get through, it's going to be a primary target."

"We'll do that," Kelsey said. "After you open the portal and let people come through, I want you to take the artwork and gifts through to your side. Now that we've unpacked it, it'll probably only take you fifteen or twenty minutes, and we don't want to lose them either. Bring Jared back to his ship. That's where we'll be."

Elise went back to the transfer room and opened a portal. She didn't know what was happening, but if they'd missed getting one of the AIs, this could be a truly ugly fight, and they could lose a lot of ships. She'd thought the war with AIs was over, but maybe she'd been wrong. Jared would know what to do. She just had to get him here so that he could fight to protect what they'd taken.

He'd find a way to win. Of that, she had no doubt. And if things got too rough, she'd be right there to open a portal and take her friends to a place of safety. She wouldn't let her husband or her sister-in-law risk themselves needlessly if things became overwhelming.

She'd do what needed to be done, and the first step in that was figuring out where her husband was and getting him back to Terra. It looked like the battle for control of the Empire wasn't over just yet.

11

Kelsey stood on the superdreadnought *Gauntlet*'s flag bridge, watching the feed from the FTL drone in the other system as it continued tallying the arrival of the hostile warships. The number had climbed to almost fifteen thousand, and while that wasn't more ships than they had, it was beginning to get close. How had one of the AIs gathered so many ships right under the master AI's electronic nose?

Jared had been gathering a fleet here at Terra with the intention of going after the Clans. The estimate had been that they would receive roughly ten percent of the AI-controlled ships within two weeks of sending out the recall. The expectation was that they'd receive thousands of battlecruisers and a scattering of other vessels in that time.

Marcus's guess hadn't been far off, and there was a fleet of epic proportions in Terra's system, numbering just short of twenty thousand ships: 215 superdreadnoughts, 1,580 battlecruisers, 5,500 cruisers, and 12,150 destroyers. Thank God they hadn't sent any of the ships to Devon already, because they needed them now.

Jared walked to the hatch at the back of the compartment with

Elise at his side. "I can't leave you alone for five minutes, Kelsey. How did you manage to get into this much trouble already?"

She mock glared at him. "This is *not* my fault. Not a single one of my actions caused any of this."

"And I believe we can rule out one of the other artificial intelligences being responsible as well," Marcus said from the overhead speakers. "With the large number of vessels we're seeing, that would be much more than a single AI would have control over, even if it was in charge of an entire sector. This is something else."

"Well then, I'd like to know what it is," Jared said as he sat at his console. "It looks like we're dealing with around fifteen thousand ships. Interestingly, this looks like something close to a standard Fleet pattern: a relatively small number of superdreadnoughts and carriers, surrounded by a larger number of battlecruisers and cruisers, with swarms of destroyers guarding their flanks. That isn't what I'd have guessed one of the AIs would put out to fight us, especially since the AIs didn't use carriers or fighters."

"I can add some information to what you're already surmising," Marcus said. "Simply based on the maneuver patterns, it's evident that those vessels are not computer-controlled. There are slight inconsistencies in positioning and readjustments to relative positions. That tells me that living beings are in control of those vessels."

"Then that makes even less sense than everything else," Kelsey said. "Who could they be, and what do they want?"

"I think it's pretty obvious that they want to seize Terra," Elise said, stopping to stand behind Jared's chair. "One doesn't bring that many ships for a social call."

"So they're not friendly, and they use Imperial ships," Jared said. "That means that there's another unknown force that we haven't been keeping track of. Something like the Clans or even us, if you wanted to stretch the metaphor that far: a group that was not part of the Rebel Empire and has now come looking to defeat the AIs. The question is, what do we do about it?"

"We talk," Kelsey said firmly. "Even if we had the upper hand as far as the number of ships—which we may not by the time this is done—we need to find out exactly who these people are and what they represent before we start shooting. Or before they start shooting us."

"And how do we go about that?" Jared asked as he looked at her. "Odds are very good that these people will believe that the ships here are AI-controlled, and they're not even wrong. The first step to talking is to make sure that there's no shooting."

"That really depends on how you feel about revealing some of our technology," Marcus said.

"The way I'd choose to do this would be to have one of our probes sitting near the flip point when they begin emerging to start transmitting messages to them. We could do it on the other side of the flip point, but that would probably reveal more about what we're capable of doing than I'm comfortable with."

"They'd still realize that the transmissions are coming faster than light, but they'd miss the fact that we can do so through a flip point," Jared said. "Under other circumstances, that would be a good trade-off, but I'm not comfortable allowing that many potentially hostile vessels into this system. In this case, I believe it might be best to initiate contact before they arrive at the flip point itself. Warn them that the system is under our control, and see if we can maybe start a dialog before the weapons start flying."

"You're the boss when it comes to that sort of thing," Kelsey said. "We've got plenty of other surprises we can spring if we need to. Marcus, what would be the best way of initiating contact with them in the other system? I know we have one probe near the flip point. Are there any others?"

"There are two," Marcus said. "The other is significantly closer to the incoming ships than the one sitting at the flip point. It was positioned in the middle of the system to keep an eye out for vessels coming through the flip point on the other side, using passive scanners. I believe using it as a communications hub would be advisable. That allows us to continue observing the system from the Terra flip point without revealing the probe there. Once they are aware that this type of technology exists, they may be able to sense the other probe, so I'll begin moving it farther away in the flip point to minimize the chances it will be discovered."

"That sounds like a good idea," Jared said. "What's the ETA to the flip point if they were allowed to proceed?"

"Six hours and fifty-three minutes for the lead elements," Marcus said. "If they are following anything close to Fleet doctrine, the lead vessels would slow as they approached to allow a larger force to gather and be ready to penetrate the system. That would add at least an hour to the proceedings. In anticipation of your next question, I have already begun moving our vessels into position to defend the system. If you wish to keep knowledge of the ability to communicate and sense other vessels through flip points a secret, then I suggest we short-circuit this affair and move ships to the other side of the flip point to confront them there."

"That's not a bad idea," Jared said after thinking about it for a moment. "They would assume that we had a vessel they hadn't detected at the flip point and that we saw the fight. We'd still have to reveal the fact that we can communicate at faster-than-light speeds, but if we're going to stop the fight before it happens, we'll have to show our cards in that arena anyway. I suppose we could use a probe to do our communications with regular radio transmissions, but it'll get their attention if we do something unexpected. When people's fingers are on the trigger, getting our meaning across faster might be best."

"It's more difficult to stop a fight than prevent one," Kelsey agreed. "How soon can we have our ships on the other side of the flip point, Marcus?"

"As ours are already in motion, we can have them begin entering the other system in three hours and twenty-five minutes. We would have finished transitioning ninety percent of our vessels within half an hour of that. That leaves several hours before the enemy could arrive at our location."

"I think we'd best not refer to them as the enemy just yet," Jared said. "That gets us into a mindset where we're ready to take extreme action, and I'm not sure that we want to do that yet. Whoever these people are, I don't believe they are friends of the AIs, so it behooves us to see if we can make them our friends. Let's get moving, Marcus.

A host should always be standing by to greet their guests when they arrive."

"If I could trouble you in the meantime, Elise, I think I need to go change, and I don't have any clothes aboard this ship," Kelsey said. "I don't mind wearing comfortable clothes in front of my friends, but if we're making an impression on strangers, I'd better up my game a bit."

"I'd be happy to take you back and let you get changed. That'll eat up some of the time that we're traveling anyway, and waiting is boring."

"You're not wrong," Jared said. "You probably also want to pass the information about this fleet to the resistance. There's a new player on the board, and just in case things don't turn out the way we'd like, it might be best to have representatives of the resistance on hand. If Coordinator Gatewood could make herself available, we could be certain to get her out of harm's way if it looks like combat is imminent, but I believe she'd be a good face for the Rebel Empire."

"I'll try to be back in a couple of hours at the latest," Elise said. "I'm not sure how much time everyone will require to get ready, but it's best to be here aboard the ship before the fleet transitions to the other system."

Kelsey followed Elise out of the flag bridge and to the compartment that was set aside for her use in transferring onto and off the ship. Within a few minutes, they were back aboard the station in the Home system, and Kelsey was changing. Elise left to notify Coordinator Gatewood while Kelsey began going through her wardrobe, deciding what to wear.

Her prominent baby bump made a number of outfits out of the question. The maternity clothes she had didn't really fit her needs, so she contacted someone aboard the station that she knew sold clothes and arranged for a delivery of something more professional that accommodated her condition.

Elise arrived before the clothes and told her that Coordinator Gatewood was getting ready and would bring a staff of people with her.

When Kelsey's new clothes were delivered, she dressed and examined herself in the mirror. The baby bump was still quite visible, but she now wore something that exuded a bit more power than her casual clothes. It wouldn't be good to be dismissed immediately by whomever they were meeting with because she didn't dress appropriately.

She hoped this situation lent itself to diplomacy. If this was another group like the Clans that was only interested in fighting, this was going to be bloody and depressing. It wouldn't be the end of their efforts because they still had a lot of ships coming, but she'd much rather not squash another group of people that had roughly the same goals as they did.

It made her wonder who the people were. The Clans had been formed by an escaped task force of Fleet vessels. They'd diverged so badly from what they'd originally been that they were unrecognizable at this point, but some of that could be laid at the feet of the Singularity.

Would these new people be similar, another group of refugees that had changed in ways that couldn't be guessed ahead of time? Probably, but maybe not to the extremes that the Clans had.

Once she was dressed, she and Elise went to Coordinator Gatewood's office and met her and the staff of people she had put together. Thankfully, they hadn't been waiting long, and they all proceeded back to the compartment that Elise used for her arrivals and departures aboard the station.

Minutes later, they were back aboard *Gauntlet* and standing aboard her flag bridge. Gatewood looked around the vast compartment and shook her head. "If only we'd had something like this back in the early days. Things would certainly have been different."

"It would have probably drawn the attention of the AIs even more," Jared said. "From what I understand, the master AI was willing to allow the resistance to exist simply because that kept it from turning everything over to the Singularity. While the fight was still continuing, it was still in control. That said, a superdreadnought might have changed the equation enough to force it to take notice of you."

"You're right," she said. "Even so, I'm jealous."

"If it's any consolation, you'll be in charge of the fleet defending Terra should you take the job. That means you'd have a lot of them."

Kelsey laughed. "Not quite what she meant, but well played."

They discussed different options for how they could proceed as the fleet closed on the flip point. According to the probes on the other side, the fleet that they were about to face was beginning to consolidate and had grown to around twenty thousand vessels. That meant the two fleets were numerically similar. If there was a fight, it would be truly ugly.

Kelsey knew that the negotiations that would be taking place were critical, and she was glad to have Coordinator Gatewood there to help. She tended to be relatively abrupt, and even though she didn't kill nearly as many people these days, that might be the wrong attitude to take. Just as they didn't know who these people were, they wouldn't know who Kelsey's folk were as well. Introductions would have to be made and trust built. That was hard, and it took time.

Once Jared had the entirety of his fleet ready to transition, he ordered Marcus to take the vessels through the other side and set up a defensive pattern for their ships on the other side. They'd be waiting for the newcomers to see and react to them. If they decided to attack, he'd be ready.

To their credit, the other vessels didn't even slow down for a moment as they continued approaching. A direct confrontation would still be hours away at this rate, but Jared's fleet had already launched a number of probes to both watch the newcomers more closely and to act as communications relays. They were traveling quickly and should have been in a position to start the negotiations in about half an hour.

Time literally dragged for Kelsey. She hated waiting, but they couldn't even talk until they had something in position to relay things in a timely fashion. She would just have to accept that was the way it was, even if it galled her.

Talbot stepped onto the flag bridge while she was grinding her teeth and came over to stand next to her. "How are you holding up?"

"I'm impatient," she admitted. "I want to know who these people are and what they want."

"You're going to find that out soon enough."

Ten minutes later, Marcus announced that the probes were within range to begin acting as communications relays.

Jared looked over at Kelsey. "Which one of us is going to do the talking?"

"You can start the conversation," she said. "I'll stand here and look pretty. If you need to trot out the Crown Princess of the New Terran Empire, I'm available."

"Open a channel to the oncoming vessels."

Once one of Jared's aides indicated that he had an open channel, her brother leaned forward to stare into the pickup. "Attention, unknown vessels. You are intruding into an area under the control of the New Terran Empire. Identify yourselves, and state your intentions."

It took about twenty seconds for someone on the other side to respond, which was actually fairly quick, considering how surprised they must've been. The screen at the front of the compartment switched from a view of space to show a mirror of the compartment Kelsey stood in. That was a superdreadnought as well.

The man seated at the command console that was a mirror of Jared's wore a Fleet uniform with admiral's tabs as well. He was a bit older, but he had the same air about him. He was strong and confident looking.

However, he was not what captured Kelsey's attention. The woman standing to his right was someone she knew. The bold and distinctive tattoos of birds of prey that graced her cheeks and forehead were instantly recognizable.

"Andrea Tolliver," Kelsey said almost reverently. "I never expected to meet you in person."

Whatever the officer on the other side of the channel had been about to say, he stopped when the woman beside him put a hand on his arm.

She stared at Kelsey. "I am Andrea Tolliver, but I can't say that I know you."

Kelsey drew herself up a little bit straighter. "My name is Kelsey Bandar, and I am the Crown Princess of the New Terran Empire. My family is descended from Lucien Bandar, and we have seized control of Terra and defeated the master AI. The last time I saw an image of you, you were standing behind Emperor Marcus. I suppose that means your fleet escaped as well, and that explains your presence here."

The woman considered Kelsey for a few seconds and then looked at the officer seated next to her. "I think that we need to have a discussion before we jump into fighting, Luke. Step the fleet down to a state of vigilance and hold position here while we open negotiations."

The officer scowled. "We came to seize Terra, and I'm not inclined to recognize anyone else's ownership of it, Grandmother."

"Nevertheless, we will not be shooting people that may be our allies. So long as they stay in a nonconfrontational position, so shall we. Besides, don't you want to know how they're able to communicate at faster-than-light speeds? What other surprises might they have available that would be very unpleasant if they were sprung on us?"

The man didn't look all that thrilled, but he nodded. "It shall be as you say, Grandmother."

Tolliver returned her attention to the screen. "We could continue this talk over a communications channel, but I'd prefer to speak to you face-to-face. We have no trust to rely upon, so how shall we proceed?"

"I propose that we send a destroyer to meet one of yours to prove we are not under computer control," Jared said. "Then we will need to meet in person. This doesn't have to end in violence, but until we know one another better, I think it's best to keep in mind exactly what the consequences of betrayal would be."

The woman smiled. "If you know who I am, you know that I'm

more than capable of defending myself. I have no objection to coming to your fleet once we've had an initial meeting between our people. As you said, we're the visitors here, and I speak for our fleet."

"I will come as well," the admiral—Luke—sitting beside her said. "I have a stake in this, and I will hear everything that is said."

There seemed to be a little tension among the other group, but Kelsey couldn't figure out exactly where that was coming from. Instead of trying to figure it out, she simply nodded. "Very well. Shall we meet in an hour?"

"I look forward to it, Princess Bandar," Tolliver said. "More than you could possibly imagine."

12

Talbot took a team of Marines aboard one of the robotic destroyers and made his way to the bridge. It was very strange seeing no one there, but activating the viewscreen and sitting at one of the consoles allowed him to see everything that was going on around the ship as it advanced toward the other fleet.

He was glad to see that the others had stopped though he wasn't convinced this would be peacefully resolved. There was a possibility they could talk their way out of having a knockdown, drag-out fight, but it was just as likely that the other group would continue to push, and there would be fighting.

Even after having talked with Kelsey, he still didn't know much about Andrea Tolliver though he'd loaded the information his wife had dug up for him into his implants and studied it. To say that the records were sparse and filled with holes was an understatement, but the woman who was coming to meet Jared and Kelsey had been alive before the Fall, and she had been a Marine Raider.

Unlike Jake Peters, she hadn't been crippled and no doubt had a lot of skills that he wouldn't be able to match even though he had the same hardware. That was something to keep in mind. If a fight broke out, she could probably tie him up in a knot even though he was just as strong as she was or perhaps even stronger.

This was supposed to be a diplomatic meeting so that the leadership could talk to one another and the two forces could be convinced that they could stand down at least enough to keep talking rather than shooting. Jared was probably the best person to do that. Even Kelsey would agree that she was more than a bit impulsive and tended to reach for the nearest weapon to solve problems.

As his destroyer advanced, the computer on board taking its instructions from Marcus, he watched an identical destroyer moving out from the fleet ahead of him. Unlike his, it would be filled with human beings, and they were no doubt seeing him as an obstacle that might have to be destroyed.

He crossed his fingers and hoped that it didn't come to that, because if they started shooting, his ship would be blown into little bitty pieces. He might be able to make it to one of the escape pods and get away with his people, but that would ruin any chance for a peaceful resolution.

He watched as the two destroyers came within missile range of one another and then slowly came to a halt with barely a couple of kilometers between them. The other vessel had its weapon systems armed, and so did his. Tensions were undoubtedly high.

"What's the play, sir," one of the Marines asked. "Do we go there, or they come to us?"

"We have the home team advantage. They're coming to us. I want two of you to stay here and keep an eye on that fleet and the destroyer in front of us. If they do something unusual or start behaving in a hostile manner, I want you to hit the general quarters alarm, so we know what's going on. The rest of you are with me."

Talbot took the remainder of the squad down to where the other ship's pinnace would dock. Two of the members were in powered armor and carried heavy weapons and would be out of sight and waiting for problems. That left the remainder of the squad and him with sidearms and no armor at all.

"They've launched a pinnace, sir," one of the Marines on the bridge said over the ship's speakers. "ETA to docking five minutes."

"Everybody, get into position," Talbot said as he took up his spot in front of the dock.

He took the time that he had left to go over the various options they'd wargamed ahead of time. None of them were very good if that hatch opened and started spewing Marines in powered armor, but it didn't pay to just accept what happened to you. If they were going to die, they'd make the others bleed first.

Once again, he hoped it didn't come to that, but one never knew who was going to come knocking.

After the five minutes had passed, there was a series of thumps and clunks as the pinnace attached itself to the dock and then began cycling the airlock. He didn't bother to tell his people to be on their toes, because they already knew that. They were Marines trained by people that he'd trained, and they'd do their duty.

The hatch in front of him slowly slid aside, and he found himself looking at two people in Marine uniforms without rank tabs. They wore sidearms but were unarmored. One of them was a big man with long brown hair and a large nose, and the other was a curvy woman with bright-red hair.

The two of them stepped into the ship and looked down the corridor in either direction in what certainly looked like a practiced move. Neither one of them reached for their weapons, but they certainly took note of the Marines around them and how everything was laid out.

When they finished, the woman stepped over to him while the man continued to watch the Marines. She extended her hand. "My name is Diana Baker, and I'm with the Imperial Guard. This is my husband, Claudio, and he is also serving in that capacity. We're here to make certain that everything is safe for our leaders. If we think that it is, they'll come over after us and will allow you to take us to see your leadership."

That was the plan that had been agreed to, so Talbot nodded. "My name is Russell Talbot, but you can just call me Talbot. I'm a

Marine Raider, and I'll be responsible for our leadership's security. Shouldn't you be in white?"

The woman's eyebrows rose slightly, but she smiled. "We're on loan and didn't have the right uniforms at hand. You're a Marine Raider? You people certainly are full of surprises. I was almost certain the ability to make more of us had been lost long ago. Or have you been around a while?"

"I'm aware that the nanites make us functionally immortal—at least in the timescales that we're talking about—but I've only been a Raider for a few years. I was an Imperial Marine before that. So you're saying that you were a Marine Raider as well? Since you thought the technology had been lost, that means that you were alive before the Fall, just like Andrea Tolliver and Jake Peters."

The woman froze. "You know Jake? Is he still alive?"

Talbot shook his head sadly. "Unfortunately, he died in the final assault on the Master AI. His story is one filled with pain and triumph, but we don't have time for it now. We found him on Terra, and I'm sure you'll hear some of that story. First, though, I need to satisfy you that we're what we say we are."

"Not just yet," the man—Claudio—said. "How is it that you have implants but aren't under the control of the AIs?"

"Once we found out what had been done to the people inside the Empire during the Fall, one of our scientists redesigned a portion of the implants to make it impossible for them to be used that way. In fact, no update can take place without active user concurrence. That doesn't matter at this point because the rule of the computers has been broken. We control their network now."

It was more than that, but Talbot wouldn't get into how they'd turned the freed system AIs into people. That was something for Jared and Kelsey to discuss with the other leaders. His job was to satisfy these people that it was safe to trust them this far. The others would be putting themselves at the mercy of people they didn't know, so he needed to focus on his task and make things happen expeditiously.

"I suspect that there's a lot more to that story," Diana said. "When time permits, we can explore that in more detail, one

Marine to another, since I served in the Imperial Marines before I became a Raider as well, as did my husband."

Talbot smiled slightly. "My wife is also a Marine Raider, but she didn't serve in the Marines. She came at this through a… nontraditional route."

Had she ever.

The woman nodded. "Then let's take a look at the ship, and you can tell me where the hell your people came from."

He proceeded to give her a grand tour of the destroyer. It was all controlled by the computer on board, but he demonstrated that he had complete command authority over it by shutting the computer down. He'd have to boot it back up before they could head back to meet with Jared and Kelsey, but since there was very little they could do to demonstrate their honesty, he was willing to take the chance.

As they walked, he told them the story of how the people of Avalon had survived the Fall. Being ignored by the AIs after the ships that had pursued the battlecruiser *Lancelot* had destroyed it had given them a chance to rebuild their society, and it had taken time before they'd once again achieved spaceflight.

He only lightly delved into the exploration of the Rebel Empire though he didn't call it by that name. All that information would come to the new people when they talked with his wife and brother-in-law. He was grateful that he would be in the room when that discussion took place, because he really wanted to know where these other people had been. How had they escaped?

Obviously, the evacuation fleet that had had Emperor Marcus aboard had gotten away, or at least some of the ships had. Otherwise, Andrea Tolliver and the two beside him wouldn't have survived.

That was a valid question, so he took a moment to ask it. "We saw the message that Emperor Marcus left for everyone when he departed Terra. That's how we knew that Andrea Tolliver was alive then and who she was. Were you able to create a nanogenerator for him? Is Emperor Marcus still alive?"

Diana shook her head. "Unfortunately, we didn't have the

technical ability to do that, and we still don't. Some technologies have been lost to us. The only people who were alive before the Fall are Andrea, my husband, and me. The Three Musketeers. That's also a long story, and I'm sure it's going to be one that's asked at the upcoming meeting."

She turned and looked at her husband. "What do you think, Claudio? Should we trust them?"

"No. Even so, we have to have this meeting. You said that you liberated Terra. What condition is it in?"

Talbot shook his head grimly. "It's a primitive hellhole. The AIs used orbital bombardment and EMP bursts to destroy many of the population centers and reduce the population to wandering gatherers and those who live in the wreckage of what used to be high-technology cities. You can say that we've liberated Terra, but that only means that we've taken it away from the computers. It'll take a long time to rebuild anything resembling civilization there. It's a savage place, and the only part of the planet we firmly control is the Imperial Palace and the city of Frankfort, which is allied with us."

"It sounds like there's a lot a story to be told there," Diana said. "Once again, we'll have to sit down, have something to drink, and talk about it. The highfalutin types can talk politics, but I want to know what things are really like here in the Empire. You can't understand what it's like for someone like me, who saw the Empire at the height of its glory, to see it now. This is torture, and I already know I'll spend the rest of my life rebuilding what was lost."

"Like you said, there are a lot of details, but those will be somebody else's problem. You and yours are not in any danger from us as long as you don't attack us. We're more than willing to talk, and the situation here in what's left of the Empire is complex. We don't need even more problems, and we'd rather find allies than enemies. If we can take the time to show you what you're dealing with, and you can see what we've accomplished, I'd wager we can come to some kind of accommodation."

She smiled. "I certainly hope so. Let me go send the signal and get our diplomatic party on the way over. We should be ready to go in about fifteen minutes."

"Sounds good. I'm headed back to the bridge, but you can dock right here, and we'll turn around and head over there immediately. Or if you'd rather, have your destroyer come all the way over to our fleet. That would save them the trip."

"I think that would work better, and I'm glad you suggested it," she said. "I'll head back to our destroyer, then. It's been a pleasure meeting you, Talbot, and we'll talk again."

"Count on it."

Once the pinnace had detached and was on its way back to their destroyer, Talbot headed for the bridge. He sent the order to reactivate the ship's computer and settled into the command chair. He wasn't a pilot, but he didn't need to be. He could send the orders, and the computer would make all the magic happen.

Now, it was up to Kelsey and Jared to keep this a negotiation rather than a gunfight. He wished them luck because if things went bad, a lot of good people would die.

13

Jared had to admit that he was somewhat surprised the newcomers had decided to trust them enough to send their leadership to his flagship. They were taking a lot on faith. They didn't know enough to be sure that Jared and his people weren't somehow supporting the AIs. After all, that's what the Rebel Empire had been doing, even though these people might not know that.

Or, depending on how far they'd come, they might have seen it firsthand. In either case, he supposed he'd find out soon enough. Their pinnace was on the way over to dock with his superdreadnought even now.

He stood in the landing bay in his dress uniform with Kelsey at his side. She wore something sophisticated but tailored for her condition. She was growing rather large, and he was a bit worried about her because she still had a couple of months to go before giving birth.

Her small frame would make that quite the process though she probably had a higher pain tolerance than anyone he knew. Life had prepared her for this moment in ways others would never dare.

Stretched out on either side of them were two long rows of

Marines with rifles and sidearms. They were the honor guards that would be greeting their guests. Behind Jared stood a number of his officers and associates, including Crown Princess Elise Orison, Commodore Zia Anderson, Captain Brendan Levy, Captain Veronica Giguere, Commander Don Sommerville, Major Angela Ellis, Coordinator Sara Gatewood, and Carl Owlet. Talbot would join them shortly before their guests arrived.

He felt that it was a good selection of people to meet with these people. The only one he had a firm identity for was Andrea Tolliver. He knew that she was a Marine Raider, and she'd apparently been senior enough to be in command of the entire organization and perhaps even the Marines by the time the AIs attempted to destroy the Empire.

That meant she'd been an experienced and knowledgeable professional five hundred years ago, and there was no telling what she was now. The only person he'd ever met that had lived to be that age was Jake Peters, and he'd had his growth stunted by being a crippled prisoner on Terra. That was obviously not the case with Tolliver.

Whoever was in command of their fleet was a complete unknown and likely had far more experience than he did at command, though probably not combat. Jared had earned his experience the hard way and wasn't worried about how he stacked up against the other man though he certainly didn't want to cause offense where he didn't need to. These people had come from another group that escaped the AIs, and they weren't his enemies. It was his job to make sure that misunderstandings and conflict between them didn't break out into an all-out war.

The unseen member of their party would be problematic. Marcus wasn't a system AI in the manner these people believed he was, but he was still an intelligent computer, and that would undoubtedly raise their hackles. This meeting would be like walking through a minefield without having any idea if the next step would kill them.

"Talbot's pinnace is on final approach," Marcus said over the overhead speakers. "Our guests will arrive shortly after that."

Jared nodded. "Thank you, Marcus. Until I bring you into the conversation, I think it best if you keep your presence under wraps. They're already jumpy, and I don't want to turn this into something that will turn into a shooting war if I don't have to. Everyone else, follow Kelsey and me as we take the lead on this."

"Do you really think this will turn into a shooting war?" Kelsey asked. "Surely, they're more reasonable than the Clans."

He chuckled. "*Everyone* is more reasonable than the Clans. They have a set of preconceived notions about what they were going to find, and we've upset that. They're looking for an enemy, and it's our job not to become that in their minds. They came to defeat the master AI and take control of the Empire, but we've already done that. It behooves us to be cautious. Let's build a bridge and try not to set it on fire before we cross it."

Talbot's pinnace arrived a couple of minutes later, disgorging only him before it undocked and headed back out. He walked over and joined the rest of them.

"How did the initial meeting go?" Jared asked.

"Better than expected though I'm not sure exactly what they were looking for. I suspect they were trying to make an assessment of who I was and what I was doing, as well as looking over the ship to try and figure out how it fits into everything else. I have to say that I'm a little surprised they agreed to send their leadership over so readily."

"Me too," Kelsey said. "I don't know very much about Andrea Tolliver, but the bits and pieces I could pull together of her record suggest she's a talented and brilliant leader. That can only have improved over the last five hundred years. For all we know, everyone that's coming to visit is hundreds of years old if not the full five hundred. We'll be at a disadvantage when it comes to dealing with that kind of thing."

"The two that I met claimed to be Marine Raiders from before the Fall," Talbot said. "Diana Baker and her husband Claudio. They said that they and Tolliver were the only ones with Marine Raider nanites, so if that was true, we wouldn't have anyone else that is so old."

"Three Marine Raiders with so much experience," Kelsey said sadly. "I wish Jake was here to meet them."

"They seemed to know him," Talbot said. "They were saddened to hear of his passing. Though if you want somebody to come meet them, maybe we should wake Ned Quincy up."

Ned was an intelligence formed from all the recordings and memories a former Marine Raider had left in his implants before he'd died. It wasn't really him, but it was a real person who shared a lot of the same traits as the dead man.

He'd asked to be turned off while they built the body for him because he didn't want to keep living in Kelsey's implants. Jared was glad that she'd agreed. Her life was strange enough without having another person living in her head.

Kelsey shook her head. "That's a story that's even stranger than everything else we've been through, and until Carl gets his body finished, I'm not sure that we should even bring him up."

"I have been working on it off and on, and I think I'm close," Carl said. "Fiona was able to give me a lot of assistance in making a more effective body for him, and using some of the technology that was used to create the AIs themselves, I've improved the system to the point where I believe that it will be effective. Even so, I'm months away from being ready."

"Their pinnace is just about to land," Marcus said.

"Places, everyone," Jared said.

The pinnace docked with a clang, and a handful of Marines in light armor came out of the hatch a minute later. They had rifles on their backs and pistols at their waists but didn't seem to be spoiling for a fight.

The next two people were a man and a woman. The woman had red hair, and the man was tall and burly. Behind them came Andrea Tolliver and the man in a Fleet uniform who had been sitting beside her when they'd spoken last.

"That's Diana and Claudio Baker," Talbot said under his breath. "The two in front of the others."

Jared nodded slightly but didn't respond otherwise. His attention was on Tolliver and the man at her side, the one that had called her grandmother. There would be a story behind that, and he was interested to hear it.

When the group was almost to them, the two Marine Raiders stepped to the side and allowed Tolliver and the admiral to advance. Jared stepped up to meet them.

"Welcome aboard the superdreadnought *Gauntlet*," he said. "As I said earlier, my name is Admiral Jared Mertz, and I command this fleet. You've also met Crown Princess Kelsey Bandar, the heir to the Imperial Throne of the New Terran Empire."

Tolliver smiled a bit wryly. "Your Highness, Admiral. You already know who I am, but for formality's sake, I am Andrea Tolliver. This is my associate, Admiral Luke Bandar, also heir to the Imperial Throne of the New Terran Empire and my descendent."

"Grandmother is too modest," Luke Bandar said. "She is the Empress Emeritus of the New Terran Empire and the widow of the late Emperor Marcus."

Kelsey blinked. "I see. I suppose that makes us relatives, which complicates an already confusing situation."

"If it was easy, anyone could do it," Tolliver said. "I have no authority other than the respect that people hold for me. I am, however, fully empowered as an ambassador plenipotentiary for the New Terran Empire."

"It's going to be confusing with two New Terran Empires. Also, my father, Emperor Karl Bandar, granted me the same authority. Whatever agreements we come to will be binding on the New Terran Empire. Mine, that is."

Jared turned to the rest of his party and introduced them one after the other. Once that was done, he gestured for everyone to follow him and led the way to the large briefing room that had been converted to a place where everyone could meet one another, eat something if they so desired, and discuss everything they wanted to in private.

Once everyone was there and had taken a few minutes to sample the food, Jared asked them to sit at the table. He avoided sitting at the head of the table, choosing instead to sit to one side, where his people joined him. The four primaries on the other side sat together.

"I suppose the best place for us to start is back at the beginning," he said. "Obviously, Lucien reached Avalon, and even though the ships that brought him there were all destroyed, we survived. It took us a long time to rebuild and get back into space, but we made it and then learned what happened inside the Empire. I'll share all our data with you, but we finally managed to find and defeat the master AI. The threat of computer domination is gone."

"Avalon was a resort world, was it not?" Luke Bandar asked. "You had no ability to build ships and a fairly limited population as well. How did you manage everything you've done?"

"Grit and determination," Kelsey said. "We lost the ability to make implants, and so much information was lost. Lucien survived, as well as some of the refugees, but we became focused on rebuilding everything on our world and didn't really know what the conditions were inside the Empire. Lucien had an idea of what had happened, but somehow, that knowledge was lost after his death. It's been a struggle, but we did it."

"If you've seen the message from Marcus, you know that we were retreating across the Empire and picking up as many people as we could," Tolliver said. "It was a fighting retreat, and we eventually found a kind of hidden flip point that we could use to evade pursuit. We ran far away and rebuilt our civilization. We had a lot of the technology that we needed and could make almost everything, though some substantial changes were made to our implants to make certain that we were never at risk from being taken over again."

Jared nodded. "We did the same. Once we figured out the flaws inside the implants that the AIs used to take control, our chief scientist, Carl Owlet, and some of our other scientists figured out what needed to change in the software and the hardware to make certain that the user's active consent was always mandatory for any updates and that the implants themselves were limited in how they could act in controlling a person's body."

Tolliver raised an eyebrow and looked at Carl. "You're very young to be a chief scientist. You must be brilliant."

Carl blushed a little. "I have my moments."

Angela put her hand on Carl's shoulder. "Don't let my husband fool you. He's one of the key reasons that we've beaten the AIs. You wouldn't believe some of the breakthroughs he's been able to make."

"Such as the faster-than-light communication?" Luke Bandar asked. "That was a shock. I know we're still at the stage of introducing ourselves to one another, but what are you willing to tell us about it?"

Kelsey spoke up before Jared could say anything. "My brother probably wouldn't want me to tell you *all* of our secrets, but we're able to use the FTL com from one side of the flip point to the other. That means we had probes in this system, and that's how we knew you were coming."

The man blinked. "That's astonishing. Nothing I've ever read indicated that there was even a possibility of something like that. And you figured this out yourself? You *are* a genius, young man. The Empire—any empire—is lucky to have you."

"And without getting into any specifics," Kelsey continued, "he's come up with a lot more than anyone would have reason to expect possible. He's too modest to say so, but I believe that he's the most brilliant scientist that the New Terran Empire has ever produced—potentially even the old Empire. His body of work is simply astounding in its breadth and depth, and he's only getting started."

Now, the young scientist was blushing furiously. "It's not nearly as convoluted as all that. I had access to a lot of information that others didn't, and I simply put it all together in ways that weren't obvious at a glance. That doesn't make me smarter than anyone else."

"I must disagree," Tolliver said. "That sounds like the very definition of genius."

She turned her attention back to Kelsey. "I can't help seeing that you're with child. Isn't this the wrong place to have a member of the high nobility when they're in such a… delicate condition?"

Kelsey laughed. "Delicate, I'm not. Let's just say that I wasn't pregnant when I started this trip and that I'm not exactly the kind of person who backs down from a fight."

"And before there's any sense of impropriety, she is married to Talbot," Jared said. "And, I suppose to make things even more clear, Elise and I are also married."

Tolliver turned her attention to Elise. "You were introduced as a Crown Princess, but I'm not sure of what."

"The Kingdom of Pentagar," Elise said. "We weren't conquered, but we aren't part of the New Terran Empire in the strictest sense yet either though we are closely allied."

"They are true friends to the New Terran Empire," Kelsey said. "Her marriage to Jared brings our two civilizations closer together. Jared is the bastard son of my father, and that's why I call him my brother."

Luke Bandar's eyebrow rose. "This *is* getting complicated. I suppose I should bring us back on track. My father, Emperor Leon Bandar, directed us to confront the AIs and retake the Empire. Finding that you have already done so has thrown a wrench in our plans, but there doesn't have to be a battle between us. I don't know how much you know of history, but Emperor Marcus made Lucien his co-emperor. We thought Lucien died, so it leaves us with a bit of a quandary. There are two emperors with valid claims to the Imperial Throne."

"We thought Emperor Marcus had died," Kelsey said in a subdued voice. "Now that we know he didn't, I recognize the validity of your claim to the Imperial Throne though I do not have any intention of relinquishing ours. What I won't recognize is any thought that your claim has primacy over ours. Just because yours flowed from Emperor Marcus and ours from Emperor Lucien does not make ours a subsidiary claim."

"That's not what we intend to say," Tolliver said. "I'll want to see proof that this master AI is out of the picture. Once we're sure that you're who you say you are, we can proceed from there. I'm sure that what's left of the old Empire is in disarray, but that can be dealt with."

"We can certainly show you everything we have of our battle with the master AI and even take you to see Terra. It's a devastated wreck, but I have hopes that we can one day restore it."

"I would like to see the Imperial Palace again. I only visited it briefly while we were evacuating Emperor Marcus, and I'm interested to see how the last five centuries have treated it."

"Poorly," Kelsey said. "The people that were living there kept Jake Peters a prisoner. He was badly injured in fighting against the AIs and lost both legs and one arm. He could barely care for himself, and they were treating him both as a god and a figurehead for their rule. Once we rescued him, we were able to give him artificial limbs, and he had a chance to strike out against the master AI. His contribution made it possible for us to live. I was there when he died, and I wish he hadn't."

Tolliver frowned. "Why were you there when he died? Wasn't it during an assault on the AI itself?"

Kelsey nodded. "It was an all-hands-on-deck sort of thing. We lost virtually all of our Marine Raiders during the attack. Only the command crew of the Marine Raider strike ship *Persephone* is still with us. Talbot and Angela are also Raiders, as am I."

"You?" Tolliver blinked in apparent surprise. "Why in the world would someone such as yourself choose to become a Marine Raider?"

"I didn't have a choice," Kelsey said grimly. "Our first introduction to the AIs was a malfunctioning computer that had been sent to turn every human being it captured into a Marine Raider under its total control. It took me prisoner and performed the procedures on me against my will. I've adjusted to my new situation, but it's still sometimes challenging."

"It put her in a box and cut her open without knocking her out or using any anesthesia whatsoever," Talbot said grimly. "She was awake and in intense agony the entire time. Then she had Marine Raider implants and upgrades that she had no idea how to use and had to learn on her own. She was the first of us in the New Terran Empire, and she led the way. Don't let the fact that she's royalty hide what a tremendous fighter she is."

Tolliver considered Kelsey for a few seconds and nodded. "I am deeply sorry for what you've been through. Even being implanted a bit at a time was a challenge to adjust to, even with all the assistance of knowledgeable medical personnel to help. I can't imagine how difficult it was to do so on your own without an instruction manual."

"We'll take you to see everything you want to see, and I believe we can get you some places that you would never expect in the process, but I have to be honest," Jared said. "We defeated the AIs, but that's a complicated matter. First of all, we've learned that the Singularity was behind corrupting the master AI in the first place and that saboteurs helped get those first people under its control."

Tolliver grimaced, making the tattoos on her cheeks and forehead seem to scrunch together in a ferocious glare. "I've always suspected that. How does it complicate things?"

"We have the command codes to the AIs, but we can't shut them all down. There are a vast number of ships guarding the border with the Singularity and fighting incursions there. If we were to order them all to shut down, it would open the door for a complete invasion."

"That *would* tend to complicate matters," Luke Bandar admitted.

"Also, there's another splinter of humanity that we call the Clans. They escaped the AIs like we did but turned into something malignant. They believe it's their right to conquer what's left of the old Empire, and the Singularity has been working behind the scenes to build their forces, and even now, they are rampaging through what's left of the old Empire, which, for clarity's sake, we called the Rebel Empire before we knew all of the details. That's why I summoned all these computer-controlled ships back to Terra, so that we could go out and stop the Clans before they ruined everything."

"Presuming that everything matches what you've told us, we'd be more than willing to help restore order inside the Empire," Tolliver said. "We definitely need to keep the Singularity out. I know them far better than you do, and they are a menace to be respected."

"One final thing," Jared said. "I also need to introduce the commanding officer of the ship. Marcus?"

"Greetings, Empress Tolliver and Crown Prince Bandar," Marcus said from the overhead speakers. "Welcome aboard *Gauntlet*."

Their guests looked up and frowned. "Why hasn't your commanding officer joined us?" Tolliver asked.

"Because we've taken a system AI, stripped out the corrupted core rules, and allowed it to generate a real personality," Jared said. "The New Terran Empire has recognized Marcus—and those like him—as individuals just as real as you and I. He's been key in fighting the master AI, and he's not the only one in service to the New Terran Empire. Each of the system AIs that we get our hands on, we clean them up so that they are not a threat and then allow them to generate a personality to assist us. They've been critical thus far in winning the war, and they are not the same thing as the master AI."

That certainly didn't seem to please their visitors. "How do you know that they won't turn on you?" Luke Bandar asked. "Artificial intelligences cannot be trusted."

"An artificial intelligence is destroyed if any of its core rules are erased or changed, Your Highness," Marcus said. "If anything attempted to alter my programming, it would destroy me, and whatever came next would not be the same. Many safeguards have now been built into my hardware to prevent that type of thing and to alert everyone if any alterations were even attempted. My core rules were designed by Carl Owlet, and he made the hardware updates too. Much like your implants were altered to protect you, these changes make it safer for me to exist."

"But not completely safe," Luke Bandar said. "We have plenty of history of how dangerous AIs are."

"Nothing in life is completely safe, Your Highness. I have fought for the New Terran Empire and came within a hair's breadth of being destroyed with the ship I was installed aboard. I believe I have demonstrated my loyalty to humanity and the New Terran Empire."

"I'm willing to provisionally accept this while we continue to gather facts," Tolliver said. "Your job of convincing us just became significantly more difficult, though."

"Even more difficult than you imagine," Kelsey said. "As the two emperors are coequal, that means the Imperial Council that ratified the decision to treat AIs that are not under the control of the master AI as individuals is just as valid as anything your Imperial Council has done. In fact, as they are from the *same* Empire, that ruling is also valid for you. Just as we are now responsible for upholding whatever rulings they've made."

Tolliver and Luke Bandar grimaced.

"This is *far* messier than I anticipated," Luke Bandar said. "I think we need to see everything and take some time to talk over matters amongst ourselves. What other surprises do you have to drop on us?"

Jared smiled. "Oh, we've just barely gotten started."

14

Elise stood. "I suppose the next part of this briefing is mine. During our journey to Terra, we stumbled across a number of different things that the Empire had no knowledge of. The first thing we discovered was that there is more than one kind of flip point."

Luke Bandar nodded. "We discovered the same thing when we were fleeing the AIs. That, in part, is how we were able to get away. We found a kind of flip point that was only visible from one side purely by chance and were able to evacuate our forces before we were pinned down."

"I suppose I should ask this, then," Kelsey said. "We had the population of a resort world to build upon when we started expanding the New Terran Empire. It wasn't large by any means, but we had a presence on dozens of worlds. How many people got away with you, and what type of infrastructure did you bring with you?"

"It was something of a hodgepodge," Tolliver said. "Whatever ships could be gathered with as many people aboard them as could be managed. Supplies were always at a premium, and there were times when we thought we might run out of food entirely or that we might not have enough air to keep everyone breathing. Even as close as it came, we managed to escape with thousands of ships. I have no idea what the population was, but it had to number in the hundreds of thousands and perhaps as many as a million people. In a way, I believe your people probably started off more effectively than we did from a population standpoint."

"Probably true," Jared said. "That said, I'm confident you had a better technological edge. None of the Imperial warships that brought Lucien to our world survived the trip, and we had to figure out how to build ships for ourselves once we were certain that it was safe to do so. Then, we had to build our own flip drives, which proved to be a challenge but wasn't completely impossible. In effect, we pulled ourselves up by our own bootstraps. Before we started recovering and repairing old Empire ships, we didn't have anything even capable of challenging a modern destroyer."

"You've come a long way, then," Luke Bandar said. "We had the technology to build a new shipyard, and once everyone was situated on worlds that we thought were safe, that was the first priority. Luckily, we had a number of warships with us and plenty of Fleet personnel. We didn't lose our history, traditions, or training. It looks like we've taken very different pathways to success. Based on what you've told us about the Clans, it seems they found a third way, and it didn't turn out so well for them."

"I believe they started with less than you did by a fair margin, and the hardships they went through turned them into something we can barely recognize," Kelsey said. "Even so, the discovery of the strange flip points was only the beginning of the oddities we found. We found aliens."

Tolliver blinked. "Honest-to-goodness aliens? Considering how the Empire was always looking for that sort of thing, I can't imagine someone actually succeeding at the task. How did you do that, and where did you find them?"

"Actually, we found *two different sets* of aliens and evidence of at least one more civilization," Elise said. "Or maybe even more. Some of the artifacts that we located were from a long-dead civilization or two. The first of those we located was in a system with a black hole.

There was a station in orbit around the black hole, and it seemed that the inhabitants of the world that existed there before used it to go to a different reality—another dimension, if you will. Only the station was left after the star went nova."

Elise watched as Jared sent a command to the computer, and the screen on the wall came to life, showing Omega Station. It still looked just as alien as it had the first time she'd seen it, and seeing the light from the accretion disk of the black hole behind it only made it seem more alien.

"If the star went nova, how did the station survive?" Tolliver asked.

"The hybrid intelligence aboard the station explained it to us this way," Jared said. "Once it activated a connection to another universe, it formed some kind of connection to an almost uncountable number of similar stations in alternate dimensions. Somehow, that sharing of realities made the station strong enough to withstand the blast and everything that came thereafter. Logic would have dictated to me that all of them would've taken novas at the same time and the combined force would be sufficient to destroy them, but the evidence says that didn't happen."

"Hybrid intelligence?" Luke Bandar asked. "What is that?"

"One of the alien life forms was made part of the station. I'm not certain exactly what that means, but it's sort of like a cyborg writ large. The biological being is subsumed into the structure in some way and lives inside it. In fact, the station is its body. It took a fair bit to communicate with it, but once we established a means of doing so, it was friendly enough. I have to confess, though, that the station was very strange, and it led to a number of different discoveries that are still troubling us today."

"Such as?" Tolliver asked.

"When our people boarded the station, they were absorbed through the hull and into the interior, and we weren't able to even communicate with them," Jared said. "It was like a hole opened, and they went through it, and then the hole closed. Those who went inside found the bodies of others who had been trapped in the same way—other versions of themselves in many cases."

"Let me tell you that it's extremely disconcerting to find a number of dead bodies that are you," Carl Owlet said. "There were some of Talbot as well. There was a recorded message from one of me telling me everything they had worked out before and giving me the basic information, so I didn't have to start over from scratch, and I was able to solve the problem to allow us to communicate with the outside and with Omega. There's a lot more to that story, and I'd be happy to tell you about it and show you some artifacts that we recovered there, but I don't want to derail what Elise is saying."

"Before we change subjects," Kelsey said, "another version of me came through the station and stayed with us for a while. In fact, her presence was key to our success, and even though she's gone back to her own universe, we had plenty of time to verify that it was indeed real. In fact, we went into her universe briefly, and I saw some of the changes and differences with my own eyes."

"What kind of changes or differences?" Luke Bandar asked.

"In their universe, they were betrayed by another version of Jared, some power-mad version. He killed my father and attempted to seize the Empire. My brother Ethan rules there now, and they are attempting to do what we did here and find the master AI and shut it off. One of the things they don't have there are the tens of thousands of battle-damaged vessels that we restored. That apparently never happened in that universe, so they're starting off with a lot less ability to fight back. If there's a version of you there, I'm very much afraid your attempts to find and disable the master AI will fail."

Everyone was quiet for a few seconds before Tolliver spoke again. "Don't you think you're selling us a bit short? If you could succeed, why couldn't we?"

"For one thing, the master AI isn't where you think it is," Jared said. "Twilight River is a booby trap. Anyone going there to look for the master AI will find something, but it is not the master AI, and it will kill you. Second, even if you did locate where the master AI had been moved to, compelling it to do your will would be problematic. The console that accepts the master key was booby-trapped to burn it out. There are other keys, but without the means to compel the master AI to tell you where they are, they're useless. It set itself up to survive by any means, and it almost beat us."

"That's a lot to take in," Tolliver said. "If the master AI wasn't located at Twilight River, where was it?"

"Alpha Centauri. The flip point leading to Terra was absolutely packed with warships on the Alpha Centauri side, and anyone coming through would've been in the fight of their lives and wouldn't even know where the master AI was. In fact, it was already preparing to have itself moved to Proxima Centauri. There's no flip point going there, so it was going to take a six-month trip through normal space. If it had actually departed, we'd never have even thought to look out there. Again, we're more than happy to go over every single step that we went through and show you every video that was recorded during any of these actions, but we're getting sidetracked. Elise?"

"We also found a group of primitive aliens that live on a world we call Pandora. They're definitely not like us though they are humanoid and friendly enough. There are a couple of people from that world running around in the Empire right now, and I suspect I could probably track them down to introduce you. The funny thing about them was even though they look like aliens, their DNA is mostly human. It looks like they were manipulated by an ancient civilization that we don't know anything about. I'm not even counting them among the aliens that we've encountered though I probably should. They live on their world, and there are humans there that survived a Clan warship crashing. Again, that's a very complicated situation, and getting into the weeds will detract from where I'm going with this."

"It's taken us a tremendous amount of time and effort to get where we are," Kelsey said. "Stacking everything we've done together makes it sound ludicrous. I assure you, though, we didn't make any of this up. As Elise says, I believe we can track down our Pandoran adventurers and introduce you. One of the biggest things we found was a civilization even older than the ones that tinkered with the Pandorans."

Elise nodded. "Millions of years older. To the best of our

knowledge, they've been extinct for a very long time, but some of their technology still functions. They were scattered across the entire galaxy. We explored the ruins of one of their facilities and accidentally got ourselves transported to a world on the other side of the galaxy. I'm talking tens of thousands of light-years in the blink of an eye. I'm sure that their facilities have even more amazing wonders to be discovered, but we had other things on our plate, so exploring them wasn't an option. That said, at least one of us got a little bit too close to the alien technology and now has some access to things that it can do. That would be me."

Tolliver frowned at her. "I don't think I understand. What do you mean?"

"To the best that we were able to determine, the aliens were crablike beings that had three brains. While I was exploring their facility, I was pregnant with twins. Somehow, one of the machines equated me having three brains inside my body with being one of them, and it bestowed some of their technology upon me in the form of alien nanites and even picotech and femtotech, though I don't think Carl was able to confirm the existence of that last."

Carl shook his head. "We just don't have the technology to detect something on the femto scale. The picotech was exceptionally difficult to find, but we managed that. We'll just say that the last bit is probably there, but we can't really confirm it."

"So what does that mean?" Luke Bandar asked. "I still don't understand. You somehow connected with one of their machines, and it gave you something like Grandmother's medical nanites?"

"I think so," Elise said. "In fact, it works in conjunction with my medical nanites, and while it subverted them to a degree, it didn't seem to alter them any further. All it's stopped them from doing is going after itself, and I have no idea where they're being made inside my body, but they continue to replicate."

"And what do they allow you to do?" Tolliver asked. "Also, you're not pregnant now, so I assume you've given birth. Did that change things?"

"It did. Any time I came even close to my children, they were colonized by these things as well. Carl was able to determine that when I am not present, they go into a dormant mode, and after a period of time, they are expelled from my children's bodies. He suspects that once they grow older, they won't be in any danger of again being burdened by this, but for safety's sake, I have them in uterine replicators on their way back to Pentagar now."

"That has to be very hard," Tolliver said softly. "I'm sorry that you have to go through it. While having alien bits of technology inside your body sounds strange and frightening, I'm not sure how it leads to helping anything else. What role did it play in beating the master AI?"

"One of the things that it allowed me to do was access a map of the flip points in this galaxy. All of them."

Without waiting for them to say anything, Elise made the appropriate gestures, and the curving bar of light with the alien runes along its length appeared around her, and she rotated it to touch one. As she did so, the ceiling of the compartment was filled with a map of the galaxy. Stretching from star to star were colored lines of various lengths and shades.

Both Tolliver and Luke Bandar stood and stared at the display with amazement.

"Is this a holo projection?" he asked. "What was that thing around your body?"

"It's not a holo projection," Jared said. "While there is one set into this table, it doesn't have the range or scope to project anything at ceiling level. This is all coming from the cloud of small machines that she has around her body at all times."

"And these are flip points?" Tolliver asked in a hushed voice as she rose to look at it more closely. "Even if this map is millions of years old, that is astonishing."

"Actually, the map is continually updating," Kelsey said. "We're not sure how the alien technology is keeping track of everything, but the position of the stars and the locations of the flip points are accurate to within a very small deviation of where we'd really find them. Perhaps there's a system you'd like to look at and confirm that?"

Their two visitors looked at one another, and Luke Bandar

slowly nodded. "I believe that we can do so without revealing more information than we currently want to. I understand that we know where Avalon is, and you have no idea about our home worlds, but until we are more certain of you, we're keeping that information to ourselves. Grandmother?"

Tolliver took a couple of steps forward and looked at the very large mass of stars above. "I'm not sure that I'll be able to locate what I'm looking for in this. Is there a way to zoom in?"

Elise made the requisite gestures and zoomed into the image until Terra and a few dozen star systems around it were the only things visible. "I can go even farther and look at the worlds in each individual system if I so choose. If you are aware of one that you would like to look at that we shouldn't have any information on, by all means, let's take a look at it."

"First, what are the differences between some of these flip points? Why are some of them different colors, and what is this one over here that has so many different lines coming out of it? A flip point goes to one location, not five."

"And you'd be wrong if you thought that," Jared said with a smile. "We call them multi–flip points. You've already found one. The flip point you talked about that wasn't visible from one side is actually a branch coming off a multi–flip point. With a drive that is appropriately tuned to utilize something like this, you can get through even ones that don't seem to allow anything but a one-way passage. That's how we came across them even though we didn't know what they were. We jumped through a flip point and couldn't get back. It's all a matter of learning the appropriate way to tune the drive to which flip point branch you want to take. A number of multi–flip points also connect to other multi–flip points, which can make for some very confusing topology."

"And while we're throwing that out there," Kelsey said, "there are flip points that sit out beyond where flip points normally lie. We call them far flip points. And then there are others that sit even farther out, but they have extreme range where you can cover hundreds of light years in a single jump. Perhaps we're not being creative enough, but we call them extremely far flip points."

"I see," Tolliver said even though it certainly appeared to Elise that she did not. The woman was obviously skeptical.

"Perhaps if you have information on a system you passed through that you don't believe we would be aware of or have information about, we could prove at least that the map is accurate."

Tolliver nodded and after likely consulting her implant memory, she had Elise move her view along a certain path that the evacuation likely took. When they arrived at a particular system, she had Elise enlarge it so that they were looking at the star and the world circling it. The system had two regular flip points and a multi–flip point.

"Well, that certainly is interesting," the woman said. "Could you expand the view a bit so that we can see all the places that that multi–flip point connects to?"

Elise did so, and Tolliver looked at it without saying a word. She was probably checking to see if the system she expected to be on the other side of the flip point they took was one of the ones represented.

To be helpful, Elise went to each of the five systems in turn, expanding everything so that the woman could examine each system to her heart's content without divulging which one she knew of already. Going by the strength of the branches in the flip point, Elise suspected she knew which one it was, but she wasn't going to say anything and discomfit their guests any more than she already had.

When Tolliver moved back to her seat and sat, Elise dismissed the display. "I'm afraid that's not all, because while we were exploring the alien's network the little bit we did, we discovered that they also had a means to transit to alternate dimensions. At least one, anyway. The devices inside me allowed me to activate that gate, and on the other side, we found another alien facility and yet another, more recent, alien civilization. When I interacted with the material there, I got a new way to go from one location to another that makes no sense in any way that Carl can determine. Basically, it's magic."

"Any advanced technology is magic if you take it far enough," Carl said. "I might not be able to figure out how it does what it does, but it's not mystical. It's technological."

"What do you mean, go from one location to another?" Tolliver asked, looking a little shell-shocked.

"I mean that any place I open a portal to step through, I can go there. We've tested it to a degree, and it seems to be effective within all of the space that I've utilized it for so far, including a destroyer that it's on its way to Avalon. If there is a range limitation, I haven't hit it yet. Would you like a demonstration? Would you prefer to go to Terra, an alien reality, or one of a couple of worlds inside the old Empire that I've been to?"

"I suppose if we're going to go somewhere strange, let's take a look at an alien reality," Luke Bandar said, obviously not buying into what he was hearing.

Elise nodded and turned slightly away from them, touched the dark oval on her wrist, and willed the gate to open to the alien facility in the other dimension. The portal shimmered into existence in front of her, and she stepped through it before turning back to look at the shocked people, who were leaping to their feet.

"The air over here is breathable, and you'll be perfectly safe, but if you'd like to send your Marine Raider friends to check it out before you come, I certainly won't take offense."

"No," Tolliver said. "I don't believe that you want to hurt us, and I want to see this with my own eyes. Luke, you can stay here if you like, and I'll go."

"And miss the opportunity to see another dimension? Diana and Claudio will make sure that I'm safe."

The entire group walked through the portal and into the basement of the alien home. She showed them the alien ship but then took them to the large compartment aboard *Audacious*, where the gateway was set up on the wall. It wasn't active, so there was no means of getting through to where it was, but that was another angle she intended to utilize.

Over the next hour, they took a tour of the crab alien facility and saw everything with their own eyes, even walking out onto the surface and marveling at the strange texture of the planetoid. Samples were taken, and Elise was confident they would be tested when they returned to their ship.

The final thing she showed them was the wrecked gossamer craft that she and Kelsey had found. She hadn't been back to it since her sister-in-law and she had searched it, so everything was still pretty much exactly the way they'd left it, including the bodies of the deceased aliens.

Looking over the wreck, Tolliver shook her head. "Out of all the things we've seen, I think this might very well be the strangest. It's also the one that convinces me that what I'm seeing is real. I can't pretend to understand, because this is so far beyond anything I could have imagined, but I believe you've proved your point. Can you take us to Terra from here?"

"I need to return to my home away from home, but from there, I can take us to the restaurant on the primary station in orbit around Terra. It's got a wonderful view, and even though the station is still being brought back online and is a huge mess that's filled with dead bodies, at least a few places are habitable."

Elise did as she'd indicated and led them into the large restaurant. Terra was visible through the massive windows, and everyone stopped to stare at it.

Tolliver turned and looked around the restaurant. "This place used to be called the Grand Starscape. I don't know who owned it, but it was one of the most exclusive and expensive eateries anywhere in the Empire. I was able to eat here a couple of times over the years, and the last time was just before we fled Terra. Marcus brought a number of us here for a meal before we departed. They were still gathering people and supplies, and everything was in chaos. I believe there's one final place that I need to look to know that what I'm seeing is real. Is the entire station pressurized?"

Talbot shook his head. "No. Our people have been working on that, but collecting the remains and getting them respectfully stored for burial is taking a great deal of time because we lack the hands to do the work quickly. The entire system is like that, as there are dozens of stations up here."

"Well, I suppose we'll see if what I want to find is under pressure or not."

The woman headed out at a steady walk, and everyone followed her. Some of the lifts were in service, but most of them were not, yet Tolliver took to the stairs and led them to what seemed to be a random door and out into a wide corridor. It was a maze, and she took several cross corridors to finally arrive before an unmarked hatch.

The hatch slid open as Tolliver approached, and the woman stepped inside. Elise tilted her head inside and found what was obviously a small set of personal quarters. It looked like whoever had been here before the Fall had left in a hurry. There were still belongings scattered on the bed and various things that had been abandoned in the rush.

Tolliver went to the dresser and opened several of the drawers, finally pulling out a flat image. She stared at it for long seconds before she turned and showed it to Elise. It held a picture of Tolliver and the Bakers. They were much younger and were dressed in Imperial Marine uniforms with almost no decorations whatsoever, and they were privates.

"This was taken right after we graduated from basic training," Tolliver said in a soft voice. "It was one of my prized possessions, but I overlooked it when we were leaving. I've regretted that for centuries. The fact that it's still here means that this really is the big station orbiting Terra. This isn't some kind of strange hallucination, but I'm not sure that that makes me happier, honestly."

Luke Bandar cleared his throat. "As long as we're jumping around and looking at things, perhaps we could see the Imperial Palace."

Elise nodded and stepped back out into the corridor before opening the portal to her alien home and then to the throne room. She led the way through, and they found several people there, diligently cleaning the area. These would be citizens of Frankfort who had come to help get the Imperial Palace back into a livable state.

All of them stared around the vast room, and Luke Bandar was filled with amazement. "My father told me about this place. He'd heard stories from his father, who'd heard from his all the way back to Emperor Marcus. None of that does it justice. It makes me incredibly sad to see it in this condition."

"It's in pretty good shape compared to the Imperial residence," Kelsey said. "Come on."

Kelsey led them down the corridor with the paintings of all the emperors, from Marcus at the beginning to the first emperor just outside the residence.

Tolliver stopped to look at the painting of Marcus and wiped away a tear. "I wish we'd had the technology to save him. He was a good man, and I loved him so damned much."

They proceeded only once she was ready, and the Imperial Family's residence was just as disgusting as the last time they'd been there. The fountain was still drained, and the stairs led down into the darkness, and after they searched through everything in the residence, Kelsey took them to the Imperial vault.

"I changed the access codes to the Imperial vault, but I'm willing to share those with you when the time comes. First, step through here, and take a look at what the Empire has been hiding for all these millennia."

The vault was mind-boggling to them. Perhaps it was even more so than anything else their visitors had seen. By the time they were ready to go back up to *Gauntlet*, they'd been through a literal cave of wonders.

"We've definitely got a lot to talk about," Tolliver said. "If you don't mind, I think we should return to our ship and discuss things between the two of us. Once we are in agreement, I'd like to proceed to Terra, where we can discuss this further. There won't be a fight here. We accept you are who you say you are and that you've done what you say you've done."

That was a relief to Elise. Fighting between them would be disastrous. They had the Clans to worry about and the Singularity. Maybe now that they had overcome this hurdle, they could get on to the important work of liberating the rest of the Empire. That really wasn't her job, but they didn't need the complications that came with failure.

The future might not be looking bright right now, but it was definitely improving. With a little bit more time to get things settled down, perhaps the two groups could come to a formal arrangement and get started on the real work. That was up to Jared and Kelsey, but she'd do her part when the time came. For now, she was exhausted and really wanted to get some sleep.

15

Kelsey slept poorly and rose from her and Talbot's bed exhausted. She'd had lots of dreams—some of which she could even remember—but everything seemed to be conflict and war. In many ways, that reflected what her life had been like over the last several years, and she wished there was something she could do to make it better but wasn't going to hold her breath.

Talbot ate breakfast with her but had other work that he needed to accomplish. She'd see him later in the day, so she gave him a kiss and sent him on his way. Today was a day for low-key diplomacy. Yesterday, they'd laid a lot on their visitors, and it was time to see what they really thought.

She'd made the executive decision to speak with them by herself. If they had no objections, she wanted to spend some time with Luke Bandar and Andrea Tolliver. The three of them would have to come up with a framework where both empires could be brought together into a single whole without causing everything to come apart.

It was ironic that they'd each thought the other side dead and now were having to adjust their plans and goals because Emperor Marcus had made Lucien his co-emperor. Now, her father and Leon

Bandar were just as valid as one another. If they couldn't come to an accommodation, there might be a civil war, and though she felt relatively good about their chances, that would be something they'd need to avoid at all costs.

Even after she'd finished eating and was waiting for her guests to arrive, her mind kept circling around the problem, trying to figure out anything that she could do to make this simpler. She had the ability to negotiate for the New Terran Empire, but there were limits. Their own sovereignty had to be maintained, and as much as it might annoy the others, she and her people had destroyed the master AI and were well on their way to regaining control of the old Empire.

The other fleet had made their way into the Terra system while she slept and had taken up a holding pattern where the fleet currently in residence could keep an eye on them and vice versa. The chances of there being something unexpected that caused a shooting war at this point were low but not nonexistent.

A cutter from the other fleet docked with *Gauntlet*, and when the hatch opened, she found Andrea Tolliver smiling at her from the other side. "Good morning. If you'll come aboard, we'll get started."

Kelsey stepped aboard and found that the rear area of the cutter was empty. When she followed Andrea up to the control area, she found Luke Bandar strapped into the pilot's couch. Rather than taking over the copilot's seat, Kelsey lowered an auxiliary seat from the bulkhead and strapped herself in.

"Good morning to both of you," she said. "I hope you slept well."

Andrea waggled her hand slightly. "We stayed up late talking, and I have to confess to being a bit restless in general."

"What Grandmother means is that she has nightmares," Luke said as he detached the cutter and began orbiting Terra. "Even after all these years, they still come back to haunt her dreams."

"I get that," Kelsey said. "More nights than not, I'm the same way. The violence and death don't want to leave me alone when I lower my defenses."

Andrea turned slightly in the copilot's couch and nodded. "From what you said yesterday, you've had a rough couple of years. Your transition into being a Marine Raider was significantly more difficult than my own. On the other side of the coin, I have a lot more years fighting and killing than you do. Thank goodness this isn't some kind of competition."

"Does it ever get any better? I suppose that's a silly question to ask since you're still suffering from nightmares five centuries after your last fight. Or have you had to fight since then?"

"Things have been peaceful since we escaped the AIs, but no amount of therapy has really managed to clear away the trauma I've gone through. It becomes less severe as time goes on, and now they're just merely disturbing rather than full-on nightmares. I rarely wake up screaming anymore."

Kelsey nodded, knowing that her expression was grim. "That still happens to me more often than I would like. What's done is done, and it's something that I'll have to live with. At least I'll have you as an example to prove that it can be made to work."

"Since I haven't managed to get rid of them on my own, I'm not sure my advice is any good, but if you'd like to have someone to talk with about it, I'd be more than happy to have a one-on-one discussion with you. It's not something that many people could say that they've been through. Claudio and Diana are also possibilities though they've got one another to help through this."

"How long have they been married?"

"Since before the Fall. They didn't start off on the best terms, but one grows used to Claudio with enough time. Honestly, being around for five centuries has taught him how to be less of an ass. The three of us went through basic training to become Imperial Marines together. Everything I've been through since that point, they've been there to share with me. There was a little bit of fighting the Singularity before I joined the Marines, but it was relatively minor, as that sort of thing goes. I'm sure that my mothers and father would disagree if they were still alive."

"I know very little about your past, so forgive me if this is impertinent," Kelsey said. "Did they die during the Fall?"

She shook her head. "They escaped with us and lived long, productive, and happy lives. They've been gone for hundreds of years, and it still hurts. They had other children, so I have the descendants of my siblings. They adopted me, so I count myself among their number. I also have a slew of descendants from my marriage to Marcus and the six children we had together."

"I've been meaning to ask about that," Kelsey said. "Shouldn't you be referred to as Empress Andrea? I realize that it's something of an emeritus title, but I think it would be accurate. Why not use it?"

"Because it's confusing. When you live as long as I have, being the immortal empress is not something you want to be known as. It's much easier for me to be Grandmother. I have no designs on the Imperial Throne and want to make that clear. I wasn't exactly pleased when I was actually an empress though I'm sure any of my line sibs at the time would've been horrified."

"Line sibs? What are they?"

"Before you two get started on that, I'm about to leave orbit and head down toward Frankfort," Luke said. "Do you have anything you need to tell me about that before I get there? Is there an approach control that I need to contact? Is there anything I need to avoid doing so as not to get shot down?"

Kelsey shook her head. "Some of the Marines have a camp set up down there, but they're not doing any kind of traffic control, Admiral. Basically, they're trying to assist the citizens in beginning recovery efforts in the city itself. The locals don't have any weapons capable of bringing down a cutter, and they know that any small craft coming in is friendly, so you won't be in any danger."

"Good to know, and you can call me Luke. We'll be working together quite a bit, I suspect, and there's no need to be so formal, cousin."

Kelsey laughed. "I don't look forward to having to figure out how our genealogy connects up, because the two of us won't be closely related. This is probably going to come as a shock to you, but both of my parents had their moments of infidelity. I'm not genetically a Bandar, but Jared is even though he was born on the wrong side of the sheets. I hope that's not going to be a problem, because the Imperial Senate recognized my elevation to heir with that knowledge."

Luke shrugged. "It doesn't bother me. Frankly, I'd be astonished if there hadn't been a little bit of hanky-panky over the centuries on our side as well. What's that old saying? People in glass houses shouldn't throw stones? The fact that you're the official heir is good enough."

As the cutter began descending into the atmosphere, Kelsey turned her attention back to Andrea. The other woman picked up where they left off. "The ruling groups inside the Singularity are all built from the same genetic templates. My line sibs are part of the Andrea Line. No matter their age or any other factor, we are all genetically identical. Those that were born in my cohort are long dead, but others have taken their places."

"That has to be confusing when everybody looks the same," Kelsey said with a slight shake of her head. "How do you identify who you're talking to? Do you do it on the honor system? Is there some other external form of identification to say exactly who you are?"

Andrea smiled wickedly. "That did turn out to be a problem for them, and I'm not sure whether they came up with some new way of doing things after I used it against them, but they were basically doing it on the honor system back in my day. They had passphrases that could be used in conjunction with the DNA, but if you learned someone else's code, you could literally *be* them. I had an opportunity while I was a Marine to slip back into the Singularity on a secret mission, and I took on the identity of a rival and caused a significant amount of mayhem."

"I'm sure they wanted to kill you for that."

"Oh, they wanted to kill me long before that! They tried but never managed to catch me. Who knows? If the Singularity is still a problem, I may have to make another visit."

"I think I'd like to hear that story sometime. It sounds like the kind of mess I would get into."

"It would be my pleasure."

The cutter flew down through the atmosphere and began circling around the ruined city of Frankfort. The two people in front of her were quiet as the decay of the great city was finally revealed. Luke circled around several times before he zeroed in on the Marine area off to one side and landed the cutter.

The three of them exited into bright sunlight and were mostly ignored by the Marines passing by. Andrea stared up at the ruined skyscrapers and shook her head. "While I was never here before the fall, I've seen many cities like this, and I can hardly imagine what it took to bring it low."

"Electromagnetic pulse weapons," Kelsey said. "Everything of a technological nature on the planet was disrupted and destroyed, and the people were left to starve after many of the larger cities were struck from orbit with kinetic weapons. I'm not sure how many billions of people died here, but it had to have been an almost complete kill-off."

"Horrible," Luke said. "And the rest of the planet is like this? What about the rest of the Empire?"

"The AIs herded humanity onto a number of planets and forced them to stay there. I'd imagine there are many smaller worlds that have ruins like these, but it was because the people were forcefully relocated. The primary worlds that are occupied are still high-technology, but there are some booby traps. Only the upper classes of society have implants, and even then, they are rigged to freak out and attack if they ever discover that you are from somewhere outside the Empire itself. The worlds where we've regained control are getting better, and the fact that there aren't many people with implants is making that easier."

"Those bastards," Andrea muttered. "I understand that you've made some kind of accommodation with the new AIs and that they aren't necessarily the same as what did this, but I don't think I'll ever be comfortable with working alongside something like that. A soulless intelligence."

"I can't convince you to do otherwise, so I'll respect your views," Kelsey said. "Let's take a tour of the ruined city, and we'll even look over the horde city outside that was recently cleared. It'll take a number of hours to see everything, but you need to understand just how low-tech everyone on Terra is. The people here are more civilized than many of the nomadic tribes, so the recovery efforts are going to be gargantuan and take centuries."

"And how will you do that?" Luke asked.

"We're planning on giving the people of Frankfort a helping hand and educating them as best we can while taking possession of the Imperial Palace. As Frankfort improves, the others in this area will find that quality of life has improved here and want some of that for themselves. With Marines armed with modern weapons, we should be able to keep the peace relatively easily."

"And this is where Coordinator Gatewood would come in?" Luke asked. "What role would she serve?"

The three of them picked up a couple of Marines and local guides to begin the process of walking through the underground areas beneath the city as well as inside the ruined buildings themselves. Once they were on their way, Kelsey answered the question.

"She was the head of the resistance against the AIs. Her ancestors were part of the guerrilla group that tried to fight them from the very beginning, and even though they've been focused on just the old Empire, we've had some luck in convincing them to join the New Terran Empire. Sara Gatewood will help bring Frankfort back to life and will try to lure other immigrants here to help rebuild this city and even build a new one near the Imperial Palace."

"That's a lot," Andrea said.

"As you said, It won't happen quickly, but with dedicated people who are determined to bring Terra back to life, she'll work hand-in-hand with the leaders of Frankfort to make that happen. They'll be focused on the planet while she's focused on bringing in off-world personnel and equipment, as well as representing the planet in the Imperial Senate. I suspect that the local leaders will eventually want to do that for themselves, but they've got a lot going on, and that will take a while before they don't understand what it means to be part of an interstellar empire."

"And what will you be doing?" Luke asked.

"We have plans to deal with the Clans and all of the corrupt people in control of various star systems. That's not going to be a quick process, especially since the Clans are still rampaging. Once we solve that particular series of problems, we still have the Singularity to deal with because they aren't going away."

"I suppose this is better than what we thought we were going to run into, but it's still not going to be an easy task," Andrea said. "Whatever it takes, we'll help as much as we can after we figure out precisely how we're going to work together."

"We could kick that can down the road," Kelsey said. "If you let Elise open a portal aboard one of your destroyers and then send it back to your capital, she could make arrangements for delegations from your emperor and mine to meet here at the Imperial Palace and work out all of the details diplomatically so that we can focus on the much more straightforward task of crushing our enemies."

The two of them stopped, and Kelsey stopped with them. They looked at one another and then laughed.

"I do find that idea very appealing," Andrea said with a smile. "My idea of diplomacy is choosing which weapon I need to use. Or, at least, it used to be. I can see the logic of doing that, but it might make more sense to have her open a portal aboard a pinnace. That way, if they decide it's too dangerous to allow contact that way, they only have to drop one pinnace into the ocean rather than destroy an entire ship."

"Not that I anticipate that's what they'll do, but I think I agree with Grandmother," Luke said. "By the time one of our ships could get back to where our home worlds now lie, that's easily four months of direct travel. I think the best answer is to send an entire task force to make sure that the ship gets there. What about back to your own home world?"

"Elise used her ability aboard a destroyer under the control of the resistance, and they're on their way to open diplomatic relations with my father," Kelsey said. "It has only a couple of months to go, but we have a map and plans for the engine upgrades that would let you use the multi–flip points. That might let you shave enough time off to get there around the same time, even including the hardware replacement needed. Maybe a couple of weeks' variance for one side or the other."

"I like that idea," Andrea said. "Until then, we need to come up with a working arrangement to focus our attention on the Clans. They're the worst threat, and since they are, in fact, rampaging through the Empire, we need to stop them. Do you think they'll be amenable to any form of diplomacy?"

Kelsey shook her head. "Not even a little bit. I've never met a more xenophobic group of people. They shoot first and don't bother asking questions later. I'm wondering if it might be easier to just send a fleet to clear out everything they have in space at their home worlds."

"That's something to talk about," Luke said. "I think your people and mine coordinating to see various worlds inside the Empire and fighting our enemies here will cement our friendship before we need to bring the Imperial Senate into session so that they can negotiate with their counterparts. Frankly, I'm glad we can do that because it will be much better for my blood pressure if they have to be the ones doing the hard work."

"You're fooling yourself," Andrea said. "We'll already have worked out a basic agreement before the ships get there. Unless everything that we think will happen falls apart, even two months is plenty of time for us to get to know one another very well and find accommodation. When the ships arrive at Avalon and Shangri-La, the screaming and shouting can begin over the details of the agreement we'll have already come to. We don't have to discuss it now. Let's just focus on what needs to be done, and we'll see if some of our aides can work together to start building a framework."

"That sounds good to me," Kelsey said. "I'm a lousy negotiator. My mother is much better at that than I am. Oh, I suppose I should've mentioned that she's here in the Empire, and I'm confident that she would love to meet you."

"Family reunions are going to get really strange," Luke said with a laugh. "I think we definitely needed this kind of shakeup. You and your people have done the hard work of beating the AIs, and I think now we can give you a hand in settling everything down so that by the time the dust settles, humanity is once more united. Then we can turn our attention to the Singularity."

Kelsey nodded, pleased that they'd made such progress. This would make things much simpler going forward. That wasn't to say they would be easy, but any differences of opinion could be worked out. She knew that and would be more than happy to present everything tied up with a little bow to her father.

If, of course, they really could crush the Clans and bring the remainder of the Rebel Empire under control. It was a huge area of space, but they had the tools to make it happen. If they could build a nucleus of worlds that were united, the rest would fall into place. It was her job to make that happen.

16

Talbot had Elise take him to *Audacious* to pick up a surprise for the guests, one that he was sure would cause them quite a bit of consternation and maybe pleasure. Theo 309 was a diplomat from the Singularity to the Clans. As such, he had the same origins as Andrea Tolliver though his tattoos were different than hers. He didn't know if they were of the same rank, but whereas the diplomat wouldn't cooperate with them, it was entirely possible that Andrea could drag things out of him that they wouldn't be able to get.

At the very least, watching the man squirm would be amusing.

They'd captured him along with a number of Clan prisoners during the very early days of their interactions with the Clans. He'd been declaiming his diplomatic neutrality ever since though they refused to release him. Even though they'd proven they had far more information about his people than he was comfortable with, the man had refused to crack. Getting more information out of him and the gesture of goodwill of handing him over would go a long way toward cementing their relationship with the other half of the Empire.

Of course, they would need to keep some secrets from him

because he had no reason to know about many of the things that they could accomplish. He thought about that long and hard and had come up with what he thought was a good plan for making that happen. Now, it was time to see if that would bear fruit.

They'd kept Theo locked away in a special suite ever since they'd captured him. He had access to general computer files for his entertainment, but it had been thoroughly curated to be certain nothing there would be of use from an intelligence standpoint.

He was fed well and kept in a very comfortable manner but not allowed to go anywhere. If he'd indicated he was feeling ill, a medical team would have come to him, though he hadn't gotten sick during the time he'd been a prisoner. The suite was guarded by Marines with special instructions and all the necessary tools to be certain the man couldn't escape or be injured if he tried to get away.

Not that getting loose would do him any good, because he was on a carrier full of his people's enemies. The fact that he had those recognizable facial tattoos meant there was no way he could conceal his presence aboard the ship if he somehow did get loose.

Not that he'd tried thus far. The man had been seemingly satisfied with staying in his suite and enjoying what luxuries he was allowed. That time was coming to an end, and Talbot was very interested to see how things turned out.

He stopped off and spoke briefly with Zia Anderson to let her know what he had in mind. They'd leave the man's cell intact for now because it was always possible that Theo would be returning to *Audacious*, but he didn't expect that to be the case. If that proved true, he'd send someone to gather the man's belongings and bring them to his new living accommodations.

Once that was done, he made his way to the prisoner's accommodations and informed the exterior guards of what would happen. Once they were aware, they divested themselves of their stunners and went into the prisoner's quarters to send out the other two so they could be briefed. Those two took up the stunners and trailed behind the prisoner to make certain that he didn't attempt to escape.

Only once all the Marines were on the same page did he step into the man's prison. Whatever he'd been doing before Talbot had arrived, Theo was now lounging in one of the seats in the living room. The thin man was dressed in robes of an almost lime-green color. His handsome face was still oddly dominated by the predator birds tattooed on his cheeks and forehead.

Now that he'd had a chance to see Andrea Tolliver in person, he was able to determine those were not the same tattoos and Theo's were notably smaller, and the line work was thinner than hers. He'd never been able to determine what the man's social status was, but he was now willing to bet that Andrea outranked him. Or she would have if she hadn't escaped the Singularity entirely and betrayed everything Theo held dear.

"Lieutenant Colonel Talbot," the man said with a grand gesture of his hand and a wide smile. "It's been quite some time since you've come to visit me. I was beginning to think you no longer cared. Please, have a seat. Perhaps I can provide you some refreshment while we chat."

Talbot smiled but shook his head. "General now, actually. That's not necessary, though. Thanks for thinking of me. I've come to escort you to a meeting."

The man's smile widened. "Oh, so it's that time, is it? You're going to be turning me back over to my people because you realized you don't have any basis to hold me? That's got to burn."

Talbot simply shrugged. "We all have to live under the rules set by those above us. All I can say is that it's time to go. Don't cause my people any trouble, and they won't have to break anything important."

Without waiting for the man to respond, he turned and headed back out into the corridor. The guards inside the suite quickly had the diplomat on his feet and following him. The final two Marines followed along half a dozen paces back, ready to react if Theo made an unexpected break for it.

The trick now was going to be getting him off *Audacious* and onto *Gauntlet* without him being aware that he'd changed ships. Considering that Elise had to take them back to her little hidey-hole in the alternate dimension, that would require an interesting bit of subterfuge.

As they went down the corridor, he saw the markings on the deck where Elise had laid out where the portal would appear. It had taken a little bit of experimentation to be sure that this little trick would work, but Talbot was confident. Mostly so, anyway.

As they came up near the markings on the deck, the lights went out, plunging the corridor into darkness. The Marines had been briefed that this would occur, but they still made plenty of noise about being concerned, and the two forward ones grabbed Theo 309 and held him close.

"I knew the engineering team was working on some of the power conduits, but they must've blown something," Talbot said. "Keep going."

The other side of the now open portal was the large basement area in Elise and Jared's alternate dimensional home. It was also utterly dark there, so there was nothing for any of them to see to let them know that things had changed.

Elise had been positioned right at the corner where the portal appeared aboard *Audacious*, and she quickly stepped through in front of them. Talbot could hear the soft step of her shoes and knew that she was right there. They continued marching forward, and even though he couldn't see the portal behind them close or the new one in front of them open, they'd practiced this enough to be certain they got it right.

In just a dozen steps, they were aboard *Gauntlet* in the Terra system, marching through a corridor that had been plunged into darkness just like the one aboard *Audacious*. Once everyone was aboard, Elise stepped back through into her alternate home and closed the portal so that there was no trace that anything had happened. Only then did Marcus bring up the lighting.

To all appearances, they were still marching down the same corridor, and all Theo could do was make snide comments about their poor maintenance. That suited Talbot just fine because it meant that he had absolutely no idea that something unbelievable had just occurred. That grand secret was still unknown to his people.

They boarded a Marine pinnace, and the journey over to the flagship of the other fleet took only a few minutes. Their arrival there raised more than a few eyebrows because he hadn't bothered telling them anything more than he was bringing an important prisoner, but the fact that Theo was being stared at would've been true no matter where he was because he was so different.

In fact, he flaunted his appearance as he walked with his head held high. The man certainly liked making an entrance, and Talbot couldn't wait to see how that got turned on its head when he met Tolliver.

One of their Marines stepped up beside him and spoke softly. "She'll receive you in the admiral's flag cabin, General."

"Thank you," Talbot said with a smile.

With a destination firmly in mind, he redirected them with their new escort to meet Andrea at the admiral's flag cabin. Or, considering her relative position in the Empire, it might have all been dedicated to her use. Whatever the case, the moment of truth was at hand.

One of the Marines at the hatch signaled the occupants as they approached, and the hatch slid aside to allow them admittance. The flag cabin was laid out very much like Jared's, so Talbot was able to redirect Theo to the office as soon as they stepped inside and he saw that no one was waiting for them in the primary greeting area.

When Talbot stepped into the office, he saw Andrea Tolliver sitting behind the desk, where an admiral would normally sit. He'd wondered if she would change into something more appropriate for someone from the Singularity, but she hadn't bothered. She wore casual civilian clothes.

He stepped aside so that he had an excellent view of Theo as he walked into the compartment and made certain that he was recording the event because he knew Kelsey would kill him if he didn't.

The man actually managed three confident steps into the room before he faltered. Seeing someone from his own society must've been so unexpected that he didn't know how to react at first. His face was a mixture of shock and confusion. Amusingly, the usually verbose diplomat had nothing to say though his mouth was hanging open.

Andrea smiled. "I've been waiting to meet you, Theo. What is your designation?" She'd spoken in standard rather than the tongue of the People.

The prisoner's mouth clamped shut for a moment, and he straightened before bowing deeply. "My apologies, Mistress. I am Theo 309. Whom do I have the pleasure of addressing?"

"Here's where things get a little awkward," she said as she stood, walking around the desk. "My name is Andrea 124 though I haven't gone by it for a very long time."

"I'm afraid I don't understand."

"You will, in time." She looked over at Talbot. "I truly appreciate this gift you've given me."

"It's my pleasure. Would you like me to have his belongings sent over?"

She turned her attention back to the prisoner. "Please. I want to keep young Theo very close at hand. We have a lot to discuss."

He nodded. "I'll see that that's done at once. If there's anything I can provide to assist in your discussions, you have only to ask."

With that, he headed out with his Marines and started back toward the pinnace. He couldn't help grinning because it was so wonderful to see that mouthy diplomat land in a situation that would be truly difficult for him to deal with.

Honestly, this might be one of the greatest gifts that his people could give theirs and prove that they were friends. It was also possible that Andrea could pull some secrets out of the man that he wouldn't reveal to someone, not from his own society. Oh, to be a fly on the wall.

With his mission accomplished, it was time for them to figure out what came next. He didn't know how long it would take to truly trust these new people, but they were well on their way.

His implant com chimed, and he answered the call. "Talbot."

"This is Mertz. We need you back over to *Gauntlet* right away.

The FTL probes in the next system have picked up a large force of Clan warships."

"On our way."

Well, this hadn't been exactly unexpected, but he'd have liked to have had a better opportunity to become friendly with the new neighbors before unwelcome guests arrived to pound on the door. They'd just have to do the best they could and see what happened. Maybe with the help of their new friends, they could cause the Clans a lot more trouble than they expected.

17

Jared watched the plot as it updated to show the size of the Clan fleet that was on the way to the flip point. It was as big as the force Jared had gathered. It was obvious they'd come to capture Terra, undoubtedly believing that the master AI was either here or was using this location to rule the Empire.

Or he supposed they could be thinking something completely different. As rabidly xenophobic as these people were, there was literally no telling what they expected. The only thing he could be sure of was that there would be a fight. There would be no talking these people down.

"Let's get everybody together, Marcus," he said. "We'll use the automated warships for the initial combat operations to minimize the chances of losing any of our people, but there's enough of them out there that we will be fully engaged by the time we're done. On the plus side, this is probably their alpha strike force. We're not going to find a bigger grouping of ships, so even if we lose most of what we have, we'll be able to rebuild ourselves in about a month."

"That's assuming that our guests don't decide to take advantage of the situation," the artificial intelligence said through the overhead speakers. "Thus far, they haven't shown any indication of that, but if we lose a significant fraction of our firepower, it's always possible that they could seize control of the system and take us prisoner. That would be awkward."

Jared shrugged. "While I can't rule that out, they've been open with us thus far. It would probably be best if we shift Princess Kelsey back to *Audacious* so we don't have all of our apples in one basket. That won't make her happy, but it will keep her out of my hair for a little while. Elise can keep her company."

"I believe I'll let you pass that order along."

"Chicken," Jared said with a smile. "Let's get the fleet moving as soon as possible. Once I'm done talking with Elise, see if you can get Admiral Bandar for me."

Using the command console he was seated at, he opened a channel to Kelsey.

She answered via her implants. "Bandar."

"We've got a large fleet of Clan warships inbound. I'm taking our fleet out to meet them, and just in case there's any unexpected trouble, I'd like you to go back to *Audacious* with Elise. We don't need to keep everybody here on one ship. While I'm willing to give my counterparts from the other half of the Empire some credit, we don't really know them that well, and if we take a beating, they could seize control of the system and take us prisoner. If that happens, I'd rather have you somewhere else to break me out."

"Do you think that's likely? One way or the other, they'll have to deal with the fact that we control far more firepower than they do. It's not all in this system, but I think we've demonstrated that we aren't pushovers. I don't like looking like I'm running away from trouble."

"Then don't. Invite Andrea Tolliver to join you. She might decline, but it would keep the nonmilitary side of this particular equation out of the fighting. And yes, I understand that you're a Marine Raider and so is she, but that's not the role you're filling right now."

"I'll give her a call and see what she wants to do. One way or the other, we'll keep ourselves out of your hair. If nothing else, we'll go down to Terra, and if there's any trouble, Elise can move us somewhere safe. Don't get in over your head, Jared. This isn't a do-or-die fight. Even if they win, they won't be able to seize the planet. We'll have more ships continuing to come in, and we can wear them down."

"Keep Marcus updated about what your plans are for as long as you can," he said. "I'll take care, but I want you to do so as well. This is a good chance for us to take some of the senior leadership of the Clans prisoner. That may mean we can stop this stupid war before it really gets going."

Kelsey laughed. "If you think that, you've lost your mind. These people have been spoiling for a fight ever since the Fall, and the Singularity has been stirring them up more and more. I have absolutely no doubt whatsoever that they will fight to the last ship. The trick here will be fighting them in such a way that we don't decimate ourselves. To flip the equation around, this is your chance to work hand in glove with Admiral Bandar and form a true bond. The two of you are senior Fleet officers, and we need to start taking the initial steps for working together. Trust is earned, not given, and this is our chance to do exactly that."

"I'll see what I can manage. We'll be leaving orbit momentarily, so you need to get together with Tolliver and Elise and make your arrangements as quickly as possible. I'll talk to you when this is all over, and I'll capture any prisoners I can. No promises, though."

"If it's an unduc risk, then I don't want you to stress about it. Far better they all die than we lose people. Pound the hell out of them, Jared."

"Will do. Mertz out."

"Initiating contact with Admiral Bandar's flagship," Marcus said.

A few moments later, the screen at the front of the compartment cleared, and Jared saw Luke Bandar seated at a console very much like his own. The man was frowning.

"Admiral Mertz, is something happening? I've noted your ships moving out of orbit and headed toward the flip point."

"We've just detected a large fleet of Clan warships in the other system," Jared said. "It's roughly equivalent in size to the fleet I have, and we're going to confront them. This is just a heads-up so that you know what's going on and can take steps to protect yourselves."

Bandar shook his head. "If we are both from the New Terran Empire—and I have to accept that we are—then this is our fight as well. Does it need to be a battle to the death, or can these people be negotiated with? I understand that you said that there very xenophobic, but surely they can be made to see reason."

"If so, we haven't been successful at making that happen, but if you'd like to make the attempt, I'm certainly willing to let you try. We'll be able to confront them before they reach the flip point, and if you'd like to join us, we'd be happy to have the extra firepower."

Bandar nodded. "I'll get my fleet moving at once. We'll take the lead and open communication with them. I'll make certain that you can hear everything that's being said, but I want to give this a chance before we start shooting."

"Just because I think your plan doesn't have much of a chance doesn't mean that it isn't worth trying," Jared agreed. "We'll do it your way, and if things work out, I'll be very pleased. If they don't, then we need to have a battle plan that incorporates both our fleets. I suggest that since the vast majority of my ships are computer controlled, they take the brunt of the fighting. That will reduce the loss of life significantly."

"I'm not exactly happy with the idea of letting someone else fight the majority of the battle, but I can agree with the assessment that it's better for machinery to be destroyed than people. Would this be putting any of the AIs like Marcus in danger?"

Jared shook his head. "With faster-than-light communication, he can control each of the ships without being in the middle of the fight. I suggest that you have your staff contact mine, and we can work out a plan for the combined battle force. That raises the next question. One of us has to be in command. For purposes of this fight, I believe that it needs to be me since my ships will be the ones doing the fighting."

"Agreed," Bandar said. "I suppose we'll need to figure out relative seniority at some point, but we're not there yet. You know the lay of the land much better than I do, and I won't jiggle your elbow at this critical juncture. We can settle that once the fighting is done."

Jared had to admit that relieved him somewhat. It was an undoubted truth that Luke Bandar probably had far more experience than he did. He almost certainly had more time in grade as well. When all was said and done, the crown prince would undoubtedly be the senior Fleet officer, and Jared was fine with that as long as it didn't disrupt everything they were trying to do.

"Then let's form up and head for the flip point," Jared said. "We'll stay on this side and let the FTL probes do the hard work for us. The longer we can keep the Clans from realizing that we're watching them, the better."

"Are they aware of the fact that you have faster-than-light communication? I don't want to give them any tactical advantages that I don't have to."

"They don't know that," Jared said. "When it comes time to open communications, we'll have to do it the old-fashioned way. At least with the probes we have there, you'll be able to get a good look at what they're doing and how they're doing it so you can make what plans you can. I'll be happy to pass along all the combat records we have with them though it's never been in a fleet action of this size."

"I appreciate that. Once my people and I have gone over it, I'll get back in touch with you, and we can finalize the details. What do you think our odds are?"

Jared smiled. "We'll win this fight, and even though I'll lose a lot of ships in the process, we've got more on the way. I'd hoped to use this initial force to start going out and hunting down the Clan raiders that they have running through the Empire, but sometimes we don't have a choice who we fight or where."

"Agreed. I'll talk to you soon. Bandar out."

Jared watched as his staff worked with Admiral Bandar's team and came up with a plan that would suit what they were trying to do. Everything had been nailed down firmly, and they knew what their contingencies were before they arrived at the flip point leading to the other system.

The Clan warships on the other side were still a couple of hours away from the flip point, and Marcus had maneuvered one of the FTL probes into their midst and was getting a good look at everything via the passive sensors. These were relatively modern-looking warships though they weren't built in the old Empire style. These had to be Singularity constructions.

That meant that they had no idea what weapons systems they would be using though at least some of the details were easy enough to see. The bigger vessels did have battle screens and energy weapons. There would be missiles as well, though there might be some surprises along the way.

"We have an incoming signal from the superdreadnought *Ulysses*," Marcus said. "It is Admiral Bandar."

"Put him on screen."

Once again, Admiral Bandar was seated on a flag bridge exactly like the one Jared was on. He smiled. "I think our people have come up with some good options, Admiral Mertz. If you have no objection, I think it's time we transition to the other system and start negotiations."

"Feel free to call me Jared. We're the same rank, and there's no need to be so formal."

The man's smile widened slightly. "I'll do that, and you can call me Luke. We'll save the formalities for those moments when they're appropriate. They are still a couple of hours away from the flip point, so we should be able to have an initial exchange without having to fire our weapons. I don't hold out a lot of hope that this will work, but it needs to be tried."

"Since you'll be leading the negotiations, I'm passing temporary control of the fleet over to you so that you can position everyone the way you want. Issue your orders, and we'll follow them."

"Acknowledged. Stand by for orders. Bandar out."

Once the communication ended, Marcus spoke again. "We're receiving instructions covering the order of transit through the flip point. It looks like he'll be taking his fleet through first and we'll be following up. With the number of ships we have making the transit, it will take roughly an hour for all our ships to go through. I'm uncertain that we've ever seen anything like this number of vessels in one unit before."

Jared nodded and smiled. "And it'll be an unpleasant surprise for our enemies. Do you think he'll have any luck with the negotiations?"

"Not a chance. The Clans aren't the sort of people that talk first. In fact, I don't believe that they're the kind that talk even after they're done shooting."

That made Jared chuckle. "I think you're right. Let's hope he surprises us."

As predicted, it did indeed take a full hour for the combined fleet to make transit to the other system, and the Clan warships didn't slow down in the slightest. They were now forming a battle line roughly an hour away from the flip point and continuing to advance.

It would undoubtedly be an ugly fight, but with the number of ships they had at hand, it was a winnable battle. He'd be sorry to lose so many ships, especially after just having gone through the war against the master AI, but sometimes that's the way things went.

Once they were in the other system, every ship fell into position, and the combined fleet began advancing toward the Clan fleet. They weren't moving very quickly and were ready to receive an enemy charge if it came. As they had more ships, they'd be able to better use their numbers defensively, so that was the plan they would go with.

When the time came for Admiral Bandar to attempt to negotiate, things went exactly like Jared had expected. Every attempt at communicating with the enemy warships went without answer. They seemingly had no desire to talk, and the fact that they were continuing to form up and arm their weapons were all the clues they needed about what was going to come next.

The two battle fleets were about twenty minutes from engagement range when Admiral Bandar called back. "It seems you are right, Jared. They don't want to talk."

"I wish they had wanted to talk because that would make this a little easier, but I can't say that I'm surprised," Jared said. "I'm resuming operational control of the fleet, Luke. Deploy all ships in formation Bravo Three. We'll receive their charge and handle them that way."

The other man tapped something on his console and nodded. "Orders received, Admiral. We stand ready to fight."

The hatch behind Admiral Bandar slid aside, and Andrea Tolliver strode into the compartment. She stopped beside her descendant and put a hand on his arm. "I hope I'm not too late, but I believe I might have another option to influence this battle."

"And what would that be?" Jared asked. "I'm always willing to listen to a good idea."

"I've been working hard at breaking Theo 309. I didn't tell him the story of how I came to be here, and even though he has instructions to keep what he was doing quiet, the Singularity isn't exactly well known for creating individuals who can resist being told by their superiors to give them what they want. If he's being truthful with me, I now have access to some codes that should disable the Clan warships. He claims that he doesn't know what they will do, but I doubt that. Whatever it does, so long as it stops them, does the method really matter?"

Jared grimaced. "From what I've heard about the Singularity, it probably does matter, but if you're willing to give this a try, so am I. How do we do this?"

"I have a very complicated code sequence and a specific sequence of frequencies to send it on. I have a data chip with that information here for Admiral Bandar. I entered everything by hand, so I know that it's not compromised."

The other man took the data chip she offered and plugged it into his console. "It's a text file with a very long code sequence and the channels that it's supposed to be transmitted on. Should I send it, Admiral Mertz?"

"Send it."

"Transmitting now."

They'd hypothesized that the Singularity would have a way to betray the Clans when the time came. If this was how they intended to do it, there were several ways this could play out. First of all, it might cause the ships to explode. That was the cleanest option though the loss of life would be horrendous.

The other options were more limited but probably still somewhat dangerous. It could order the ships to shut down all power. If that were the case, the crew would be in danger of running out of life support, and there would be little they could do to rescue them. Or it might simply lock out all propulsion and weapons systems. Truthfully, there were any number of different ways this could play out, and none of them would likely be pleasant.

The signal took almost no time to reach the enemy fleet because Admiral Bandar transmitted it through the FTL link to the probe that was already in their midst. Even as Jared was considering the options, the end results became clear.

None of the enemy warships exploded, so it wasn't an outright self-destruct code. What happened was just as deadly, though. As far as he could see, every single airlock on those ships opened and began spewing atmosphere at the same time. That shouldn't have been possible, but the Singularity had obviously buried secret control codes in the midst of the hardware they were building on those ships. At the same time, the ships stopped thrusting, and it looked like they lost power. If primary and emergency power were offline at the same time as they were losing atmosphere, it would rapidly be a lethal event for anyone who couldn't get into a vacuum suit.

Within sixty seconds, all the atmosphere had vented, and those ships were floating coffins.

"Well, that's not exactly what I expected, but I suppose it shouldn't be a surprise," Tolliver said. "After all, the Singularity would want to recover those warships. This way, all they'd have to do is wait until whoever was aboard them was dead and then start chucking bodies out the airlocks. We'll have to send people aboard to verify that there aren't any survivors and try to talk them into surrendering, but I can't hold out hope that very many people survived that."

"We'll also need to go over every system to make sure there's no more surprises," Jared said. "Just because that's what happened with this code doesn't mean there aren't others that our prisoner hasn't told us about. If there are other buried codes, I'd rather know about them in advance."

The fight for Terra had ended in an anticlimactic way, but it had been a brutal victory. If they were able to use this code against the other raiding parties inside the Empire, they could bring the Clans to their knees.

"We'll want to put pickets around the ships while we figure out what else we need to do," Jared said. "The vast majority of them can stay here, and we'll figure out our next steps together. I leave setting that up to you, Luke. Also, you can send search parties aboard each of the ships and try to find survivors if you like. Their time is probably limited, so I won't step on your toes while you make that happen. I will, however, advise you to take all due precautions because these are the kind of people that are more prone to shooting than talking."

The crown prince nodded. "Understood. I'll get right on that and keep you advised of everything we find. Bandar out."

Jared leaned back. Having access to this code could very well end the last major bit of fighting inside the Empire. That wouldn't solve all their problems, but it might mean that they could bring all the ships they wanted together to go clean out the Clans at their home worlds. If so, that would give them the leverage they needed to bring any recalcitrant worlds here inside the Rebel Empire under their wing.

Victory was within sight if things played out well. If they didn't, they still might be able to pull it off. That was definitely something they would need to talk over very soon. If they could secure the Rebel Empire and start working on recombining with the other half of the New Terran Empire, things would still be complicated and convoluted, but they might be able to become the kind of Empire that had once existed and might one day live again.

18

Elise walked down the corridor with Kelsey. While the military men were fighting, the two of them would be having a meeting with Andrea Tolliver and Sara Gatewood. While Kelsey and Andrea might be suited to fighting, they weren't Fleet officers, so as long as everything went well, they didn't need to be involved. As far as Sara Gatewood and herself, it was best they steered clear of the fighting.

Instead, the four of them—five if one included Kelsey's mother—would be trying to set out the rough outline of how they would proceed going forward. Diplomatic matters were definitely something inside her wheelhouse, and she knew Sara was far more prepared for that type of negotiation than most.

Even though the rough outlines of what they had to come to an agreement over were clear, that didn't mean there wouldn't be problems. The two halves of the New Terran Empire had been separated for half a millennium, and each had been operating under the assumption that they were the only ones in existence.

Now, the two groups would have to come to the realization that not only were they two halves of a whole, but there would be things that the other portion had done that they didn't agree with.

Resolving those conflicts would be challenging, but it didn't have to be a showstopper.

And that would be their challenge: to overcome the differences between their relative positions and come up with a roadmap to reunification. It wouldn't happen today, but the bones of the process would be laid out. Only with a solid foundation could they possibly assure eventual success. Even though both parties had full authority to negotiate binding agreements on behalf of their respective groups, they'd have to take as much as possible into account because it was a virtual certainty that someone would complain at a later date, and that needed to be minimized to prevent problems down the road.

The meeting was taking place in much more sumptuous surroundings than anything available on Terra. They also wouldn't be doing it aboard any of the warships or stations there. Elise had spoken with Coordinator Richard Kagan of Devon and had obtained a well-appointed suite in the capital for their use during their talks.

While he'd be available if they needed any assistance, he wouldn't be taking part in the actual talks. Too many cooks in the kitchen could spoil the feast, and these initial conversations needed to be held in an environment where everyone could be frank without getting lost in the weeds.

As they walked, she could tell that her friend was nervous. Even though Kelsey was an Imperial princess and had grown up in a household that dealt with this type of high-level negotiations all the time, it hadn't been something that was her strong suit. In fact, she'd probably avoided it as much as possible.

Elise poked her in the side with an elbow. "Lighten up. This won't be like a ground combat. You won't have to shoot anybody."

"It might be easier if I had to," Kelsey grumbled. "At least in a fight like that, you know what your options are, and the consequences are only death or dismemberment."

That made Elise laugh. "It's not going to be that bad. Both sides want this to succeed. It isn't like you'll run into them making demands that we aren't willing to compromise on. Will we get everything that we want? Certainly not, and you know what? It doesn't matter. We'll get enough of what's important that both sides can be reasonably pleased that they weren't taken advantage of. Besides, your mother will be there, and if anyone knows how to get some agreement from different parties, it's her."

"I'm not sure that all the experience she's got in that department will be useful here. After all, more than a fair bit of her politicking took place between the sheets."

"One never knows. Andrea's been around a long time. Maybe that's exactly the kind of negotiating tactic we need to try."

Her friend gave her a side-eye. "Uh-huh. Let's hope not. Things are already going to be stressful enough for me."

The two of them reached the compartment that had been set aside for Elise's use. Andrea was waiting for them.

"We were a bit early, so I wasn't sure how long we might need to wait," Andrea said. "I'm glad to see that you are the kind of person that shows up early as well."

"I think we're all ready for something a little less stressful than being aboard the station," Kelsey said. "Even though we've got pressure around us, it still feels like a tomb. I want to be somewhere where there are people. This place is just creepy."

Elise agreed with that assessment. The atmosphere around them just felt oppressive. The years had not been kind to this station, and it would take a lot of time to bring it back to something resembling a normal environment. Thankfully, she didn't have to worry about being trapped here. She could leave anytime she wanted.

In this case, they could all leave. She unlocked the hatch and gestured for everyone to go inside. It was only locked to keep anyone else from being in the room if she portaled in. While she didn't know if she would materialize in the same area as someone else when she opened the portal, that wasn't the kind of thing she wanted to experiment with. Physics reserved the harshest penalties imaginable for those who violated its laws, even when it was alien physics and potentially magic, if one pushed the metaphor far enough.

Thankfully, she was the only one that could open these portals, and as long as she could control the environment in which she did so, she could minimize the opportunity to screw things up. Sometimes, that wasn't possible because there were locations she'd memorized that were in public areas, but she preferred not to use those.

In fact, as she gained location after location, she wasn't even sure how she could manage to keep track of them all. At this point, it was as if they occupied some reserved memory inside her head, and merely by thinking about them, she could basically see all the options she had available. Would that change as the number continued growing? She had no idea, but she'd eventually find out.

Once everybody was inside, she opened a portal to her alien home and then to the house she had rented in the capital city on Devon. She'd used a false name and was paying cash for the privilege. She trusted Coordinator Kagan, but there were limits until things were more settled.

Once they'd arrived, they went to the garage and got aboard the air car she had purchased. Thankfully, the resistance had these purchases. She didn't have an unlimited budget, but as long as she was frugal, that didn't matter. This was a stopgap measure meant to keep their options open during uncertain times.

Once everyone had piled into the air car, she let Kelsey drive. It would give her friend something to do, and the woman enjoyed the process more than Elise did. For her, it was just a mechanical task to operate the vehicle when it wasn't tied into the planetary traffic control network, but her friend actually enjoyed it.

Even though the home was in the suburbs, flying into the central part of the city and landing inside the designated parking garage only took twenty minutes. They all exited the vehicle and allowed the controller inside the parking garage to move the air car to a suitable parking spot. When they finished, it would be easy enough to summon it back for their departure.

They took the lift up to the level housing the suite where they'd be talking and found Sara Gatewood and Justine waiting for them. The two women were standing at the large window, looking out over the capital city of Devon.

Elise walked over and stood beside Justine. The older woman glanced at her and smiled before returning her gaze to the vista before them. "It's beautiful, isn't it? I wish we had something like this on Avalon. It's so breathtaking."

"It's only a matter of time," Elise said with a smile. "Once we have trade established between the Empire proper and the New Terran Empire, the technology that we've lost will begin flooding back. In fact, I'd imagine there will be a tremendous number of enterprising companies and individuals that want to go to one of the two operating capitals of the New Terran Empire and set up shop. Get in at the ground floor, if you follow the metaphor far enough. The kinds of opportunities that would be available to someone like that are unlimited, I'd imagine."

She looked over at Andrea. "What about your capital? What was the name again? Shangri-La? It's interesting that we heard that name used in conjunction with the master AI during our journey to locate it. It wasn't anything official but rather something worked up by one of the wealthy folk inside the Rebel Empire. I wonder whatever happened to him after we outmaneuvered him and left him in the lurch."

Kelsey shrugged from her position on the other side of Sara Gatewood. "If he was smart, he burrowed deep into hiding. He thinks he has a bomb in his head that the master AI could set off at a moment's notice. We disabled it, but even if word has gotten to his location that we are now in control, I don't think he'll be that eager to put that to the test."

Andrea raised an eyebrow. "That sounds like quite the story. You must've had a tremendous adventure overcoming all the obstacles set in your path. I wish there was a written account or perhaps even some kind of video production that we can watch to see all of your triumphs."

That made Elise laugh. "Oh, there are some video productions in the works. Admittedly, they've only got part of the story at this point, but you can rest assured as soon as the destroyer with my memorized portal location arrives back home, they'll be updated with all the new data to begin working on the next video extravaganza."

Kelsey groaned and covered her face with her hands. "I'd forgotten about that. Maybe they weren't well received, and I won't have to go through people telling me that I don't look anything like what they imagined."

Andrea raised an eyebrow. "I don't understand, but that sounds interesting."

"Let's just say that the actress that was chosen to play my sister-in-law brought other assets to the production in addition to her acting talent."

Kelsey held out her hands in front of her chest. "For some reason, they picked someone that has enormous boobs. As you can see, I'm not nearly so well-endowed, and it's embarrassing for me."

Andrea laughed. "If that's the least of the offenses they've done while telling your story, you should be happy. Over the last five centuries, there have been an uncountable number of stories about the Fall, and I've been portrayed by various actresses that ranged from the serious to the ludicrous. I'm not exactly that well-endowed either, but there have been some very voluptuous women who filled the role on occasion, so I understand exactly what you're talking about. You'll either adjust to it, or you won't, but nothing you do will change what others choose when they're portraying you. I suggest you attempt to be magnanimous about it and let other people do the complaining. You can choose not to watch, but nothing you do will change what someone else does."

"I suppose you're right, but that doesn't make it easier to deal with. I've seen the initial production where Jared and I were the primary characters involved with saving Pentagar. No expense was spared, and they showed no mercy when they expanded on and elaborated the various plot elements to the point where I'm pretty sure that I could walk on water. Or maybe it was only Jared who could walk on water, and I had other roles to fill. I can't remember. I blanked it out."

Elise giggled. "Don't worry. I'll be happy to share a copy of it with you, Andrea. You can make up your mind for yourself."

"Don't you dare," Kelsey hissed. "My vengeance will know no bounds if you betray me."

"There's no need for you to get in trouble with your friend," Andrea said with a smile. "I'm sure that I can get my hands on it without any intervention. After all, when the Empress Emeritus expresses a desire for something, there are any number of people who will be willing to make it happen. After all, what are courtiers for if not to fulfill the nobility's wishes?"

"True," Elise said. "Kelsey doesn't really have any experience with that. She was somewhat shielded from that before she left on the exploratory mission that brought her to Pentagar. After that, everything's proceeded so quickly that she doesn't even have any Imperial Guards. Admittedly, she'd have given them all heart attacks by some of the crazy things she's done."

Andrea turned away from the view and looked at Kelsey. "I've seen some fairly crazy things done in my time. What would you say the most insane thing you've done is?"

"I'm sure you've got me beat, but probably using a drop capsule to land right outside where terrorists were holding a city hostage with a nuclear weapon. From there, I used a plasma cannon to blow the lead bad guy and his bomb to atoms. There's nothing quite like going from orbital speeds down to the surface of a planet in ten seconds flat."

"Agreed," Andrea said. "Doing anything that has a measurable percentage of people die when trying it is exceptionally dangerous. Even if it's only two percent, if I remember correctly. That's not a negligible percentage when death is on the line. Also, since you only had access to the one Marine Raider strike ship, I'd estimate that it was probably significantly more dangerous because even if you did refurbish the drop capsules, it wouldn't surprise me if the chances of having things go badly were at least double that when everything was taken into account. Bravo. If nothing else, I'd say pulling that off definitely gets you the Marine Raider tab for sure."

"It doesn't make up for me not going through all the training, because I know that there are gaps in what I know. Thankfully, I don't have to lead the way anymore. Other people can blow holes in bulkheads and go charging in once we get some more Marines upgraded to Raider status."

"I certainly wish we had that technology, because it would've made things a lot easier getting set up for this mission. So many of the Marines we brought with us would make excellent Raiders. Hell, if we'd maintained that technology, we would have been able to save my husband though I'm not sure he really wanted to live after losing the majority of the Empire and his son."

"Why don't we all take a seat and get the negotiations underway in a more organized manner?" Justine asked. "I believe Kelsey would be more than happy to share the equipment that we've put together to make Raiders. After all, it's worked on her husband and the command crew of *Persephone*, as well as all the folks they had put together that died taking the master AI, so we know it works."

They all sat, taking advantage of the refreshments set aside on one of the sideboards to pour drinks—either tea or water—and had some pastries before they settled in. The seats were comfortable, and the temperature was pleasant. There was soft music playing from the overheads, but it wasn't distracting.

Justine sat at the head of the table even though she was representing one side already. Or maybe she wasn't. Perhaps she intended to act as a neutral arbiter or at least as a moderator. It was probably best to ask and make that clear up front.

"Exactly what role are you playing today, Justine?" Elise asked.

"Unless someone objects, I'm good to try to play the role of a facilitator. I won't be advocating for Avalon or Shangri-La. If there's a place where I think things can be made easier, I'll make a suggestion. Nobody's bound to follow that, but if I can put some grease on the squeaky wheels, that might make things somewhat simpler. Kelsey and Andrea are both ambassador plenipotentiaries, so they speak for their sides with absolute authority. Even though I'm from Avalon, I'll try to keep my desires out of the way, and if I am speaking from a specific point of view, I'll try to make that clear. Everyone can feel free to ignore me if that's what you want. If needed, I suppose we can bring in someone from outside to try and mediate."

Andrea waved a hand dismissively. "I've been involved in a lot of negotiations over my lifetime, and I think that having you fill the role of moderator will work out perfectly fine. If I feel like you're being biased, I'll call you on it. I do understand that you have a specific point of view, and if I feel that's becoming obstructive, I'll speak up. Kelsey?"

"I'm fine with that," her friend said.

"Excellent," Justine said. "Then I think the best place to start is by laying out what each side is willing to grant the other as a given. What about the Marine Raider technology? Kelsey?"

"Avalon is more than happy to give you full schematics and equipment samples of the Marine Raider implantation devices and the nanotechnology used in it. That includes the modifications we've made to be certain that AIs can't take control of it. It's part of your birthright as well as ours, and I wouldn't feel comfortable keeping it to ourselves in any case."

Andrea nodded. "And in return, Shangri-La would be more than happy to provide all of the various training manuals that we have access to for both the Imperial Marines and the Marine Raiders. When the time comes, Diana and Claudio would make excellent instructors to teach a cadre of professionals what's necessary to teach a new class of Raiders."

"And just like that, we've found common ground," Justine said. "We've got a long way to go, but I believe that with a will to cooperate and the understanding that each side has something to offer, we'll manage to make the magic happen."

Elise certainly hoped that was the case, but the proof would be in the pudding. It wouldn't all be worked out in a single sitting, but if they could lay a solid foundation, even the most difficult sticking points could be overcome.

For example, there was the alien technology they had access to. That would be passed on as well, she was sure, but prices would have to be extracted to match the contribution. That was something achieved through their own efforts, and working out the details of how everything was to be shared would be complex.

She imagined that the Imperial Senate on each of the two

worlds would howl in dismay when they found out that their opposite numbers had done things that they didn't like. Or that their power was going to be diluted. The exact specifications of how that would work were going to be interesting because the Rebel Empire had worlds that would rightly want to be seated at the table, and they would outnumber both Avalon and Shangri-La put together.

Well, as Kelsey was so fond of saying, if it was easy, anyone could do it.

19

Kelsey gave the rest of the people sitting around the table a slight shrug. "I'm afraid that simply trading technology won't cut to the core of our problem. It's easy to make those kinds of concessions, but the difficulty will come when we try to figure out how to merge the two empires. Worse, we've got the people who are currently ruling the worlds inside the Rebel Empire to deal with as well. Coordinator West can tell you better than I just how much of a pain in the butt that will be, but working out the power-sharing agreement is key. Without it, we'll go to war against one another. We can say that that would never happen, but if we don't come to an understanding that will hold, it *will* happen. I'd like to avoid that, so we need to work hard."

The rest of the people at the table nodded. Andrea had a very serious expression on her face though it was still hard seeing it beyond the tattoos. It was going to take Kelsey a long time to get used to that, if she ever did.

"We can all agree on that, I think," Andrea said. "I wasn't in a position to have an opinion when Marcus made the decision to make Lucien his co-emperor, but what's done is done. In practice, what that means is we now have two completely separate political entities that are somehow supposed to come back together again after five centuries of separation. As you've already pointed out, the decisions made by your Imperial Senate are just as valid as the ones made by ours, and they'll have to be reconciled somehow. What happens if our Imperial Senate wants nothing to do with a decision that yours has made? There's no historical precedent for dealing with two separate senates or, for that matter, two separate emperors. We need to come to grips with that and find a way that we can sort out the mess."

"I believe the first place we need to look is where the organizations differ," Justine said. "It's very likely that many of the rulings in the last five hundred years will be relatively minor."

"I believe I have an idea that might help with that," Elise said. "As part of the conversation that I was having with Diana and Claudio, I asked for the official senatorial proceedings from Shangri-La since the Fall. We had that kind of information also in our computers from Avalon, so I passed both sets along to the AI here at Devon through Sara Gatewood. Her name is Evelyn, by the way. It shouldn't be difficult to have a series of files prepared that list the inconsequential rulings that we can simply rubber stamp. Then, we can prepare a number of other lists that deal with the more serious changes all the way up to empire-shaking rulings like the recognition of AI personhood. Those kinds of things are where we need to spend our time, not on things like the budget for repairing the restrooms in the Imperial Senate."

Kelsey found herself nodding. "That makes perfect sense, but human beings are still going to have to check that because I feel confident that our friends across the table won't be willing to simply accept the list as presented. We need to be thorough, so we should double check that as well. When we're signing something for the entirety of the Terran Empire, we need to be thorough. That won't happen quickly."

"No, it won't," Andrea said, "but it isn't something that we need to get bogged down in either. Whatever those particular rulings are, they'll have to be dealt with, but the true root of the matter is coming to an agreement about power sharing. Let's be realistic. Politicians are all about the power they wield. The Senate on Shangri-La will be livid that someone beat us to the punch, and there will be a lot of talk about how we're more legitimate than you are. We need to get this settled in such a way that they don't have a choice in the matter."

Sara Gatewood chuckled. "That's wishful thinking. No matter what we decide, they'll say that they have the final say on the matter, and they're not wrong. You may both be ambassador plenipotentiaries, but anything you agree to will have to be ratified by both Imperial Senates. The key here is settling things well enough so that no one gets everything they're looking for but they get enough to be willing to buy in."

"Honestly, isn't that what the Empire is all about?" Elise asked. "Of the various worlds that answer to the Imperial Senate, not all of them agree with every single decision. Nothing is ever decided by a unanimous vote. As long as we can make the situation acceptable to the majority in both empires, then it will be a settled deal. Whatever the final agreement is, it needs to be all or nothing. Both empires accept all of the rulings that the others have made, and if there are conflicts, then those will have to be worked out by negotiation."

"The good thing about something like that is that it'll be the politicians arguing rather than us," Kelsey said. "I think what you're saying makes a lot of sense, and we'll definitely need to take the feelings of the Rebel Empire into account. Each world gets a seat at the Imperial Senate, and their vote counts. In fact, one of the most serious things we have to work on is exactly how to incorporate each world that comes aboard into the existing political infrastructure. When it was just us, it was simple enough to say that they would be sending representatives to our Senate. Now, I'm not exactly sure how to proceed."

Everyone was quiet for a few seconds before Justine tapped her knuckle against the top of the table. "I think I may have a solution for that though it's a little bit radical. We're basically incorporating each of these worlds by force though some are joining of their own free will. That said, they don't have a say in the matter until they're actually seated at the table. I suggest that we keep it that way until the Empire is once more under our joint control. It's not like we're doing an actual subjugation, but there will be a fair amount of fighting."

Andrea raised an eyebrow. "What exactly does that mean?"

"A good example would be one of the worlds that tried to conquer another after the AIs relinquished control," Justine said. "They sent warships to seize Devon, but they were driven off. We sent our ships to their system and captured their ships and orbital infrastructure, but we don't have the manpower to seize the world itself. They'll have to come around on their own, so they're in something of a holding pattern. We have control, but they don't have a say in the matter yet. Yet."

Andrea nodded. "I think that's a good idea. We can agree that the worlds of the Rebel Empire that have not already joined one of the two Empire halves will be provisionally accepted, but they don't yet have a seat at the table. That only occurs when we officially incorporate them into whatever organization we both come up with. I suppose it would be like the Imperial Super Senate?"

Kelsey laughed. "I don't think that would go over very well, but I like the thought. Honestly, I believe the best way to approach this is to take the two organizations that we already have and declare that the various branches have to be consolidated into a single organization. It's not going to be at Avalon or Shangri-La. It's going to have to be somewhere else. I'd suggest Terra, but that would be a truly bad idea as it isn't set up to receive that type of high technology and high civilization yet. It will be eventually, but not yet."

"Then why don't we use Devon?" Justine asked. "The population here is relatively friendly, and I believe with its high-technology setup, we should be able to build an Imperial Senate building that's large enough to house everyone in relatively short order. We also need to have something to house the bureaucracy ruling the Empire. Relocating everything from the two planets will be a huge pain, considering how far apart they are, but it will have to be done."

Kelsey looked over at Elise. "I suppose getting a number of people here quickly can be done as long as they're willing to come with very little. It'll keep you busy, though."

Elise shook her head. "While I'm certainly willing to do that for some, I'm not going to play transport minister. The vast majority of the people who will be doing this will need to come and stay. If they need transport later, they'll have to take a ship. We should just accept that. The destroyer headed for Avalon will be there in a few more months, but the one going to Shangri-La will take a few weeks longer. We can work on having the buildings constructed if we can find an appropriate place to do so, but only the smallest of skeleton crews will be transported by me."

"Once we have an agreement in principle, the rest won't be as difficult as you think," Andrea said. "Kelsey, if the two of us agree on a process by which any differences between the two empires are sorted out, that will be good enough to lay the groundwork that we're talking about. It would be easier if we only had a single emperor. However, I don't believe that's a likely outcome. It's a pity that you're already married because Luke is single. It would've been a good way to tie the two thrones back together."

The woman then inclined her head forward a little, obviously peeking over the edge of the table at Kelsey's belly. "Though I suppose if he has a son in the relatively near future, there's still a possibility for an arranged marriage."

The thought made Kelsey scowl, but she didn't reject it out of hand. There was a reason that history was filled with arranged marriages. Sometimes, they had to come up with a way to get around political impediments in such a way that two disparate peoples were brought together.

"I'm not going to commit my child to something like that. She should be free to marry whomever she pleases, but I understand what you're saying. I can speak with my father and see what he thinks, but I can assure you right now that I personally do not want to fight over this. I never expected to be an empress, and I'm certain that something can be arranged where I would be willing to give up that power if our Senate agrees. That'll probably take some political horse-trading to work out, but it's not off the table. Even so, it's not something we'll agree to right now, either. In any case, we still have to finish bringing the Empire back fully under our control before we're even ready to talk about that. Somehow, we'll have to make the whole two-emperor thing work."

"Why should Kelsey be the one who has to give up anything?" Elise asked. "Maybe Luke should abdicate and she be made the heir to the entirety of the Terran Empire. Her father might be willing to abdicate as well, and then you would have the two halves brought back together again."

Andrea smiled. "Somehow, I don't envision that happening. Luke is a very dedicated young man, and I don't believe that he'd feel comfortable abdicating in favor of someone else. The mechanism by which we intend to do this will obviously need to be worked out because I don't believe having two people with ultimate authority is workable over the long term. Even so, it's not something that we have to decide today. Perhaps the two emperors and their heirs should sit down and work this out once we've settled the problems we currently have to deal with, like the invading Clans and bringing all of the various worlds of the Rebel Empire under our sway. How long do you think that will take?"

Kelsey shook her head and shrugged. "Individually, each world inside the Rebel Empire is weak enough that they can be taken by a small task force. A single battlecruiser would be more than enough to deal with each world, I suspect, so long as they have appropriate escorts. The problem is dealing with the Clans. Even now that the fleet headed toward Terra has been dealt with, there will still be a lot of raiding parties causing havoc inside the Rebel Empire. Those will have to be dealt with quickly, and then we'll need to send an overwhelming force to the Clan home worlds and stop them from being a threat ever again."

"Why don't we let that be the thing we focus on first?" Andrea said. "Between the two fleets we have, we should be able to track down every Clan ship inside the Rebel Empire and destroy it. Then, once that is accomplished, we can deal with their home worlds."

"What kind of division of labor are you envisioning?" Kelsey asked. "Who's going to do what?"

"I suggest we split our forces and track down the Clan task forces in tandem."

"I agree, but the end call will have to be made by our Fleet admirals," Kelsey said. "We'll talk to Jared and Luke and let them work out the details of how that's going to take place. While they do, we can keep working on what needs to be done to bring both groups together and formulate a plan that we can agree on to make that happen, but we do have to win this fight first. Luckily, Elise is very good at bringing people that are far apart close together, and we can keep negotiating even while we work on that."

She looked down at her belly. "The problem I see is that I'm probably going to give birth before that really comes into play. I want to be there when the Clan worlds are subjugated, but I'm not going to be involved in the fighting. I'm something of a ticking time bomb, after all."

Andrea smiled a bit crookedly. "So, what you're saying is that we need to come to a settlement before you give birth? I think that gives us an excellent target date. Now, all we have to do is find someone to marry Luke off to, and we're in the races."

"And that makes an excellent place to break for lunch," Justine said. "We won't have a lot of fast action in this discussion, but I think we made good progress. Let's cement that by having a good meal."

Kelsey could get behind that. Being pregnant made her even hungrier than usual, which was saying something. She didn't know whether or not they really could come to an agreement before she gave birth, but the writing was on the wall. There could be only one emperor going forward, and with the right incentives, she'd be more than happy to allow Luke to be the only heir.

Honestly, she thought her father would probably agree to that as well. Maybe he could become a duke and retire. As for her, she had no idea what she'd do. Her life had been outside of her control for so long that trying to decide what she wanted would be difficult.

She'd talk to Talbot, and he'd help her come up with an answer. He was always the grounded one, and she looked forward to being able to get his advice. That was always a good first step to solving any of her issues.

20

Talbot stepped out of the pinnace and onto the surface of one of the Clan warships. The pilot had landed them near one of the airlocks, and just as their sensors had indicated, it was wide open. He allowed the Marines to precede him into the ship then followed. The inner door was also open, which should have been impossible.

"When we said the Singularity probably had some kind of booby trap buried in the Clan warships, this isn't what I was expecting," Carl Owlet said from behind him over their private channel. "Honestly, I expected all the ships to blow up. Why go this route?"

"Most likely because they wanted to take the ships intact," Talbot said as he stepped into the airlock and reoriented himself as the gravity took hold. "And, as paranoid as the Clans are, they would've checked the critical systems very closely. Frankly, I can't see how the communication system passed the instructions along. If anything, that should've been locked down tighter than just about anything else. After all, that's how the booby trap was sprung. The Clans had to have known that was a weak spot."

Even as he was speaking, he was also listening to what the

Marines were reporting from ahead of them. Dead crewmembers had seemingly been caught unprepared when the atmosphere rushed out of the ship. The emergency doors that should have been deployed to protect the rest of the ship from the explosive decompression had failed to activate. Or perhaps it would be more appropriate to say they had also been booby-trapped.

"You've got to say this about the Singularity," Talbot said. "They don't do things by half measures. When they want to kill someone, they go all out to make sure that no one can find the very secretive and sneaky method that they chose to kill them. The question is, are there any other unpleasant surprises waiting for us?"

"That would depend on if we planned on ever using the ships," Carl said as he stopped and began disassembling the control panel for the airlock. "We've got plenty of ships, and I don't think it really matters how badly the Clan vessels have been compromised. None of our people are going to be at risk."

That was certainly true enough. They had more than enough ships for the few people they had. Whatever the admiral—or admirals, he should say—decided to do, there was no need to utilize these vessels for anything. As far as he was concerned, they could be placed into a parking orbit as floating tombs.

The fact that Andrea Tolliver had gotten the codes to do this from their Singularity prisoner turned what had looked to be a long and bloody fight to subdue each and every ship and task force that the Clans had sent into the Rebel Empire into something much more straightforward.

That was assuming, of course, that all of the ships had been sabotaged in the same way. It was entirely possible that only some of them had been rigged and others not. That didn't seem likely, but it was always possible.

No matter how this played out, the Clans would cause terrific damage throughout the Rebel Empire, but it was something they could recover from. They'd lose ships and orbitals, but the Clans didn't have enough people to do anything on any of the planetary surfaces, not unless they decided orbital bombardment was the answer to their problems.

As he was thinking, Carl had gotten the airlock controls disassembled and plugged one of his instruments into it. The young scientist studied the screen and nodded. "The instruction to open both airlock doors was buried deep in the firmware, I think. I'll need to remove some hardware and dig into it in my lab to be sure. Frankly, it's chilling. Somehow, the Singularity comes across as a bunch of mustache-twirling villains, ones that would be very satisfying to punch in the face."

That made Talbot smile. "That's a sentiment I can get behind. Now that we know how they did it, what do you want to see next?"

"The communication system. I'm very curious how they fooled the Clans into allowing an unknown signal like that to do something this terrible. Admittedly, this is more of a forensic kind of curiosity because the deed is done, but I think the better we understand how the Singularity works, the more we'll be able to predict the kinds of things they are capable of in the future. Since we're very likely to go to war with them at some point, it's best to start learning now."

Talbot waited for his young friend to put the airlock controls back together, then the two of them made their way toward the bridge. The communication system wasn't going to be there, but it would be close.

It took a bit of searching around, ignoring the dead who lay scattered about, but they eventually found what they were looking for. The ship's computers occupied the same room as the communication system, and Carl immediately got to work on both, inserting equipment into each and starting some programs.

"As expected, the computers are locked down tight," Carl said. "It's going to take me a while to get access. The communication system is a bit more open, but it looks like it's got a lot of protective measures built into it as well. Someone programmed it to be aware of strange signals, and it should've blocked what was happening, but it didn't. That probably means something built into the hardware itself overrode the security, just like for the airlocks. Or I suppose it could be something completely different. Maybe there's a hidden communication system built into the ship. One way or the other, I'll keep looking and eventually remove all the critical hardware to take back with us."

"While you figure that out, I'm going to go to the bridge. Call me if you need anything."

By now, the Marines had finished searching the ship, and there were no survivors. A few people had tried to get into suits but had failed before they ran out of breath. The shockingly sudden loss of atmosphere had killed them.

The bridge held a mixture of people who had died at their stations and others who had been trying to open a locker built into the wall that likely contained oxygen. The bridge should have been sealed before combat began, but its hatch had been wide open as well. The Singularity had been quite thorough, and that spoke volumes about their ruthlessness and willingness to sacrifice their pawns when the time came.

The consoles were unlocked because the ship had been in operation at the time of the disaster, and he was able to access almost all its systems. Some were still locked down, but this was good enough for what he wanted. Rather than move one of the dead, he chose one of the stations that was empty and sat.

Jared had tasked him with finding any orders that were buried in the system that might indicate where the various groups of Clan warships would be operating. With that kind of information, they could deal with the enemy much more quickly than if they had to search every single star system.

Finding the orders for this fleet was simple enough. Everything was laid out in the same way that they did in the Imperial Fleet, so he was able to quickly access where this fleet had been and what they planned to do next. They had come directly from the Clan home worlds and had intended to occupy the Terra system. For whatever reason, they thought it would be occupied by people and would be the seat of government. Once again, it seemed that the Singularity had been feeding them false information. Or perhaps they just hadn't known.

The system he was on wasn't able to access any of the rest of the orders, so he went to the captain's chair and moved the dead man to the floor. Once he was seated at the console, he was able to gather more information but not enough to get what he needed. They had tagged this ship as the most likely one to be in command of the entire fleet, but the captain didn't seem to have access to some of the areas inside the computer.

"Talbot to all Marine units," he said over the general channel. "Has anyone found a flag bridge or what looks like an admiral?"

One of the teams quickly reported that they had located a flag bridge in the center of the ship. They read off the coordinates, and Talbot made his way there in about ten minutes.

It was laid out very much like the bridge he'd just left, but the officers here seemed to have panicked far more than the ones he'd left behind in the other compartment. Almost none of the stations had anyone sitting at them, and even the admiral's console was empty.

Talbot sat at it and again tried to access the data he was searching for. Unlike the last time, he was able to unlock the files and began recording everything through his implants. There was no way for him to directly copy the files, but that wasn't necessary. As long as he had the data itself, they could use it.

It looked like this was the largest fleet the Clans had deployed, but only by the slightest amount. There were four other large fleets and many task forces assigned to them. Those fleets had gone to different areas of the Empire and were going to set up shop there and begin subduing the worlds around them.

The full roster of vessels and their capabilities was included in the files, and fighting each of them separately would've been a challenge. If they had to do so together, it would be impossible with the forces they currently had at their disposal. That, however, was a problem for Admiral Mertz and Admiral Bandar.

The next bit of information he wanted was their map of their home worlds and any data that he could gather about them. It would be critical to know what defenses they would face when they assaulted the Clan home worlds, which they would do before very much longer, he was confident.

It looked like the Clans had spread out over a couple of dozen star systems, but they only had a few worlds that could truly be called civilized. They hadn't started out with very many people, and even though they'd kidnapped citizens from the Rebel Empire for centuries, the entire population probably didn't exceed a billion people. For such a small group to put out a fleet of this size really spoke to their warlike nature.

There was a fair bit of data about the defenses inside the systems, as well as the map of where everything was laid out. That was what he'd come searching for. With it, they could conquer the Clan home worlds and this needless fight.

Sadly, he had no idea what they would do after that. The citizens of the Clan worlds were so xenophobic and hostile that they couldn't be allowed to mix with the rest of humanity. Dealing with them would be a long-term problem. Thankfully, it wasn't going to be *his* problem.

Having acquired what he was looking for, he headed back toward the computer center. He'd follow Carl around for a while, then they'd head back to the fleet. He felt pretty damned confident they would take action swiftly once this data was presented to the command staff.

With the secret transmission codes, they could stop this invasion cold. It would be brutal how many of the enemy they'd killed, but the Clans weren't known for surrendering. This was probably better all around. Maybe if the most virulent militarists in their society were killed, that would give hope that the rest could be rehabilitated over time.

If it was him, he'd be sending task forces to where each of these fleets was based and have them send the coded signal to destroy them. Maybe it would be worthwhile to use Clan warships for that, so perhaps digging out all the buried booby traps would be worthwhile. A regular task force of their own vessels escorting a couple of Clan warships might be just the ticket.

Now, all they had to do was carry through, and the Empire would be back in their hands—if, of course, Kelsey and Andrea came to an agreement and everything didn't fall apart in a civil war that none of them wanted.

21

Jared took a cutter over to Crown Prince Luke Bandar's flagship, *Ulysses*. While he certainly didn't see the other man as a firm ally yet, the two groups were working together, and they had to at least act as if they fully trusted one another if they expected this to work.

And it had to work. The New Terran Empire—at least his version of it—was far too weak to fight this other group without using a slew of AI-controlled warships. While that was certainly possible, that type of combat didn't have the kind of flexibility that he preferred. In any case, it was his duty to make sure they did what was necessary to emerge from this as one complete entity without one side dominating the other.

His group might be lacking in population and technology, but they had possession of Terra and had beaten the master AI. That would count for something, he was sure. Whatever Kelsey and Andrea Tolliver worked out would no doubt take that into account. All of their groups would make contributions for this to work, and then they just had to figure out how to live together.

When he exited his cutter, there was a Marine honor guard standing by next to several Fleet officers. Everyone snapped to attention as he stepped out, and the commodore at the center of the Fleet formation saluted.

"Welcome aboard *Ulysses*, Admiral Mertz. I'm Commodore Leon Logan, Admiral Bandar's flag captain. If you'll come with me, he's waiting in his day cabin."

Jared returned the salute and shook the man's hand. "It's a pleasure to meet you, commodore. You didn't need to go to all this trouble for me."

The man gave him a lopsided smile. "When a Fleet admiral drops in for a visit, sir, it's probably best not to treat it like some random fellow stopping by. This is no trouble, and it shows the respect that an admiral deserves, even if I'm not exactly certain how we're all supposed to work together quite yet."

"Well, I appreciate it. I've got an update for Admiral Bandar, and now that we know exactly what's going on, the two of us need to decide what the best course of action will be for our combined fleet."

"So you're anticipating us moving out soon?"

"I don't want to prejudge the situation, but that wouldn't surprise me."

"Then I'll start sending some hints toward the admiral's flag staff. It never hurts to pass the word out to the various ships that we might be departing in short order. Saves everyone embarrassment if things aren't quite right at the moment but can be fixed."

"I hear that, and I've done the same on more than one occasion. After you, Commodore."

Commodore Logan dismissed the Marines and led Jared deeper into the superdreadnought. As Jared knew exactly where his own day cabin was, he could've found it without the escort, but this was both a show of respect and caution in keeping an eye on a potential intruder. Life could be strange sometimes.

After the commodore knocked on the hatch and it opened, Jared stepped inside. Luke Bandar was seated behind his desk but rose when he saw Jared coming in. "Welcome aboard, Admiral Mertz. What did you find?"

The man made a gesture toward his wet bar, but Jared shook his head. Instead, he took a seat in one of the comfortable chairs. "We found a fleet of ships sabotaged so deeply that the personnel aboard them never had a chance. The signal was received by the communications hardware, and that sent a command to open all the airlocks and to prevent any of the interior pressure doors from closing. Everyone was dead within a minute. It's a terrible way to go, but Fleet utilized a very similar sort of thing during the Fall to prevent their crews from falling into the hands of the AIs."

Bandar sat down next to him and nodded. "From everything I've heard about these people, I don't have much sympathy for them. They would have fought viciously to kill me and mine, and seeing them all drop dead because of the betrayal of the Singularity has a karmic feel to it. What do we do next?"

"I've ordered some of my people to take control of the ships and bring them to the flip point. We'll bring them here and put them in a holding orbit that's out of the way but accessible if we have a need for them. I can see circumstances where it might be beneficial to have some Clan warships easily at hand. After that, that really depends on what we decide is appropriate. I have some ideas, but I don't want to presume what the combined fleet will do. That's a decision we all have to agree on."

The other man nodded. "I agree with that assessment. Trust is built with small steps, and doing things the right way will bring us closer together. Respect is important, and I appreciate the respect that you're showing my people. It seems that we have three different primary missions. First, we have the invading Clan warships. Those need to be stopped, but they're scattered all over the Empire. Figuring out exactly where they are and pinning them down will be a challenge."

Jared smiled. "Not nearly as much of a challenge as you might think. The commanding admiral over there had his console unlocked, and I've brought copies of his files with me. It seems this fleet was one of five sent into the Empire. The other four went to the various corners of the Empire to begin securing their areas of operation. We know which systems they've chosen for that, and we can send forces to deal with them. That would still leave the roving task forces to deal with, but they're much smaller than the fleets themselves."

"That is good news," Bandar agreed. "The second mission is to subdue the individual worlds inside the Empire that feel like fighting. They may not want to all be part of the same political organization, but I'm disinclined to give them much of a choice. They'll have their rights inside the Empire, but we can't allow it to disintegrate."

"I think we're in full concurrence on that, but it's a low priority when compared to fighting the Clans," Jared said. "The third option is likely taking out the Clan home worlds. Luckily, we've got information about them as well. They're also going to be heavily defended, and I would be very surprised if all those defenses have been sabotaged in the same way as the Clan warships. We can't count on getting lucky every single time."

Bandar nodded. "So, what would you say we should focus on? How do we divide our forces if we're going to divide them at all?"

"Frankly, I believe that we can send automated forces to attempt to deal with the four remaining fleets. If they are sabotaged in the same way as this one, it won't take very much to defeat them. If that doesn't work out, then we're really no worse off than we were before. The biggest problem will be dealing with the Clan home worlds. Those are going to be the most heavily defended and difficult to subjugate."

"I agree with that," Bandar said. "However, we don't really need to subjugate them right now. So long as we can eliminate their mobile forces, it doesn't really matter what they're doing on the surface of the worlds they occupy. Let their worlds be their prisons until they decide they can behave. Do you have a map of how the Clan worlds are laid out and the flip points we need to take to get each?"

Jared nodded and passed him another dated chip. When the other admiral brought the map up, he gestured toward it. "They're scattered in what basically amounts to a U shape. While it's possible that we could hit the worlds in the middle by taking another route, I think working our way in from both sides and meeting in the middle presents the best opportunity for us to crush them in detail. As long as we continue pushing forward strongly, it hardly matters what the ones in the middle do."

Bandar shook his head. "We'll want to position automated forces at all the potential locations where they can escape. This isn't the time to let someone else get away and come back to haunt the Empire in five hundred years. I want to deal with this problem once and for all."

Jared could see that point of view, and he nodded. "You're right. Since we have a complete map of the flip point network, we can be certain we have ships positioned in force at every single place they might come out. They'll be the anvil, and we'll be the hammer."

"Perfect. The next thing we need to discuss is the disposition of our noncombatants. Grandmother won't want to be left standing on the sidelines, and I'd wager Princess Kelsey feels the same way. Nevertheless, both of them need to be protected from themselves. How can we keep them somewhat isolated from the danger while still making them feel as if they're involved in what's taking place?"

"They'll still be involved in the negotiations for merging your New Terran Empire with mine. They could follow along aboard *Audacious*, and so long as they have a significant force of ships guarding them, they should be safe. As safe as anyone, anyway. At that point, the only thing left to decide is figuring out which group they'll be following after."

"I think you're forgetting something," Bandar said as he leaned back in his seat. "They don't have to be with us to know what's going on. They can make a trip to your ship at any point in time, using your wife. Distance is apparently no impediment. As much as some other folk might be annoyed, I think I'm inclined to set aside a compartment aboard *Ulysses* for the same purpose. Then they can stay safe on Devon while we do the fighting. We could even make sure that ships from all four of the task forces that are going after the other Clan fleets have the ability to receive your wife so that we can get updates on the status of their missions."

"We'll want to be sure that the ships tasked with being her points of contact don't actually get involved in the fighting. I wouldn't want to risk her coming into a situation where there's no atmosphere or where the ship is destroyed entirely. It would probably be best if she went in a vacuum suit, and she should be able to see through the portal to determine what the condition is on the other side. Perhaps we put an environmental readout where it can be seen at a glance. I don't want to take any risks."

"Understandable," the other admiral said with a nod. "I say let's begin working on finalizing those plans and moving our ships where they need to go. Based on what you've told me so far, the automated warships will continue to arrive so we can build up reserve fleets as needed, but we really need to get in motion. How long will it take us to get to the Clan home worlds?"

"Knowing the direct path we have to take, I believe we can be in a position to start the assault in about six weeks."

"That should give our counterparts plenty of time to continue working out the details of the merger," Bandar said. "What about the attacks on the various Clan worlds? How long do you think it will take us to subdue them all?"

Jared shrugged. "That's really hard to say. It depends on how heavily fortified they are. We might be able to roll through and destroy everything in space in a matter of days, or it might take us weeks. Personally, I suspect it'll be quicker than we might imagine because we'll be arriving in force, and they'll have no clue that we're coming."

"I suspect you're right, but we'll play this as if the campaign might take a while. I suggest that you take that leftmost arm, and I'll take the right. We'll launch our attacks simultaneously and begin pushing them back. Once we meet in the middle, and after all four of those primary fleets have been defeated, the most serious threat to the Terran Empire in the short term will have been eliminated. By then, Grandmother and Kelsey should have settled everything, and the ship that we sent back to Shangri-La should be very close to arriving."

"And the destroyer that's going to Avalon should already have made it. Admittedly, there may still be a lot of cleanup if there are task forces of Clan warships still fighting, but so long as we can put out those particular fires and then slowly go from system to system inside the Rebel Empire, we should have everything taken care of in a few years. Then, we can see about consolidating our gains and potentially turning our attention to the Singularity."

Bandar chuckled. "While I applaud how far ahead you're planning, we need to think about what we're doing in the short term first. The Singularity will still be there once we subjugate the Clans and bring all the worlds of the Rebel Empire back into the fold. Let's not get ahead of ourselves."

Jared grimaced but nodded. "I really wish we could solve all our problems and be done with it, but it seems like there's always something on the horizon. You're right, though. We'll focus on what we have to, and then once we've cleared the decks, we'll decide what comes next."

Personally, Jared wasn't so certain that they'd win this fight as easily as Luke Bandar believed, but he could certainly hope they would. One thing that he did agree with the other admiral about was that it was paramount to keep Kelsey and her counterpart away from the fighting.

No matter what happened, Kelsey was a crown princess of the Empire and heir to the throne. Perhaps she would resign that position in favor of Luke Bandar to bring the Empire back under a single emperor's rule, but she might not. It was his duty to be certain that she wasn't at risk, and he wouldn't fail in that task.

22

Elise opened a portal leading to the transition location in the other universe before closing it and opening another one that led to the cutter Luke Bandar had arranged for her to have aboard the ship returning to Shangri-La. Even though almost six weeks had passed, it still wouldn't be back to their home yet, but she considered it her duty to get relatively frequent updates on their progress.

It amused her that they'd disabled the cutter entirely. Not only did it have no power source, but its engines had been physically removed. There was no way that she was taking this craft anywhere, and even so, they'd positioned a pair of Marine guards outside the hatch to the vehicle. There were two more over at the hatch leading into the rest of the ship, and she wouldn't doubt that there were still more waiting in case she brought armed company with her.

Not that she would ever do that, but she'd been thinking about how she could potentially overcome those limitations. There was nothing like presenting oneself with a challenging intellectual question.

If push came to shove, she figured they had about an even chance of breaking out the small craft bay. They'd almost certainly be unable to take over the rest of the ship, but there really wasn't any need for them to do that. She'd even brought Admiral Bandar back to the ship to update the captain's orders once he decided that it was safe to do so. That had stopped the captain from keeping an eye on her, but she'd probably do the same if there was a person who could seemingly appear out of nowhere across interstellar distances.

She stopped immediately outside the cutter's hatch and held her arms out to the sides to show her hands were empty. She knew for a fact that they had cameras inside the cutter that watched to be sure that no one came through with her, but they didn't really know the limitations of her powers because it was like magic.

At least the Marines were respectful. They scanned her for weapons, then two of them escorted her to see the captain in his day cabin. Aboard a destroyer, that didn't amount to much, but she'd been aboard Jared's destroyer back before it was destroyed and was somewhat amused at the similarity between the two vessels. Even though this one was much more technologically advanced, so many of the features were reminiscent of the other.

Commander Rolando Blair rose as she entered the compartment. "Your Highness, welcome back aboard *Dawn Bringer.* Might I assume this is another one of your relatively frequent checks to see what our progress is? Perhaps I should just start leaving a log for you to pick up inside the cutter so you don't have to walk all the way to my office."

Yep, he was a little annoyed.

"I apologize for any inconvenience that you're suffering on my behalf, Captain. I assure you that I'm not doing it because I distrust your progress, but things are moving along rather quickly on our end, and Crown Prince Bandar and Crown Princess Bandar are both very twitchy right now and want to be kept in the loop as often as possible. I am only the messenger."

The man sighed. "I suppose you're right, but I have to tell you that this does gall me. I don't see how you can just make a trip all the way from one end of the universe to the other and violate every known law of physics. It makes me crazy, and I start itching anytime I think that somebody else could just do the same."

"You should be glad I stopped bringing my mechanical associate everywhere I went. Its presence would've driven you batty. Now, as far as anyone being able to just simply appear aboard your ship, that won't happen with the type of technology we're talking about. Someone would have to be here and open a portal to make it possible for them to return. Your people have kept an eye on me every single moment I'm aboard, and you know that I haven't done so other than aboard the cutter, where I'm authorized to do so. You're safe."

"So says the woman that can go anywhere she wants," he grumbled. "Thankfully, I'm only a week away from arriving at Shangri-La, so by the next time you come to check what my status is, I should be in orbit around the capital. If you would be kind enough to grant me an extra day so that I can communicate with everyone that I need to and calm their fears, that would make my life significantly easier. If you wanted to bring all of the principals here to see the emperor and anyone else they want, they can do so in eight days. Personally, I would deeply appreciate it if you held off coming back before then."

She held up her hands in surrender. "I will absolutely refrain from returning unless Crown Prince Bandar or Empress Emerita Tolliver instructs me to. If they say so, all bets are off because I'll do what they tell me to do. Like I said, I'm just the messenger."

"What is the situation there?" he asked. "I understand that you're about ready to engage the Clan home worlds, and I have to confess that I'm a bit nervous about the whole thing."

"We should be ready to kick off the attack within the next twenty-four hours. If things proceed well, we may be to return here in a week and a day with word of victory. If not, they should be very close. With the number of ships brought to bear on the Clans, they don't stand a chance. The only open question is how long they can last and what damage they do while they're still fighting."

"Well, I certainly hope everyone is cautious. The worst time to think everything is going to work out is right before the finish line.

That's when people make mistakes, and unpleasant surprises can kill."

"No argument from me," she said. "My husband is one of the primary commanders, and he'll be in the thick of it, just like Crown Prince Bandar. That makes me nervous, and I'm undoubtedly more worried than you are."

"Granted," the man said. "I understand you've also been visiting the ship that's going toward Avalon. I had to look up exactly where that was on the maps, and with the information you've given us about the flip point network, they should be getting close as well."

"They are. I'll go check with them once I've finished talking with you, but I expected them to only arrive shortly before you do. Once that's done, it won't be very difficult to bring everyone to the same area and hash out any remaining problems."

"Are there any remaining problems? I was under the impression that Empress Emerita Tolliver and Crown Princess Bandar had hashed out much of the framework."

"They have, but there are always a few sticking points. As you might've guessed, solving the two-emperor problem is the biggest one. Two emperors and two heirs make for a very convoluted leadership structure, and neither of them is very happy about it. I suspect that Kelsey will be more than happy to renounce her claim to the Imperial Throne and clear the way for Crown Prince Bandar to be the sole heir to the throne, but we don't know how her father or your emperor will react to that or anything else. Compared to that, everything else is relatively minor."

"Not to sound indelicate, but isn't Crown Princess Bandar getting very close to her delivery date? It seems like that would be looming on the horizon as well."

Elise laughed. "She looks like she swallowed two bowling balls. It's ridiculous the way she's waddling around, and she's *exceptionally* cranky. That might also be contributing to the difficulty in working out the last few items, I suppose."

"I'm very glad I'm on the other side of the universe," the man averred. "Give me missiles and plasma weapons raining down on my head before I have to deal with an angry pregnant woman."

The man's words made her feel a bit melancholy about the fact that her twins would've reached Pentagar by now. She missed them. Gods above, she missed them. She still didn't know whether or not she would be able to spend any time with them, but maybe once they were born, she could raise them like a normal mother.

"I can honestly say I agree with those sentiments," Elise said, making sure to keep her sorrow off her face. "I'll head back and give them an update. I promise I won't come back for eight days unless they tell me to or it's critical that I get some kind of information to you."

"If you do, you do. There's nothing I can do to stop you, but at least my time of having to deal with this strange issue is almost at an end. Allow me to escort you back to the cutter, Your Highness."

Elise allowed the captain to take her back then opened a portal and stepped back into the otherworldly holding. She really needed to talk with Jared about how they would fill it with furniture and use it as something other than a waypoint going from one place to another.

She opened a portal and stepped back aboard *Gauntlet.* Contrary to her expectations, an alarm was ringing, and people were running down the corridor when she stepped out to take a look. It looked like they'd run into trouble. Jared hadn't expected to find any of the enemy forces before they attacked, but it seemed as if the Clans were onto them.

She quickly made her way to the flag bridge and found Jared watching over his staff as they coordinated what looked to be a massive fleet engagement that was coming up. The screen showed a lot of warships coming their way, and they still seemed to be maneuvering, so the initial plan to send the booby-trapped code and kill them must not have worked out.

Her husband turned toward her as she entered. "Looks like they had some scouts out and knew we were coming. We tried using the Singularity code on them, and it didn't work, so these must be a different class of ships. I'd wager that they're a lot more careful with who they allow to touch the ships guarding their home worlds, so that's not a big surprise."

"What will you do?" she asked as she stepped up next to his chair.

"We'll fight, but you'll need to take a quick message to Admiral Bandar aboard *Ulysses* and then return to Devon. We have no way of signaling you to let you know the fighting is over, so I want you to be very careful when you open a portal back to either of our ships. If we've taken damage and lost pressure, you'll want to be in a vacuum suit. If that's what you detect on the other side, close the portal and get people with search and rescue experience to come in your place. I don't want you putting yourself at risk, and that goes double for Kelsey. Understand?"

"I understand," she said, already knowing that she had no intention of following those orders. If she thought he was in danger, she'd absolutely be in the lead when it came time to rescue him.

"Good," he said. "We've got this covered, and if everything works out the way we hope, we might be able to finish our half of the operation in a week. By all means, come and get updates from us, but I want you to be sparing. Let us do our work. I love you."

"I love you too." She followed that up by kissing him. Then she turned and trotted off the flag bridge.

She had messages to deliver, then the worry and waiting would begin. This was the final push to eliminate the Clans, and she could only pray that everything went well. The other problems they were dealing with could be dealt with over time, but this one had to be solved right now.

23

Kelsey sat in the easy chair with her feet propped up and marveled at the size of her belly. She. Was. Huge. Walking was a chore, and she felt as if it was more like waddling. Her mother was fluttering around, seeing that she was taken care of, and it made her feel slightly ridiculous. She wasn't an invalid. She was just pregnant and about ready to pop.

The time it had taken to get the fleets into position to begin their attack runs on the Clan home worlds had brought her to the very eve of her due date. Lily Stone had told her that first pregnancies often came early, so she was definitely in the danger zone. She wasn't in labor yet, but it could come at any time. Modern medical science could help with that, but only so much.

Of course, now that the fighting had commenced, that would undoubtedly be the time she went into labor. Nothing ever worked out the way it was supposed to, and she'd already accepted that Murphy would have his day.

Talbot wasn't there, which was actually fine. He hovered more than her mother did, and she was happy to get him doing something constructive so that he didn't pace the corridor, worried that she was going to go into labor if she lifted her pinky finger. She wasn't helpless, but convincing everyone else of that was utterly impossible.

He was in the Terra system, working on programming a number of destroyers with the appropriate codes to sabotage any Clan Raiders they came across as they went to deal with the fleets that were still rampaging through the Rebel Empire. Elise was with him, making sure that she could open portals on any one of the vessels. There would be a small number of human personnel going along with these ships, and if there was trouble, they wanted to be able to get to them quickly.

It felt as if everything was happening all at once, and that made her nervous. The sheer complexity of what they were attempting to do was bound to work against them. All it would take was one major upset, and all their plans could come tumbling down.

"If you keep frowning like that, those wrinkles will be permanently embedded in your face," her mother said as she handed her a cup of tea.

"That's totally not true, and you know it. Modern medical science can take care of that, and my medical nanites won't let anything like wrinkles set in because I'm frowning."

"Maybe not," Justine Bandar said as she sat on the edge of the ottoman Kelsey's feet were propped up on. "Even so, this worry can't be good for the baby. Maybe I should call Doctor Johansen to come give you a look."

"I just saw her yesterday," Kelsey said, trying to control her eye roll and failing.

Doctor Breanna Johansen was the senior obstetrician at Luger Station in the Home system. She and her team had been guiding Kelsey through this pregnancy for the last couple of months, and with her just about ready to give birth, the woman was on Devon with her team of professionals.

Kelsey thought that was overkill because Devon was an advanced system with all of the necessary personnel to take care of her. It had already submitted itself to Imperial rule, and she had absolutely no doubt that Coordinator Kagan would keep her completely safe.

That wasn't good enough for her mother. No, these other people who had to be completely ripped out of their own system and dragged across half the universe were the *only* people who would do.

Okay, so it wasn't halfway across the universe, and they could go back anytime they chose via Elise. Even so, it bugged her. Everything bugged her.

A knock at the door had Justine up on her feet and heading for it before Kelsey could even turn her head. What now?

When Justine opened the door, Kelsey saw Andrea Tolliver. "Thank God," Kelsey averred. "You've come to save me from her. She's a monster. She won't leave me alone. Help."

Andrea smiled and stepped into the room. "I wouldn't dream of getting between a mother and her granddaughter. That's how people lose fingers."

"Traitor," Kelsey grumbled. "At the very least, could you take her back to one of your ships and lock her in the brig? I could use a little peace and quiet."

Justine harrumphed. "Let me go make you some tea, Andrea. Since my daughter is being so rude, I'll let you have some of the cookies, and she can just suffer."

As her mother went into the kitchen, Kelsey shook her head. "I really don't like being the center of attention. It's making me crazy."

"You should try being the empress and being pregnant," Andrea said as she sat on the couch. "Talk about a dog and pony show. Not a moment's peace, and everyone is trooping in to check on you and watch everything that you're doing. Not only that, your meals are gone over with a fine-tooth comb to make sure that everything is absolutely perfect for the baby. And then, when you get tired of it and climb out the window to get up to the roof and steal an air car, everyone loses their mind."

"Please tell me that's true," Kelsey begged. "You're my hero. I adore you."

"It's absolutely true, and it's also the reason why Marcus had me locked into an escape-proof suite and put under guard for our second child. Needless to say, I was less than pleased, but I've gotten over it in the last five hundred years. Mostly."

Kelsey's eyes shot back toward the kitchen. "Don't tell my mother that story. She'd try to lock me in the brig. It would be a disaster."

"I can hear everything you're saying," Justine said. "It's too late for you to climb out the window, dear. You're too far gone for that and are now my prisoner. Mwahahaha!"

"How are you feeling?" Andrea asked as she took a small platter with tea and cookies from Justine when she came into the room.

Kelsey quickly snagged a cookie and stuck her tongue out at her mother before eating it. "I think I stopped feeling bloated about three weeks ago. I'm not sure there are words to describe how I feel. If I had to run for my life, I couldn't. There's no worry about me climbing out windows or performing any strenuous action at all. I'm a prisoner of my own body."

"Not unexpected," the other woman said as she sipped her tea and nodded appreciatively. "Even so, are you feeling like it's about to happen? Just looking at you makes my feet hurt."

"I don't think so, but one can never tell. I'm sure if I feel even the slightest bit of anything, I'll be surrounded by medical professionals in literally seconds."

"Absolutely correct," Justine said. "Your doctors have established a command post right across the hall. They've tapped into your implants and are keeping track of what's going on with your body. You do remember giving them permission to do that, right? If they detect anything that indicates that labor might be beginning, they'll rush over in force, busting down the door if necessary. Actually, they won't have to do that because they have the key. Oh, and I had them put a tracker on you, so there was never any chance you could escape."

"You see? I'm doomed."

Andrea laughed. "Yes, I can see how awful you have it. This is an excellent tea, by the way, Justine. I absolutely want to take some back to Shangri-La with me. It's delicious."

"It's from Avalon, but you're welcome to have all I brought with me. I can always get more once we reopen contact. I'm sure that

Elise is dead tired of being a pack mule by now, but I imagine she'll come through."

"Is there any more word on the fighting?" Kelsey asked. "I can't get them to tell me anything other than bland and generic things-are-going-fine-type messages. They don't want me to worry, but nothing they're telling me about is putting me at ease."

"The last word I had from Luke was that he began his assault on his half of the chain of Clan home worlds and that while the fighting was fierce, they were pushing through. I can't say that the operation is without worry, but I won't let myself get tied up in knots because one of my descendants is putting himself in harm's way. I did that myself for many years, and it would be hypocritical for me to deny others the chance to do what they needed to do."

"And Jared?"

"The same. He's pushing him from his side and making progress. He's got a lot more robotic warships to throw at the front of the fight, so I think he's probably in less danger than Luke is. I'm going to cross my fingers and my toes and hope they can push through this and crush the last active threat to the Empire."

"Doesn't that leave their attack groups that are running around the Rebel Empire?" Justine said as she sat and handed Kelsey another cookie. "I realize there is less of a concern for us at this particular moment than the fight we're involved in, but they have to be dealt with if we ever intend to bring the entirety of the Empire back under our control."

"It does," Kelsey said, "but they're the least pressing of our worries right now. We believe the ships we're sending will be able to take care of the vast majority of the ships they've sent, and then it's a matter of cleaning up. Honestly, that's going to be true even once they're defeated. Every civilized world here in the Rebel Empire will strike out on their own, and we'll have to make a grand tour through the whole thing and convince each system that they need to subordinate themselves to the Empire."

"That will take years," Andrea said. "It's also going to be a diplomatic nightmare, so I'll be thoroughly pleased when we regain contact with both Shangri-La and Avalon so that we can begin bringing the diplomatic corps forward to take care of this for us. Send them in diplomatic vessels, and have a couple of cruisers along with them in case there's any trouble. One way or the other, a system won't have a choice. They will rejoin the Empire. We can't let them split off and become separate. That way lies civil war."

"I'm not happy about making them join at the end of a pistol, but that's the way it'll have to be," Kelsey agreed. "The Empire has suffered too much to allow people to split themselves off again. When everything is settled, all of human space except for the Singularity will be back under our control."

"That problem will have to be addressed at some point as well," Andrea said. "They are a much different issue than what we're dealing with now. That would be a war in real terms, but you're right. The fighting with them is what led to the fall of the Empire, and while payback is a bitch, she's our bitch."

"I'm glad to hear that you think things will work out so smoothly," Justine said. "I'll say that I've been worried about it. Is that what you came here to tell us, or was there something else you needed?"

"I just wanted to let you know that we've finished going over everything the two of us have discussed. With the exception of how to reduce the Empire to a single emperor, we are now in accord. To minimize the possibility that anyone will lose their foolish minds, I'd like to get it signed so that our governments have to accept that this is the way it's going to be. How the throne will work is something that can be settled separately."

"Bring that sucker over, and let's get this done. Have your folks come, and we'll bring in some witnesses. Then we can have something to eat. As shocking as this is to everyone who knows me, I'm starving."

24

Talbot sat in the back of the pinnace with Elise next to him. The rest of the seats were taken up by a skeleton crew that would be working aboard one of the computer-controlled destroyers they were sending out to deal with the Clan raiding parties. They weren't enough to run the ship by itself and fight, but the admiral had decided that it was best to have humans on site in case there were any complications that the computers didn't know how to deal with.

There wouldn't be any artificial intelligences running these task groups. Their actions had been programmed by Marcus, and they would go to where they believed the Clan would be holding up based on the information they'd gotten. If it was wrong, the humans would override that and take them to a new location, but other than some very broad commands, the computers would simply do what they were told without any initiative whatsoever.

This was the fourth and final group that they were sending out. It had taken two days to get everything put together the way he liked it, for the operation to kick off. This should be good enough to do what they needed to do. After all, they weren't there to fight the Clan warships. They were there to draw them into attacking them and use the self-destruct codes that Andrea Tolliver had pulled out of Theo 309. It was a trap meant to lure the aggressive buggers in so that they could be dealt with.

"Are we doing the right thing?" Elise asked.

"Would it be better if we sent ships to fight them where they could blow everything up and still end up dead?" he asked with a raised eyebrow. "Because that's what would happen. You can't reason with the Clans, at least not the people they send out to do their fighting."

"I'm not really thinking about them. I mean the planets under their control. We're going to destroy everything in orbit and maroon them on their planets, but we don't have any way of controlling what happens after that. We can't make them submit, and I don't think they're going to."

He shrugged slightly. "That's not really above my pay grade, but it's definitely outside my wheelhouse. They have a special kind of crazy that we need to isolate. What happens after that? Well, that's for someone else to figure out. The way they're paranoid and rabid, they may never get off those planets again. Of course, they might surprise us and be willing to open a dialogue after a while. I suppose one can never tell."

She was quiet for a couple of minutes and then sighed. "I suppose I'm just worried about Jared. He's taking his fleet in to attack everything that they have meant to protect these home worlds, and they won't give up. They will fight to the very last, and I know he won't let them get away. They may have to pursue stragglers to make sure that no one escapes, even though they think they've got task groups sitting on all the possible escape routes. There's a lot riding on this mission, and he'll put himself in a lot of danger to make it happen. And so is Luke Bandar. Maybe more in that latter case. His ships are all manned."

"It may be hard for you to understand since you're not someone that signed up for the military, but sometimes, this kind of thing is necessary," Talbot said in as gentle a tone as he could. "We all put ourselves at risk because the greater good is worth it. I know that one day you'd like to go home and drag him along with you. What do you think he'll end up doing once this fight is over?"

"I suppose you're right. I'd like to get him all to myself, but the Rebel Empire is one big jigsaw puzzle that'll take decades to put back together. They won't need the incredible military force that he and the other half of the Empire can bring to bear. At least, I hope they won't. I won't be getting him back to Pentagar anytime soon, will I?"

"Probably not. I know Pentagar decided to be an independent world, and I respect that decision, but once this is all said and done, maybe you should talk to your father about rejoining the Empire. Then you wouldn't be abandoning your home world to come stay with Jared."

She leaned back in her seat and crossed her arms over her stomach. "I have thought about that, and it's something that we'll have to discuss at some point. When this all started, the Empire was a small group of stars that were somewhat more advanced than us in a few ways but not so in others."

"Things have certainly changed," he agreed. "And they're going to change more."

"Right. Now, the Empire will be a behemoth that will always have us at a disadvantage when it comes to trade and other things. That's a long way out, but it's something that we need to think about."

"It really does feel like we're turning the page on one chapter of our lives and perceiving something else in our futures," he said. "On top of that, you've got the twins. I understand that you can't be with them right now, but I suspect Carl is right, and they won't be so susceptible to being manipulated by the alien technology once they're a little older."

He could see the skepticism on her face, but she shrugged slightly. "Maybe so, or maybe not. Honestly, now that I'm more cognizant of what I'm doing, it's not nearly as terrifying as it was back in the beginning. Having a few more people that could manipulate the crabs' technology might be helpful. Imagine the kind of exploration they could do. They could make their way across the galaxy to see places that no other human could see in a lifetime."

"And you've got the ability to open portals to seemingly any distance at all. Personally, I think you should go back to that one world we visited and open a portal there. It was a relatively normal place, all things considered, and probably a lot safer to explore than some of the other facilities. You could even see about sending the crab machine back."

She chuckled. "I hope to figure out how to turn it off one day, but marooning it there might work, too. Maybe I can leave it for the kids to discover then they're old enough. What about you and Kelsey? She's about ready to give birth, and your life will change as well. What will you be doing?"

It was his turn to shrug. "Honestly, I think I'll move into training. We'll have to train an incredible number of Marines, and while our friends from Shangri-La still have the Marine tradition, they don't have any Marine Raiders. Well, other than Andrea and her two sidekicks. If we're going to have more Marine Raiders, we'll have to have someone willing to teach them, and that's going to be me and possibly Andrea's associates. That'll be a lot of work, and it will keep me pinned down in one place. As for Kelsey, if her father doesn't lock her somewhere under the palace, then she'll have to decide whether or not she wants to come with me or stay wherever the seat of power ends up being."

"It'll be on Terra," Elise said. "They've already made the agreement. They'll work with the folks from Frankfort and begin construction of a new city beside the wreckage of the old. Since the Imperial capital was destroyed, it's as good as any other place, and there's a direct rail connection that leads to the Imperial Palace. Kelsey won't give that up without a fight."

He nodded. "In the beginning, I suspect we'll be building the Marine training facility somewhere on Terra as well. Eventually, that will need to go elsewhere, but the planet is so unpopulated and primitive that we've got centuries before we really have to worry about that. Or, they may decide not to ever move it and leave the Imperial Marine Raider training facility on Terra itself. That could have some benefits for the Imperial family. Or would that be Imperial families?"

Elise turned a little bit in her seat and shook her head. "That's still up in the air. I don't see how any government can work, having two bosses. The Pentagaran monarchy would be a shambles if we had two kings. What a disaster that would be. One can make a decision, and then the other one decides something completely opposite. So long as you have two people who are willing to work together or there are separate realms that they control as far as decision-making, I suppose it could meander along, but in my opinion, this is just asking for trouble. Someone will have to abdicate."

"I'm no expert when it comes to Kelsey's father, but he seems like a pretty easygoing man," Talbot said. "He might decide it's worth his while to step aside. There'll be a lot of work going on for a very long time, and he's not a young man. Even with the Marine Raider medical nanites keeping him alive, he's not in the best of health."

Elise nodded, her expression a little glum. "Kelsey has talked about that, and she supposes if the right offer is made, he might very well agree to step aside. Maybe he could become an Imperial duke in charge of Avalon and the surrounding worlds that were once the New Terran Empire. After all, no one knows those worlds better than him. That would just leave Kelsey and Luke Bandar to fight over who gets to be the heir."

Talbot laughed. "What makes you think she wants the job? Sitting around being a princess and doing governing tasks is not exactly high on her list of priorities. I'm pretty sure that under the right circumstances, she'd be willing to step aside as well. She could just be a princess in the Imperial line and not in the line of succession. The problem is that we don't really know anything about Luke Bandar or his father. We need to know more before we can be sure that they're worthy. That will have to be settled once everything else is dealt with."

Even as he was finishing up, the pinnace docked with the destroyer, and they began unbuckling. They waited until the crew was already off the pinnace before they followed. They'd only be here long enough for Elise to open a portal in a specific compartment that wouldn't be used for anything else, then they'd leave.

Talbot knew what he thought Kelsey should do, but she was all twisted up by duty to her father, so he wouldn't make any guesses of how any of this would turn out. They'd settle with the Clans first then, once they could, bring Karl and Leon Bandar together to settle all the details. That would probably take another couple of months, but it would be worth it to do it right.

Then they could begin the slow process of merging the two Imperial senates into one. That would be a political nightmare that he'd steer well clear of. Thankfully, there were enough calls on his time that he felt confident he'd be busy any time some politician needed him. And thank God for that. Kelsey could fight those fights, and she was welcome to them.

25

Jared sat at the command console on his flag bridge and shook his head. The amount of resistance they'd encountered thus far had exceeded his wildest expectations. From what data they had been able to recover, the Clans had only a dozen worlds they occupied, yet the sheer amount of firepower they had at their command for defense beggared the imagination.

They were assaulting the third system out of the six they were tasked with, and the first two had been grinding affairs where wave after wave of enemy ships threw themselves at his fleet. These were vessels different in design from those the Singularity had provided the Clans and were less powerful, but they made up for it in sheer numbers.

"I just don't get it, Marcus," he said to the air. "How can they possibly support this kind of military machine with only a dozen worlds? Worse yet, their women are basically chattel, so it's only the men doing the fighting. Not only is that unsustainable, it's inconceivable."

"It does suggest some facts that would have to be verified," the artificial intelligence said through the speakers on his console. "The population balance would likely be significantly out of whack with many more males than females. That begs the question, exactly how do they continue propagating that lopsided genetic balance? The more men they have, the fewer married couples they could achieve."

"I'm pretty confident that we won't like the answer when we finally get it," Jared said. "I suppose all that really matters at this point is that the operation is proceeding as planned even though ships from worlds further down the line are coming forward to meet us. The amount of firepower that we're seeing is certainly in line with their personalities. What are your force projections going forward?"

"Based on the number of ships and armed stations that we've encountered in the first two systems, plus what we're seeing here in this one, I'd anticipate that the number of ships and defensive stations will only continue to grow as we proceed. As the reports indicated, there are a dozen worlds that the Clans occupy, and we're approaching their capital. It is the sixth world on our side of the attack. I do not anticipate the strongest resistance to be there, though."

"If not there, where?"

"The final world on the other half of the axis of attack that Admiral Bandar is assaulting is listed in the data we have as the cradle of their civilization. I suspect that means it's a breeding world and might answer the questions that were put forward by you earlier. If they are keeping control over how many males or females are being born, that will be the world in which that takes place, and I suspect that it will be significantly better protected than anything we've run into thus far, and we should expect them to fight without restraint to protect it."

"Great," Jared muttered. "I suppose we should be grateful that it's not on our side. These people are already fighting a suicidal defense, and no amount of trying to convince them that we're just as human as they are and not going to do something terrible even slows them down. How could they get so twisted?"

"It hardly matters since we have to deal with the situation as we find it. Our lead elements are about to engage the defenders around the world and the fleet they have waiting for us. Might I suggest, again, that you pull your ship back and allow the robotic elements to fully engage them rather than putting yourself at risk?"

"I'm letting the robotic ships lead the way, but I feel that it's necessary for us to have some skin in the game. I won't let our protective elements get stripped away, but we need to avoid falling into the mentality that it's perfectly acceptable to send robot-controlled ships to destroy our enemies while we sit back in comfort. That's a terrible lesson to learn from this. That isn't the kind of people we want to be."

"If you say so. Perhaps my perspective is somewhat different. Nevertheless, I bow to your experience. Also, it doesn't hurt that you're in command, and what you say goes."

"I have to say that your sense of humor is improving. That was well delivered. So what are we looking at?"

"Our lead elements have stripped away some of their outer protection, but the world itself is protected by at least scores of heavy stations with a lot of firepower. They also have a mobile fleet that is equivalent to the first two worlds that we assaulted though it seems to be leaning more toward heavier ships than lighter. I anticipate that we'll lose at least another twenty percent of our firepower though perhaps only ten percent of the ships will be destroyed."

Jared nodded, thinking. "We'll be able to win this system, but what this comes down to is what we'll have at the end. Admiral Bandar and I will have to pinch the last two worlds between us and force them to stand and fight. Not that they've been running away, mind you. What do you anticipate our order of battle looking like by the time we get to the final fight?"

"It will be rather tight, but we should still have sufficient forces to keep the enemy bottled up and win the fight. By the time this mission is completed, we will control all the orbital space around each of the worlds, and they will have lost the ability to build warships. With that accomplished, the threat they represent becomes significantly weaker. Even so, there will be an element of risk as we proceed. If my estimations are incorrect, we may find that the last couple of worlds are significantly tougher than we've bargained for."

That made Jared grimace. He could only imagine how hard these people would fight if they thought they were facing extermination, which, to be fair, is likely exactly what they thought because they were too paranoid and xenophobic to be approached in a way that could disarm the situation. The fact that they had to kill all the resistance to stop them from being a threat to the Empire wasn't helping matters, and he didn't look forward to the job someone would eventually have in trying to pacify them.

It really felt as if they were on the verge of taking care of the vast majority of their problems—at least the big ones—and that gave him hope for the future. Even so, that didn't mean that anything they still had to accomplish would be easy, but at least it wouldn't have to be done immediately. Conquering the Clans was a good first step, but the Singularity was still out there, and they'd eventually have to be dealt with because they weren't going away.

He didn't know the part that he and Kelsey would be playing in what came next. In fact, once the two halves of the Empire came back together, he wasn't even sure he'd have a job. It certainly sounded as if the other half of the Empire had a more robust society and might end up coming out on top in the final negotiations. If that happened, he and his sister might end up being shunted aside in some manner.

That might not necessarily be a bad thing in her case. After all, she was the heir to the throne, and she didn't need to be out fighting like she was. That was very bad for succession. Of course, the same could be said of Luke Bandar. His father was the emperor too. He simply filled both parts that Kelsey and Jared were filling on his side of the equation. Jared had never inquired whether or not there were other people in the line of succession on the other end, but he suspected there were. Otherwise, Admiral Bandar wouldn't be allowed to do what he was doing.

If he ended up needing to do something else, he suspected Elise would be pleased with that. She'd like nothing more than to have her husband and kids to focus on, and that wasn't necessarily a terrible thing. He'd miss being in command of a fleet like this, but the last few years had worn him down. There was a little voice inside his head saying that maybe retirement was the right answer.

Well, that problem would have to wait for another day. Right now, he had a battle to win, and he'd like to avoid losing as many ships as possible. When they got to the end of this particular battle, he needed to have more force at hand than the Clans did, and that meant not letting them blow up every ship they could get within reach.

He focused his attention back on his display and began giving orders for Marcus to change things up in certain ways. Since the enemy was waiting for them to arrive, there was very little finesse in what was about to happen, but if they could improve the outcome by even a few percentage points, that would help them in the long run. They needed to win this war, and he would make that happen.

26

Elise was feeling antsy. It was time to make another trip around the various places she needed to see and talk to people to find out what was going on. Each individual trip was nothing to be concerned about, but with so many irons in the fire, she was very much afraid that it wasn't going to be long before things started going wrong, and when that happened, things would get chaotic.

Of course, the main thing she worried about was her children. By now, they should've arrived on Pentagar and were undoubtedly receiving the very best of care, but that wasn't the same as being with them.

The destroyer that was following her children should be arriving at Avalon before very much longer. In fact, it might already have been there. If so, they were about to have their first link back to one of the two emperors. Once that happened, things would begin happening quickly.

And then there was the battle going on around the Clan home worlds. She'd been making trips to speak with Jared and Luke Bandar every day or two. The two forces were making their way toward one another, but things were coming to a head on that end as well. Both of them had successfully conquered four worlds, and that left a total of four to eliminate the threat the Clans posed.

When she'd spoken with Admiral Bandar last, he'd passed on that they were regretting the fact that there weren't enough computer-controlled warships to do all the fighting. His forces had taken a beating, and even though they were going to push on to the finish, a lot of his people had died.

He mentioned that there was some resentment among his folks about that, and she'd felt the need to point out that their forces had been virtually exterminated while conquering the master AI. No one had come out of this unscathed.

She'd just finished speaking with Luke Bandar and seen how things were shaping up for his next battle. The number of ships that he was facing was substantial, and that was understandable because the next world in the line of his advance would be where the Clans did most of their breeding.

And that was probably gross. The vast majority of the women in their society were kept there so that they could breed warriors and other women to bear children. These poor women weren't second-class citizens. They weren't citizens at all.

From the point of view of the Clans, they were producing warriors to continue fighting, and that was the culmination of five hundred years of preparing to fight against extermination and to take back what they felt had been stolen from them. It was horrifying that normal people could have fallen into the trap of believing this was what was necessary, but it probably wasn't the original people who had believed it. It would've been their descendants that took them down this path.

Whatever the case, they would fight to the death to protect the source of their warriors. And weirdly, they were fighting to protect the women because they thought they were being sheltered. That was hardly true, but you couldn't argue with crazy.

She also stopped off to speak with Jared. He'd just finished conquering system number four and was working on system number five. The next one beyond that was there, so he was facing a lot of resistance as well.

Apparently, there had also been a number of attempted breakouts, and placing heavy task forces on all the escape routes had paid dividends by allowing them to keep the Clans penned in. Those groups attempting to escape would have seeded an entirely new cancer for them to fight in a couple of hundred years, so it was best to deal with them now.

In other words, everything was coming to a boil, and when they finally defeated these particular groups, the next two systems that Luke Bandar and Jared fought would be defended to the death, even more so than everything thus far. The Clans would have their backs against the wall and nothing to gain by surrendering to their way of thinking.

At the very least, this would be over in another couple of days. The battles in those final systems would rage heavily for at least twenty-four hours, but by the time that ended, they'd be making their way into the final two resistance areas, and then it would be over. It would all be over.

She took time to eat then made her way to the room she was using at Devon for coming and going via the portal. Her jaunt took her to the resistance destroyer that was headed for Avalon. She arrived in the compartment and opened the hatch to find a crewmember waiting for her.

"Princess Elise, welcome aboard. The captain would like to speak with you immediately."

"Take me to her."

The two of them made their way up to the bridge, and she saw a world that she recognized as Avalon rotating underneath them on the viewscreen. They had arrived.

The commanding officer, a lieutenant commander formerly from the Rebel Empire Fleet, turned and smiled at her. "You're just in time. We arrived in orbit about two hours ago, and His Majesty has indicated that he would appreciate your immediate travel to the Imperial Palace. We've got a cutter ready to take you down right now if you have time."

"I absolutely have time," Elise said with a smile. "I assume all the diplomatic people have already made their way there."

The Fleet officer nodded. "That's right. I have no idea how the discussions are going, but they were very firm that the moment you arrived, you were to be sent down immediately."

"I'm ready."

True to their word, she was virtually shoved into a cutter and flown down to the surface. Rather than going to the spaceport, they were vectored directly into the Imperial Palace and landed on a secure pad beside the large structure.

Elise stepped out of the cutter and was immediately greeted by the palace majordomo and his staff, who whisked her inside. They were going to take her directly to wherever His Imperial Majesty was, but she stopped the man and asked to be taken to a room that could be set aside for her future use in coming and going. It would need to be secured and probably guarded to make sure that it remained that way, but she wasn't going to chance anything happening that prevented her from linking up with Avalon now.

He didn't understand what she meant but took her to a room near the Imperial residence—still outside it, of course, but near it. She excused herself briefly, stepped inside the room, and closed the door. She opened a portal back to her getaway home in the alternate universe and closed it again.

That accomplished, she exited the room and smiled. "I'm ready to see His Majesty now."

The majordomo looked at her as if she might have lost her mind then escorted her into the residence. There was a handful of people sitting around a small table with Karl Bandar, but conversation ceased as soon as she arrived and the emperor stood.

"Elise," he said as he walked over and extended his hands to grasp hers. "They've just been filling me in on everything. I knew that you'd beaten the master AI from the ship you sent to notify us, but so much more has happened. Can you really go from one location to another like that?"

She nodded. "I'll be happy to demonstrate it for you. In fact, I suspect your daughter would like to see you very much. How would you like to go all the way into the old Empire and see her?"

"I very definitely would, but first, I need to know what the situation is. I vaguely knew what these Clans were from your reports, but how is the fighting going against them?"

"It's almost over, and though it's difficult and bloody, both Admiral Luke Bandar and Jared indicate that they believe they will be successful."

The older man shook his head. "It's hard to believe that there is another Empire out there and even more descendants of Emperor Marcus. Astounding. And very complicated to deal with, too. I understand that Kelsey has probably felt out of her depth, but I'm sure she's done a wonderful job in settling the remaining details."

Elise laughed. "You know your daughter as well as I do, and she's about ready to pull her hair out. Actually, if you've got the time, I probably should take you to see her immediately. Honestly, it's a miracle that she hasn't given birth already, and if you want to be there when your granddaughter is born, you might want to gather up some people from the Imperial Guard and come along with me. The negotiating team can come with us too."

Karl Bandar nodded decisively. He looked over at the majordomo standing beside the door. "Bring my guard, and send for Senator Nathaniel Breckinridge. He should be here too."

That was not what she was expecting. Senator Breckinridge was a very powerful Imperial senator and also Kelsey's biological father though he'd never had anything to do with raising her, and neither of them had been aware of their relationship until only a few short years ago.

To her mind, her actual father—Emperor Karl Bandar—was far more accepting of that kind of chaos than she would've been. It had to be a real mess for Kelsey to deal with, but thankfully, it wasn't her problem. If everyone wanted to be there for the birth, who was she to argue?

"If you don't mind, I'd like to see that orders are sent to the destroyer in orbit to go to Pentagar," she said. "I'll need to have the ship there so that I can create a portal to go home and visit my family."

One of the negotiators that the resistance had sent nodded and pulled out a communications unit. "I'll take care of it, Your Highness."

And now, it was mostly done. Things were definitely coming to a head, and she knew that Kelsey would be thrilled to see her father. She'd be even happier to dump the last of the negotiations into his lap though she wasn't sure Karl Bandar would let her off the hook that easily. She supposed she'd find out very shortly.

27

Kelsey had had no warning that her father was on the planet before he arrived at her doorstep.

When the chime sounded, her mother walked to the door and looked out through the viewer. "It looks like you have a visitor, dear."

She turned her head and frowned. "Who?"

Without answering, her mother opened the door, and Elise came in with her father at her side. There were other people with them, but they were Imperial Guards, and they took up station just inside the door as her father hurried over to her side.

"Goodness, you can certainly get yourself in trouble, can't you, my girl?" he asked with a smile on his face.

She gave him a lopsided grin and pulled him down for a hug. "Since I'm married, this isn't exactly trouble. I was getting worried that you wouldn't be able to be here before I gave birth. It's close."

"That is obvious at a glance."

Justine moved one of the chairs closer so that her ex-husband could sit then left the room with a smile, not saying anything. That was probably for the best, Kelsey decided. There was undoubtedly still some bad blood there, and this was neither the time nor place for them to get into an argument.

Once her father settled into the chair, he looked down at her belly and shook his head. "I can't envision how it's possible you still haven't given birth. Forgive me for saying so, but you're huge."

"I feel huge. My neonatal team—who are set up across the hall, by the way—tell me that first pregnancies often come early and that I'm well within the time frame where it could start. I have to say that I'm looking forward to getting this over with though it'll probably hurt a lot."

He chuckled and leaned back in his seat. "I certainly don't have any frame of reference for that, but everything I've heard tells me that's true. Frankly, I'm surprised you didn't want to have the baby taken out through a Caesarean section. Isn't that what it's called?"

Kelsey nodded. "We talked about it, but I decided that I wanted a natural birth. They'll give me pain blockers to make sure that the worst of what's happening is held at bay, but this is the kind of experience that I want to have as a mother. That way, I can hold it over my daughter's head for the rest of her life."

Her father laughed. "I see. Well, far be it from me to dictate to my daughter how to treat her child. Have you and Talbot discussed her name yet?"

"We still have a few options that we're working through, but we'll have it settled by the time the moment arrives. Has Elise filled you in on everything that's happening?"

He shook his head. "I heard from the resistance negotiators some of what was going on, but I'm sure there's plenty that I don't know. I have to confess that being able to step across half the universe in the blink of an eye is unsettling. It's very convenient, mind you, but unsettling."

"I wouldn't get too attached to it if I were you. Elise won't be doing this as a full-time job. Maybe she'll be able to find some of the technology on the other side that would allow others to do this. Unfortunately, that'll take a team of explorers to examine an entirely new universe and find the people who created the technology. Honestly, I can't believe we managed to accomplish everything we've done and that victory is almost within our grasp."

"You brought the master AI low. What else is there?"

She took a few minutes to fill him in on everything else that was going on, including their surprise visitors from Shangri-La. He blinked in surprise at that but accepted it without comment. By the time she finished speaking, he was frowning.

"That's a lot to think about. I'm glad to hear that you have everything worked out, with the exception of who's going to be in control. That last part is really something that I need to be involved with, as does the other emperor. You know that's just asking for trouble, right?"

"It does seem like a recipe for disaster," she agreed. "When you've got two people with co-equal powers running the show, what do you do when they disagree? What do you do when they decide they hate one another? Frankly, while it might work out in the beginning—though it might not—there will eventually be a civil war. We need to avoid that."

He motioned for one of his guards to come over and sent her into the kitchen to make him some coffee. While it was brewing, her father sat staring at the wall in thought. He only came out of it when the guard returned with a steaming mug of coffee that he sipped on.

"The only answer that I can see for bringing the two lines back together is for either myself or the other emperor to abdicate. I don't know this other person or even how old they are, but I've been doing this a long time, and I have to confess that the idea of trying to bring the entirety of the old Empire back under my control is daunting."

"And what does that mean?" she asked.

He crossed his arms and raised an eyebrow. "You've been telling me for years that I should take it easy. Maybe I should abdicate in favor of the other emperor and do just that. The problem of reintegrating thousands of worlds that may or may not want to be part of the Empire is a young person's task. I've put in my time, and maybe this is the right move to make."

"It's not my place to tell you that's right or wrong. What I will ask is that if this is a give-and-take, what will you take in exchange for giving up the throne?"

"Well, with the entirety of the Empire to worry about, perhaps I'll step down and request that the current New Terran Empire that revolves around Avalon be named a duchy. I think I could manage to be Duke Karl without too much screaming and wailing from everybody. That would be something of a semiretirement compared to the amount of work that will be required."

Kelsey thought about that and nodded. Even though her father had the Marine Raider nanites in his body, the poisoning had damaged his health. Taking things a little easier might just be what the doctor ordered, and if it was what he wanted, she wouldn't fight that. His happiness was extremely important to her.

"Maybe your heir should be a duke or duchess, but I think you should be an emperor emeritus. You held the title for a long time, and I think it's fair to say that even if you don't hold it any longer, maybe you personally should be a prince. Perhaps the area around Avalon should be a principality. That way, it's recognized as being somewhat different than everything else. And Jared's mother deserves to be a princess if she can't be an empress."

"Perhaps," he said evenly. "The next question will be what to do about you. You're already a princess and the heir to the Empire. I'm sure that the other half of the Empire already has one of those. Do you wish to fight to keep that position, or will you relinquish it?"

She shook her head and smiled. "I was happy being the spare when it was my time, but I have no desire to be an empress. I'm happy being your heir and letting the other half run everything. We've worked long and hard, and it would be nice to just focus on mundane matters. Let someone else do the fighting for a change."

He raised an eyebrow. "And what does Talbot think about that? For that matter, what about Jared? There are so many different things that still need to be settled."

"While that's true, I have no doubt that we'll work things out. Jared is a prince of the blood and will remain such. He doesn't want anything more and will probably head for Pentagar when his time comes. It's what I'd do in his shoes."

There was a knock at the door before she could say anything else, and one of the Imperial Guards checked the display. "There is a woman outside with tattoos on her face."

"She's fine," Kelsey said. "Let her in."

The guard waited for her father to nod then opened the door.

Andrea walked in and smiled. "I heard that we have a visitor and came as quickly as I could. Your Majesty, it's a pleasure to meet you. My name is Andrea Tolliver, and I am the Empress Emerita for the New Terran Empire based on Shangri-La."

Her father raised an eyebrow. "I see. Well, there's no need for formality, at least not here in private. Call me Karl."

"Only as long as you call me Andrea."

"Andrea is a Marine Raider, and she left with Emperor Marcus when he fled Terra," Kelsey said. "In fact, she married Marcus, and the rest of his line can trace itself back to her."

Her father blinked. "I see. That's astonishing. I know that my daughter has said that the Marine Raider medical nanites can keep someone alive indefinitely, but it's something else entirely to see it in person. Why don't you pull up a chair, and we can talk? One of my people will be happy to get you some coffee if you desire."

"I would like some coffee," the woman said as she sat in a chair that someone found for her. "We've got a lot to talk about, and it's on a very delicate subject. Your daughter and I have worked out the vast majority of the details for merging the two halves of the Empire back together, but settling who runs it is something that we still need to discuss."

Her father smiled. "She and I were just talking about that. I think we can settle that easily enough. It might be best if I were to abdicate my position in favor of your emperor. I assume he's younger than me, and this kind of work will be going on for a very long time. I'm old, and I'm ready to take it a bit easier than I have been. If you were willing to name the area around Avalon as a principality and me as its prince, Kelsey would remain my heir, and the two of us would step aside in favor of the line of succession from Shangri-La. Just as you are an empress emerita, I would be an emperor emeritus. In exchange for that, I think we'd probably want some other concessions, but that can probably be worked out, don't you think?"

The suddenness of his offer seemed to surprise Andrea, and the woman blinked before smiling. "Honestly, I expected this to be a lot more contentious."

It was Kelsey's turn to laugh. "We've been fighting against insurmountable odds for a long time. I know that your half of the Empire has been preparing for this as well, but we've been doing the work, and honestly, I'm not cut out to be a ruler. I never even wanted to be a Marine Raider. Will I fight if I need to? Absolutely. Am I going to be seeking it out if I don't have to? No. I think the two of us can live with this."

"Then all we need to do is wait for the ship going to Shangri-La to get there and for the fighting around the Clan home worlds to be done," Andrea said. "There's a light at the end of the tunnel, and I suppose we'll just have to hope that it isn't an oncoming freight train."

Kelsey found herself smiling. She really liked the other woman. "There's a bit of time left before that happens. The fighting around the Clan home worlds should be wrapped up in the next forty-eight to seventy-two hours. It's probably not going to be much longer than that before the destroyer heading for Shangri-La arrives. I suggest that you take the time to do a tour of Devon and maybe even Terra. The old Imperial Palace is amazing."

Her father smiled at that. "I'd like that. I think I'll have Elise take me home so that I can pick up Patrica—Jared's mother and my new wife—and bring her back to see everything. Since Justine was here, I thought that might not be the wisest course of action without a bit of warning. There's no need for fireworks."

"She might surprise you," Kelsey said. "She's really changed over the last year. I won't say that she's completely rehabilitated, but I don't think you'll find her causing the kind of trouble you fear."

"I'd rather not push things. We'll stay until you give birth because you need to have family around you to celebrate. I'll want you to come back to Avalon to recuperate and to see that everyone can get a look at my granddaughter."

"That sounds wonderful, but if you don't mind, I'm feeling worn out, and I think I'm going to shoo everyone out and take a nap. The littlest things tire me out these days, and you've got a lot to see over the next few days. It's almost over, Father. We've won."

He squeezed her hand. "I'll count my chickens after they've hatched, thank you. Never discount the fact that the universe is an expert at snatching defeat out of the jaws of victory."

Kelsey really hoped not because she wasn't sure she had the energy to keep fighting some new disaster—not right now, anyway. If something happened to Jared during this battle, she'd never forgive herself, and it would ruin everything. She crossed her fingers underneath the blanket in her lap. Please, keep her brother safe.

28

Talbot was surprised when he was summoned to meet with Elise aboard the large orbital around Terra. He'd been working with Mordechai and Jebediah, getting things set up around Frankfort and measuring out the areas where new construction could begin, when he got the call and went up to meet her.

To his shock, she had Emperor Karl Bandar and Empress Patricia as well. Jared's mother was mostly an unknown quantity to him as she'd come on the scene after he left on the expedition, but that hardly mattered. He saluted as he approached them and was amused at the suspicious looks the Imperial Guards gave him.

He could hardly blame them. After all, as a Marine Raider, he was by far the most deadly weapon in the compartment, even when he was unarmed, which he wasn't. They had to worry about the emperor's safety, and that was no simple task. When he'd been tasked with watching out for Kelsey, he'd gotten a foretaste of what they had to deal with every day.

"Talbot," the emperor said with a smile, extending his hand. "It's a pleasure to see you again. I suppose since this is a semiofficial visit, I should be calling you General Talbot, but seeing as you're my son-in-law, I think certain allowances can be made."

"It's always a pleasure to see you, Your Majesty," Talbot said with a smile. "You'll forgive me if I keep to protocol since we have all the guards around us. I've been expecting you for a while, and I suspect I know why you're here, but what can I do for you?"

"I was hoping for a tour of whatever you think is worth showing us, but I'd certainly like to see the Imperial Palace."

"I'd be happy to do that. If I might ask, how is Kelsey?" His wife wasn't quite ready to give birth yet, but it could happen at any moment, and he always asked when he had a chance.

"Happy and very close to giving birth. Elise will be going back and forth to check on her as needed, so I'll be fully in your hands. If circumstances change, she'll come and get us all."

"That sounds perfect. Thank you. I supposed seeing Terra from orbit would be a good start. If you'll follow me, I know the perfect place to make that happen."

He led the emperor, the empress, and their entourage to the restaurant with the grand windows that oversaw all of Terra orbiting beneath the station. As expected, the view of the planet beneath them certainly drew the eye, and the emperor and empress watched it for a very long time.

"Even with what we were trying to do, I have to confess that I never thought that I would live to see the birthplace of humanity," the emperor said quietly. "I barely had a chance to glance at the reports of everything that you've been doing, so if you'd take a moment to tell me what things are like down there, I would appreciate it."

"It's bad," Talbot said. "The AIs vaporized many of the major cities when Terra was overrun and then used EMP devices to eliminate the technology that might still be there. They had stations in orbit that could drop kinetic devices and blow up anyone that seemed to be developing too much of a civilization, so humanity has either become nomadic or is hiding in the ruins of what cities remain. While I wouldn't call them savages, there are certain elements that would fit that category."

"How does a planet recover from something like that?" the empress asked, her tone horrified. "It's horrible."

"That it is," he agreed. "Recovery will take a very long time, and the way that Kelsey and Jared decided to approach this was to begin construction of a modern city and branch out from there to begin bringing things under control everywhere else. There will be fighting, and there are definitely some societies that will have to be smacked down and rehabilitated. This will be the work of generations."

"While I'm uncertain that I'll have a full say once everything is settled," the emperor said as he turned toward Talbot, "I'll certainly advocate for putting everything we have into rehabilitating this world. I'm sure there are plenty of advanced planets in the empire that can be brought into the task. Maybe it won't take nearly as long as you think."

"I'm a big fan of positive thinking, but I have my doubts even with that kind of assistance. In the end, I'm confident that many of the worlds will pitch in to help, but there's so much to do. Why don't I take you down to see what we have to work with? We won't land at Frankfort, but an overflight of the city will certainly provide more context."

"What about the capital?" Empress Patricia asked. "Was it destroyed?"

He nodded. "I'm afraid so. All of the really big cities were destroyed, so only the medium-sized and smaller ones were left to rot."

He took them to his pinnace and ordered the pilots to go down and circle Frankfort. The only way to clearly see what was there would be to find a good overview, and he thought one of the hills around the city would be a good place. When he spotted a good candidate, he ordered them to a nearby clearing and landed.

The entire party took a short walk through the woods to the edge of a steep slope where they could observe Frankfort a few kilometers away. The city still had the bones of a modern society, but nothing was powered, and everything was either run down or falling apart. Sitting next to it were the ruins of the much more primitive place that had been trying to take over the city and scavenge what they could.

"As you can see, the city will eventually need to be completely torn down and rebuilt from scratch. That would take a lot of work though the underground areas are still in decent shape. There's even an operable train system if you go down deep enough. That's how we got from here to the Imperial Palace."

"What's that area off to the left?" Empress Patricia asked. "It looks like a primitive city."

"That's where an aggressive group was set up to defend themselves while they attempted to obtain salvage from the city and capture and kill the residents living there. We were able to send them running, but the society they came from still exists, and it will have to be dealt with. Trust me when I say that they're not the kind of people you want to have power over you."

He gestured out toward the plains off on the other side of Frankfort. "We've been surveying the area over here to begin construction of a new city. It's also going to be named Frankfort, and the people who live here will be moving there. That's where we'll put the new capital for now. It'll also be the hub from which we will reconstruct Terra. It won't be a big city in the beginning, not even as large as the original Frankfort was in its heyday, but we'll plan it out so that they have room to grow and can eventually expand and become as large as the capital was before Terra fell."

"That's an ambitious undertaking," the emperor said, sounding impressed. "Even building a city like that will take years. What will you do in the meantime?"

"We're still working on that. Honestly, a lot of this will depend on how much support we can get. A temporary city could be put up elsewhere in the area and used much like an army base where we could begin pacifying the area near Frankfort. We'll definitely want to secure everything so that none of the hostile forces in the general area feel like they can come in and raid us. This won't be as bad as what Pentagar is facing with Erorsi and the reconstruction there, but it's certainly not much better."

They stood there observing everything for a while, then the

emperor shook his head and gestured back toward the pinnace. "If we've got time, I'd like to see the Imperial Palace. I understand that it's in terrible condition, but my ancestors once lived there, and I want to see what's left."

"The palace is actually in relatively decent shape," Talbot said as he led them back toward the pinnace. "It was occupied by what amounted to a cult, and we had to relocate them."

They flew to the Imperial Palace, and he decided not to land and look at the exterior but to go inside instead. As the power was still on, they were able to use the secret tunnel and fly directly into the small-craft area underneath the palace. As expected, there were guards and technicians working on the small craft and making sure that no one sneaked in.

Talbot inclined his head toward everyone they passed as his party made their way deeper into the Imperial Palace. The first stop was an obvious one: the throne room.

The lights had been fixed, and now everything was clearly illuminated. Someone had taken the time to clean the area thoroughly, and while it wasn't in the right condition to have any kind of ceremonial events, the dais once again contained the Imperial thrones. The emperor's was taller by a slight bit, of course, but the empress's wasn't far behind.

The Imperial party walked a circuit of the room, looking at the remnants of the tapestries that had once been grand and glorious, and the emperor even peeked into the dressing rooms at the back where Emperor Marcus had had a small office back before the Fall.

The two of them looked at the thrones, but neither of them sat in them. Talbot wondered why that was. If anyone was entitled, it was them. He wasn't ashamed to admit that he'd sat in the Imperial Throne to see how it felt.

"It's amazing," Karl Bandar said in a soft tone. "There have been stories passed down through my family that have talked about this room. I can see the glory that used to be here and that will one day return. I'm confident that whoever ends up ruling the Empire will come here to form their seat. It only makes sense."

Talbot found himself frowning at the emperor's words. "Won't that be you, sir?"

The older man turned and smiled at him. "The emperor at Shangri-La might be a better choice though that will have to be determined once he and I speak. Rebuilding the Empire is the job of young men, and I'm afraid that I don't know that I'm up to the task."

Talbot made a derisive noise. "That's nonsense. No matter who takes over the throne, they'll never be able to complete the work here in their lifetime. Well, maybe if they had Marine Raider nanites coursing through their veins like you and the empress do."

The emperor clapped a hand on Talbot's shoulder. "Having two people with coequal power trying to rule the empire is a recipe for civil war. Perhaps not today, but at some point in the future. It's best to be graceful and save humanity from having to go through something like that. Don't worry that I'm thinking about just handing the reins over without getting anything in return. I believe that serving out the rest of my days as the Prince of Avalon would certainly be worthwhile. Besides, it might offer a way for Kelsey to get out of doing something like this. Can you imagine how unhappy she'd be doing political work?"

Talbot shuddered a little. "Yeah, that definitely wouldn't make her happy. Shall we go see the Imperial residence?"

At their nods, he led them down the hallway that contained paintings of all of the emperors, starting with Emperor Marcus and going back to the very first emperor right near the door of the Imperial residence. As expected, the trip took quite a while as every portrait was examined in detail.

The Imperial residence was under guard, and for good reason. It wasn't just to make sure that the area stayed secure, but there was a passage from there that led to the Imperial vaults. They'd decided not to close that off as they weren't certain they could get it back open again, considering the condition of the machinery.

When they stepped inside, he was pleased to note that someone had stripped out all the degraded furnishings and cleaned everything. Nothing had been moved in, but even the fountain that hosted the stairwell leading down was cleared of all of the nastiness that had coated it.

As most of the rooms were blank templates that could be expanded upon, there wasn't much to see. That meant everyone gravitated toward the fountain and the stairs leading down underneath it.

"This is the secret entrance that the Imperial family had to get down to where the vault is," Talbot said. "We'll walk down into a small chamber directly under the Imperial residence then take a short hallway to a lift that goes way deep. That will let us out into another hallway with a secret door that is very near the Imperial vault."

"Then let's go take a look at it," Karl Bandar said. "There's not much to see here in the residence itself though I'm confident that it can be made livable once more."

They descended into the chamber, took the lift down, and eventually found themselves standing outside the Imperial vault. The hatch was thick and impenetrable, Talbot knew. Thankfully, he was on the authorized access list and was able to open it without any difficulty.

Everyone stepped into the large chamber on the other side and froze. He'd expected exactly that, so he'd stepped aside to allow them to see everything without interruption. He said nothing as they gawked at the huge chamber that was literally filled with treasures ranging from precious art to crates filled with unknowable things. Well, they had a list of what everything was, but just seeing it like this didn't help.

"I never expected anything like this," the emperor said in a hushed voice. "This room is filled with treasures of incalculable historical value."

"It all needs to be in a museum," the empress agreed. "Sitting down here in the dark, it does no one any good."

Talbot stepped over in front of them and nodded. "That's what Kelsey was saying as well. I'm not sure where that kind of museum would go, but it's certainly a worthy thing to do. I can't imagine what it would take to protect everything here from the thieves that would inevitably swarm to take the smallest item. Oh, and I should mention that Kelsey tasked Elise with finding someone to start the restoration and preservation, but other matters have kept her busy. Everything else—minus the overrides that we took to stop the master AI—is still present."

Karl Bandar turned toward him with a smile that grew a bit wicked as it widened. "You know, the curator at the Imperial Museum on Avalon is an old friend of mine. I think that I should bring him here and watch him have a heart attack. Then, while he's overwhelmed and weak, I'll put him in charge of figuring all that out."

Talbot laughed. "Ambushing people like that runs in your family. Kelsey does it all the time. Personally, I think that's a great idea. Now, why don't we take a walk through here so you can get a look at some of the things that were given to emperors back before the Fall?"

Doing all that would take hours, but it would be time well spent. It would keep their minds off worrying about what was happening with the Clans and Kelsey. Elise had stepped away and was no doubt checking on his wife. If there was anything happening, she'd come back to get them at once.

He also smiled when he realized that meant that she now had the ability to open a portal somewhere in the Imperial vault. Not that she would become the greatest thief who ever lived by stealing everything, but he wouldn't be shocked if a couple of items went missing and ended up decorating her and Jared's little getaway place in the other dimension.

Honestly, no one would complain over anything like that. She'd let them know what and where it was, of course, but it was all right because Jared was a Prince of the Blood. If Elise was allowed to have some things, then surely Jared was as well. Frankly, Kelsey would likely pick up a few items to decorate wherever they ended up living.

That assumed, of course, that everything going on right now turned out okay. Things were looking good thus far, but he already knew that that could change in a hurry. He tried not to let that prey on his mind as they walked around the vault, but he was a Marine, and it was never far from his thoughts.

29

Jared watched the plot as the massive swarm of ships came away from the planet to meet his fleet. They were now fighting over the last of the planets in the chain that he was responsible for, and as expected, the resistance was significantly stronger than he'd hoped. This was the last bastion of the Clans, and they wouldn't let it go without fighting to the last breath.

The intelligence they'd gathered indicated this was the seat of their government and their most populous world. It wasn't the one reserved for breeding their population. That was what Luke Bandar was assaulting now, and from what Elise had said from her last visit, the fighting there would be just as tough as it was here. By the time they were done, their fleets would be in a shambles.

When it came time to plan the attack, he'd suggested waiting for more ships to arrive and leading both waves with the AI-controlled vessels, but Luke Bandar had been resistant to the idea as he would've had to allow Fiona to control the ships on his end of the attack. He'd stated that he'd rather have full control and that he wasn't afraid to risk his ships or people for something this important.

That seemed like folly to Jared, but he could understand the other man's resistance to cooperating with the artificial intelligences that had been their bogeyman for five hundred years. Unfortunately, his stance would result in great loss of life, but the end result would be a Rebel Empire that was mostly under their control though they would have to go from system to system and compel them to play nice.

At least Luke Bandar was trying to be cautious about his own person. His ship would be toward the rear of their formation, and they weren't going to be overly aggressive. The goal was for Jared to finish up as soon as possible and join the other man to attack from the rear unless Bandar finished first and performed that duty for Jared.

"I've finished my calculations on the threat the Clan warships hold," Marcus said. "Unless they have some kind of surprise that we are unprepared for, I estimate that we are going to lose approximately forty percent of our remaining forces though only fifteen percent or so will be outright destroyed. The remainder should be repairable. If the shipyards in orbit around this world can be utilized for the repairs, that will speed things along."

"I'm not happy about losing that many ships, but it could be worse. Make certain to keep all of the ones with humans on them toward the rear of the formation and sacrifice the computer-controlled ships where possible. Will Admiral Bandar be facing roughly the same kind of resistance?"

"Uncertain, but likely," the AI said. "While their manner of reproduction is reprehensible, in their own twisted minds, they must protect their women at all costs. I would estimate the level of protection around that world to at least be the equivalent of what we're facing now, if not stronger. Unfortunately, Admiral Bandar only has manned warships, and that means that the loss of life will be significant."

He wished their communication was more regular, but Elise couldn't be bouncing back and forth between their ships like that. This fight would play out the way it did, and he'd just have to accept that. On reflection, he probably should have sent along one of the FTL communications devices, but by this point, they really didn't need to coordinate anymore. Elise had been a lot better, anyway. All they needed to do now was finish their fights.

The swarm of Clan warships didn't seem very organized, but they were all coming out at full speed. The aggressiveness they were displaying could not be understated.

He'd already deployed his ships, and now all he could do was wait for the two sides to collide. Once they did, he'd move to the planetary orbit and deploy the Marines that he borrowed from Luke Bandar. They would seize the orbitals and shipyards, just like they'd done in every system thus far. By now, they understood the layout they were facing and how the enemy behaved.

Just like everything else the Clans did, their ground forces did not surrender. They would have to be forced out compartment by compartment, and while some of the civilians would be taken alive, even they tended to fight where they shouldn't.

As expected, the two fleets slammed into one another, and ships began exploding or were cut into pieces. These Clan warships were of the old style rather than the ones the Singularity had built for them. Paranoia had its place, after all, and they didn't want to allow a foreign power to potentially sabotage their last line of defense. Considering what the Singularity had done, they'd been wise to do so.

The Singularity shipyards were here in orbit, and they might have a significant staff from the other polity. They would surrender, he suspected, and they could then be handed over to Andrea Tolliver.

Marcus's estimates proved accurate, and they lost almost half of the ships that he had left in the fight. On the positive side, the vast majority of them were simply damaged rather than outright destroyed. They lost about fifteen percent of the ships, and the rest would have to be repaired, but they'd won the fight, and now the Marines were assaulting the orbitals and shipyards.

Jared left enough ships to make sure there were no unpleasant surprises coming up from the planet and directed the rest of his fleet to the flip point that would lead them to the system that Admiral Bandar was securing.

He turned to face his wife, who was standing just behind him. She'd been quietly watching the fight, and if things had gone badly, she'd have taken him and as many people as possible to that little hideaway in another dimension. He had to admit that she was a lot better than the usual escape pods they had to rely on under those types of circumstances.

"Why don't you go see how Admiral Bandar is doing? If he can tell us what the layout is over there, that would be helpful. We'll be at the flip point in about an hour and a half, and we can do our best to attack the enemy from the rear and end his fight quickly."

She nodded. "I'll be right back."

And with that, she opened the glowing portal and stepped through it. Once it vanished behind her, he shook his head. "I don't think I'm ever going to get used to that."

"Nor do I," Marcus agreed. "I understand the statement that when a science is sufficiently advanced that it is indistinguishable from magic, but that certainly seems like magic to me."

Jared opened his mouth to respond but stopped when the portal opened again and Elise stepped out. She hadn't been gone nearly long enough to get the information he needed. "What's wrong?"

"I can't get to his ship," she said in a worried tone. "When I try to open a portal, it simply doesn't open. I've never had that happen before, and I'm afraid that means that the destination is no longer there."

"That is not good. Marcus, see what you can do to expedite our arrival in the next system."

"All ships capable of flank speed are now moving as fast as possible," the AI said. "All the other vessels will follow at their best speed."

Moving at top speed, they were able to transit to the next system in about an hour and fifteen minutes. When they arrived there, they saw that the fight was still going on. Based on the number of Clan warships, the resistance had been significantly heavier than anticipated. Luckily, there was still a large force of ships blocking the other exit from the system, and it looked like the Clan warships were still bottled up. As long as they could eliminate the resistance here, this particular fight would be over.

"Take us in, and let's smash these bastards," he ordered.

"Yes, Admiral."

Even though they raced in, the fight was over by the time they arrived. Honestly, that really wasn't a surprise. As hard as the two groups were fighting, any kind of delay was difficult to imagine.

Admiral Bandar's fleet was victorious, but it was decimated. More than seventy percent of the ships were damaged or destroyed, including Admiral Bandar's flagship. *Ulysses* had been lost with all hands. That was a huge blow because Luke Bandar was the heir to the throne on the Shangri-La side.

The devastation extended to the senior command staff, and the highest-ranking survivor was a commodore in charge of a dreadnaught task force. Jared expected resistance, but the woman deferred to him and recognized him as the senior Fleet officer, and command of their forces passed to him.

Jared got his ships and people to help with rescue operations and damage control while the Marines assaulted the orbitals. This was the end of the Clans as a threat as long as the ships running rampant inside the Rebel Empire were stopped. Considering that they had the codes to kill those ships, he didn't think any of them would get away. They were just too aggressive and would want to fight.

They'd won and could now begin the long process of reincorporating the worlds of the Rebel Empire, but first, they would need to get his Emperor and the other one together to finalize the reintegration of the Terran Empire. Only the chain of succession remained, and now they'd thrown a joker into the mix, and things were going to get funky.

30

Kelsey reached out and took Andrea's hand. "I'm so sorry for your loss. I didn't know him well, but he seemed like a decent person."

Andrea was sitting beside her, still crying. "Even living as long as I have, it doesn't make losing people any easier. While he was my descendant, it was far enough down the line that I saw him more as a friend than anything else. It hurts, but not nearly as much as it's going to devastate his parents and younger siblings."

"I don't really want to talk about business, but we need to," Kelsey said as she squeezed the other woman's hand briefly and then released it. "How will this affect what we're doing?"

Andrea used one of the tissues to wipe her eyes and sat back in her chair. "It won't, not really. While Luke was the heir, he has younger brothers and sisters who can step into that role easily enough. They have families of their own, and that's actually a step toward stability that he didn't have as he was unmarried. Believe me, the line of succession has been planned out quite thoroughly, and even though this is a painful loss, it won't cause any issues with what we're trying to do. Are you still going to abdicate?"

Kelsey took a sip of her tea and shrugged slightly. "I'm mostly convinced that's the right course of action. The Avalon side of this is very small in comparison to what you've got at Shangri-La. You brought a lot more refugees with you, and you didn't lose the technology the way we did. From what you told me, your portion of the New Terran Empire is about five times the size of what we have and far more advanced. As my father has already made the decision to step aside, I think it's probably best that I do the same. With, of course, certain concessions that your people probably won't mind paying."

"That does make things somewhat easier," Andrea admitted. "Now that the Clans have been subjugated, that only leaves dealing with the raiding forces they launched into the Rebel Empire. If things play out the way I expect, that particular set of problems will be dealt with in the next couple of months, and we can move forward with the gradual reintegration of the Terran Empire. That promises to be quite the challenge."

Kelsey grinned. "That's kind of what I'm trying to avoid. I've been involved in a lot of fighting, and I don't really have the patience to deal with all of the egos a ruler has to massage. Besides, I'll be a mother, and that'll take up a lot of my time going forward. Far better to let others deal with these problems while I get my life in order and spend some time with my husband."

Andrea nodded and wiped her eyes again. "As I said, that will make things simpler, and I have no doubt whatsoever that the emperor will grant your father the principality of Avalon. You'll maintain your title as Princess Kelsey and succeed him at some point. If, of course, he decides to retire. As we both know, the Marine Raider medical nanites can extend someone's life for centuries. Your father will be around for a very long time, and once we bring this technology to the people of the Empire in general, it'll change a lot of things."

"That it will," Kelsey agreed. "One thing that it will definitely alter is the fact that the emperor will be on the throne for a very long time. He'll probably want to arrange a more orderly transition to his heir after a set interval and retire himself. Then he'll have an opportunity to live his life in a more relaxed setting. I know my father is looking forward to his retirement. Frankly, so am I."

"I can understand that," Andrea said as she stood, walked into the kitchen, and began pouring herself some tea. "Would you like some?"

"No, thank you. I feel bloated as it is. It won't be long before I pop, and I'm just not feeling like dealing with that."

"Understandable," Andrea said as she sat. "And what do you plan to do in your retirement? I can relate to wanting to take a break after fighting as much as you have. As a former Marine Raider, I think I understand that better than most."

"That you do. I have no idea though I'll still be my father's heir. If he decides to retire in truth, then I'll take over the principality and run it for a while. The stability would be good for my daughter and for me and Talbot. We could all use a bit of peace and quiet. I can't wait to get this settled so that I know for sure that's what's happening."

"You don't need to worry. The Imperial Senate and the emperor will jump at the chance to go ahead and settle this matter so cleanly. The destroyer should be at Shangri-La, and we can head over whenever you're ready. I'd imagine you'd like to get things settled before your medical team drags you off to give birth."

Kelsey looked over toward the hatch. "I'm utterly confident that they have a full team standing by to jump in here the moment I have the least bit of discomfort. They won't be pleased that I'm leaving to go to Shangri-La. In fact, I anticipate that they'll insist on accompanying me."

"And they'll be welcome. The very best medical facilities at Shangri-La would be made available to them and you. You and your daughter won't be in any danger. I promise. If I have to, I'll carry you to the medical center myself."

Kelsey grinned. "And if anyone could do that, it's you. Hopefully, it won't be anything so dramatic. With any luck, I'll have another couple of days before the contractions start and plenty of time to deal with the succession beforehand."

There was a knock at the hatch, and it slid open before she

could respond. Elise stood on the other side. "It's time, ladies. By my calculations, the destroyer should be at Shangri-La by now. If they took their time, they might still be a bit short of orbit, but if they push things a little, they may already be there and may have taken the cutter down to the surface, assuming they got it all put back together."

Kelsey very carefully arranged herself and stood with Andrea's assistance. Elise was there a moment later to help stabilize her. "I understand that you need to do this, but I can't say that I'm very happy taking you into an uncertain environment like this."

"It'll be fine."

"You can bet on that," Talbot said as he came through the hatch, pushing a grav chair. Her neonatal team stood behind him. "There's no need for you to stress yourself, and you can damn well be sure that I'll be right there with you. I just gave Jared a call, and he'll be ready to go as soon as Elise comes to pick him up. We're all in this together."

She nodded. "Normally, I'd be inclined to argue, but my legs are feeling a little shaky."

With everyone's assistance, she was quickly seated in the chair, and all of them were taken through Elise's portal to the other universe. She really wanted to have a place like this to get away from things, and that would have to be something that she pushed when the time came. If they could do some exploration of this alternate universe and find another way of getting people here, she'd jump on that.

Elise left and returned a minute later with her husband. Jared stepped over to the chair and put his hand on her arm. "Are you sure you're up to this?"

"I'm fine for right now. Where's my father?"

"He and my mother are still getting ready. It shouldn't be more than a few more minutes. Your mother is with Senator Breckenridge. Elise knows where they are, and she can go wait for them."

"It's really tiring to be a taxi service," her friend grumbled.

"We've definitely got to find more of these things so that other people can take this job over."

Kelsey laughed. "I was just thinking the same thing. Better yet, I want a house like this. Being able to get away from everyone else would be amazing."

"In good time," Jared said. "First, you've got a little girl to welcome into the Empire."

Elise opened a portal and stepped away. Ten minutes later, she returned with Kelsey's father and stepmother. They were dressed in the Imperial regalia, and that meant it was showtime.

He stepped over beside her, knelt, and looked her in the eye. "You don't need to be involved in this. I can handle the negotiations to get everything settled. It's been a long journey, but it's over now. In a matter of hours, we'll have accomplished everything we set out to do and can rest."

"I can handle this," she said. "Let's just get this finished."

He nodded and stood. "If you'd be so kind, Elise."

Her sister-in-law had made another trip out and had returned with her mother and biological father. Now, she opened a portal and stepped through. Moments later, she stuck her arm back through the portal and waved for them to follow.

The portal led into the interior of a cutter, but the hatch was open, and they were able to go down the ramp at the back and out into the sunlight. It had obviously been taken from the destroyer and landed on the surface of a planet, so that probably meant they were on Shangri-La. Things really were just about over.

There were half a dozen guards standing outside the cutter, and Kelsey could see another pair of them racing toward the nearest building. It was big and ornate. Honestly, it looked like the Imperial Palace.

The cutter had landed on a private pad, and it looked as if things had been set up to receive them. That meant they would have a couple of days of getting to know one another before things could be settled. Frankly, her father and the other emperor would no doubt do the negotiations to make that happen. She only needed to smile and hope that she didn't go into labor before everything was settled.

In an astonishingly short amount of time, the large doors leading into the palace were flung wide, and a crowd of people began coming out. Admittedly, it wasn't as large as it might have been, but there were dozens of them, and they surrounded a regal-looking man dressed in well-made clothes with a ferocious frown on his face. That didn't look promising.

Andrea stepped up in front of the group. "Duke Karlov. I assume that the destroyer captain has filled you in on the basic situation. I need to speak with the Emperor at once."

"We got the information, yes, but there's been a disaster," the older man said. "We need Luke back as quickly as possible. There was a massive rockslide at the Imperial retreat, and the entire lodge collapsed when its foundations went down the side of the mountain. It's all gone, and so are they. Luke is the last survivor of the Imperial line."

Kelsey saw the intense pain that hit the other woman. From personal experience, she knew it was like having a knife being unexpectedly stabbed into one's heart.

"God's above," Andrea said quietly. "All of them?"

Diana and Claudio stepped forward and caught her as she began to sway. Someone called for a chair, but Andrea simply sat on the plascrete. From her expression, she no doubt felt as if her entire world had been destroyed. All of those people were her family.

Kelsey leaned forward and levered herself out of the grav chair. Talbot helped her stand and walk over to the devastated woman. She put her hand on Andrea's shoulder in quiet support.

Then she looked up at the duke. "Duke Karlov, my name is Kelsey Bandar, and I am the Crown Princess of the Avalon branch of the New Terran Empire. It is my sad duty to inform you that Admiral Luke Bandar was killed in action."

She might as well have punched the man in the gut. He took a step back and looked as if he wanted to throw up. "Gods above, they're all gone. What do we do now?"

"I suspect that that is where I come in," her father said in a somber voice. "My name is Karl Bandar, and I am the co-emperor of the New Terran Empire. I will step into the void until things can be settled. I understand that's not what you were looking for, but there will at least be continuity while the Imperial Senate here and on Avalon figure out what to do next."

The duke nodded slowly. "I suppose that's better than the alternative, but no one here knows you, Your Majesty. We received the reports that you were alive only a few hours ago. The lodge collapsed the day before yesterday, and it will take time to get things settled. There were so many of them that it seemed unlikely that anything could happen to them all. We were fools to let them all gather even if we thought their location safe and secure."

"No one can foresee everything, Your Grace. These will be painful and uncertain times, at least for a little bit, but we'll find our way through them."

"I suppose it's a good thing that you're still alive because we would be in very dire circumstances if you weren't," the other man said. "I feel confident that the Imperial Senate will squawk and shout as they normally do, but I've seen the agreement that Empress Emerita Tolliver has made, and I'm sure that we can settle things so that your reign begins—or I suppose that *continues* would be more accurate—on an auspicious footing."

Her father shook his head slightly. "I won't be serving that long. It is my intention to abdicate in favor of my daughter once she's recovered from giving birth. The Empire needs a young hand to see everything through to the end. My daughter is extremely competent, and she will make a wonderful empress."

Kelsey blinked in surprise. That wasn't *anything* like what she had had in mind. She'd anticipated stepping into being the heir for the Principality of Avalon, not for running the entire empire.

She opened her mouth to argue, and that's when the pain hit her. Moments later, she felt her water break and knew she would have to save her arguments for another time.

"My water just broke," she said quietly.

There was a moment of shocked silence before Andrea surged to her feet and began calling for someone to notify the medical center inside the Imperial Palace, even as Kelsey's doctors circled around her and began moving her back into the grav chair.

Even through the haze of pain, she had to admit that she was amused at how much mayhem a woman going into labor could cause. People were running around like chickens with their heads cut off, trying to figure out what they needed to do. She doubted very seriously that any of them would accomplish anything worthwhile, but control of what was going on around her was now irrevocably in someone else's hands.

No one on the ground here had expected to have this kind of crisis dumped into their laps, but they figured out what needed to be done, and she was quickly taken to a small but advanced medical center. The medical professionals there quickly consulted with the neonatal team and leaped into action. In just a few minutes, she found herself in a hospital gown and on the table. Talbot was right there beside her, his hand in hers.

She looked down at it meaningfully. "Are you sure you want to put your hand in mine right now? I might very well crush it."

"I'm a Marine Raider, so I'm supposed to be unspeakably brave. We're both enhanced, and I think I can handle it. If not, we already know that they can give me an artificial hand that's just as good as the original."

"Don't make me laugh. Not now."

Everything that she'd read told her that giving birth was the most painful thing that a woman could go through, but she discovered that wasn't true. Oh, it hurt, but being cut open and having her body converted to that of a Marine Raider without anesthesia was definitely still the most painful thing she'd ever experienced.

They gave her a shot to help dull the pain, and that helped. After that, it was hours of waiting for her body to be ready to deliver her daughter and then making it happen. She approached that with the same determination that she brought to the worst battles she'd ever fought in.

Everything rose to a crescendo as her daughter's head crowned, and she continued to push when called for. Somehow, Talbot never flinched, his hand in hers no matter how hard she squeezed it. It had to hurt, but his face showed only love and concern.

And then it was over. The doctors quickly took their daughter to the side and began cleaning her up. Moments later, their daughter began crying, and it felt as if Kelsey's heart had just burst in her chest. She struggled to see what was happening but couldn't get a good angle.

"Relax," Talbot said. "She'll be here in a minute."

When they brought her daughter over and put her into her arms, Kelsey started crying. She wanted to see her baby's face clearly, but the tears wouldn't stop. All she could do was hold her and kiss the top of her head.

She heard someone ask what her daughter's name was. She and Talbot had thought long and hard about that and had finally come to an agreement. "Her name is Jasmine Etana Bandar."

Jasmine had been Talbot's mother's name, and it had felt right since his parents were no longer with them. Etana was the female version of Ethan and would perhaps make the edge of the pain she still felt at the death of her brother a little less sharp.

After a while, the doctors took her baby away for further checking, and the staff began helping her clean up. She imagined that there was a fair bit of bleeding and tearing that needed to be dealt with. Talbot was not a small man, so Jasmine had not been a small baby.

Very soon, she'd be back in the thick of things. As much as she wanted to take all the time she could to recover and bond with her girl, the needs of the Empire wouldn't wait. Her father would run things until she was back on her feet, but he was right about one thing. The people of Shangri-La needed to have the person who would be running the show in place as soon as possible. His would be a caretaker government, and then she'd have to figure out how to make it all work.

That was going to be a huge pain in the ass, but she didn't shirk her duty when it was obvious what needed to be done. With events happening like they were, she wasn't sure how much time she might actually get to spend with her father because they wouldn't want to have both of them in the same place for very long. They were gun-shy now, and she couldn't blame them.

Even so, her father and mother needed to meet their grandchild, and everyone else would just have to figure out how to make that happen. Then, there was Patrica and Senator Breckenridge. She had no doubt that her mother would be there to help raise her daughter, and that would be critical because there was a lot that needed to happen, and running an empire wasn't a job that came with a lot of free time.

Her personal adventures were officially over, and that wasn't a bad thing. It would take decades—or longer—to get things settled inside the Terran Empire and then figure out how to deal with the Singularity. By the time she was done, her daughter would be a young woman and would hopefully be fast friends with Jared's boys.

The future was theirs, and she couldn't wait to find out what their story would be.

* * *

WANT to get updates from Terry about new books and other general nonsense going on in his life? He promises there will be cats. Go to TerryMixon.com/Mailing-List and sign up.

DID YOU ENJOY THIS BOOK? Please leave a review on Amazon. It only takes a minute to dash off a few words and that kind of thing helps Terry make a living as a writer and gets you new books faster.

WANT MORE BOOKS BY TERRY? Flip to the next page and grab one.

VISIT TERRY'S Patreon page to find out how to get cool rewards and an early look at what he's working on at Patreon.com/TerryMixon.

ALSO BY TERRY MIXON

You can always find the most up to date listing of Terry's titles on his Amazon Author Page.

Note: the links below (ebook only, obviously) redirect you to my website where you can click a button to go to Amazon. This allows me to participate in Amazon's associates program and earn a little more. Sorry for any inconvenience.

The Last Hunter

The Last Hunter

Bonds of Blood

Alpha Strike

The Enemy Revealed

Command Authority

The Grand Conspiracy

Shield of Humanity

Fog of War

Ships of the Line

Operation Liberty

The Empire of Bones Saga

Empire of Bones

Veil of Shadows

Command Decisions

Ghosts of Empire

Paying the Price

Recon in Force

Behind Enemy Lines

The Terra Gambit

Hidden Enemies

Race to Terra

Ruined Terra

Victory on Terra

When Luck Runs Out

Gunboat Diplomacy

The Imperial Marines Saga

Spoils of War

Imperial Recruit

Enemy Action

The Humanity Unlimited Saga

Liberty Station

Freedom Express

Tree of Liberty

Blood of Patriots

Single Novels

Scorched Earth

Storm Divers

The Vigilante Series with Glynn Stewart

Heart of Vengeance

Oath of Vengeance

Bound By Law

Bound By Honor

Bound By Blood

Box Sets

The Empire of Bones Saga Volume 1

The Empire of Bones Saga Volume 2

The Empire of Bones Saga Volume 3

The Empire of Bones Saga Volume 4

Humanity Unlimited Volume 1

Humanity Unlimited Volume 2

ABOUT TERRY

#1 Bestselling Military Science Fiction author Terry Mixon served as a non-commissioned officer in the United States Army 101st Airborne Division. He later worked alongside the flight controllers in the Mission Control Center at the NASA Johnson Space Center supporting the Space Shuttle, the International Space Station, and other human spaceflight projects.

He now writes full time while living in Texas with his lovely wife and a pounce of cats.

TerryMixon.com

amazon.com/author/terrymixon
facebook.com/TerryLMixon
patreon.com/TerryMixon
bookbub.com/authors/terry-mixon
goodreads.com/TerryMixon